Countess Tatya Kalinskaya resigns herself to a bleak future as she watches her friends one by one fall in love and get married. She is still beautiful, but who would want a widow who is unable to walk or dance?

Then Vassily Karachev returns to St Petersburg and suddenly Tatya finds a kindred spirit. He tells her that she needs a lover, someone to talk with, to bring her flowers and gifts and a little excitement, perhaps even a few kisses . . .

What possible harm can there be in this innocent game—unless one of them should *really* fall in love?

By the same author in Masquerade

FLIGHT FROM THE EAGLE
THE ICE KING
THE EAGLE'S FATE
WHEEL OF FORTUNE

Tatya's Story

Dinah Dean

MILLS & BOON LIMITED
London · Sydney · Toronto

First published in Great Britain 1984
by Mills & Boon Limited, 15–16 Brook's Mews,
London W1A 1DR

ISBN 0 263 74590 2

Set in 10 on 10½ pt Linotron Times
04/0384

Photoset by Rowland Phototypesetting Ltd
Bury St Edmunds, Suffolk
Made and printed in Great Britain by
Cox & Wyman Ltd, Reading

For George and Michael

NOTE

Some readers may find that the Russian system of naming people takes a bit of getting used to. The principle is that a person's name has three components: the name given at baptism, the father's name and the surname. The two last, furthermore, are modified to show whether the child is male or female. Thus, in this story, the son and daughter of Mikhail Kalinsky are Boris Mikhailovich Kalinsky and Olga Mikhailovna Kalinskaya. In conversation, people are often addressed by their first two names. This applies even to the Czar, in this case Alexander Pavlovich—Alexander (I), son of Paul.

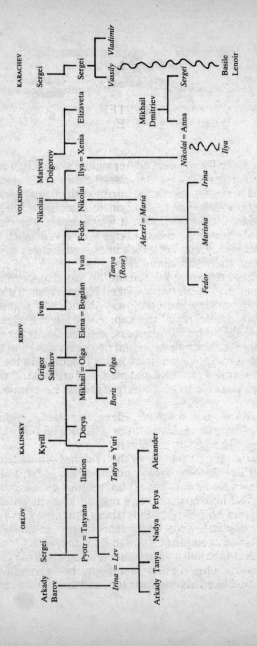

CHAPTER
ONE

TATYA Kalinskaya tweaked her widow's cap into a more becoming position on her dark, glossy curls and regarded her reflection in the mirror with critical appraisal. Her oval face was still smooth and not badly lined for a woman of thirty-two, but it was too pale, the mouth had a slight droop, and the large grey eyes looked sad. She attempted a smile, which improved matters a little, but it felt stiff and unnatural.

Perhaps the embroidered muslin morning-gown was too youthful. It certainly looked incongruous with the cap—or perhaps the other way round. On a sudden impulse, she removed the cap. After all, the General had been dead for fifteen years, and she'd only taken to wearing caps since her accident five years ago. 'I'm old,' she thought, looking at the forlorn reflection in the fine gilt-framed mirror. 'Old and plain and crippled. It was a mistake to come to Petersburg. I should have stayed at home.'

'Shall you go down now?' Elena, her maid, enquired. She opened the bedroom door and looked out on the landing. 'There's no-one about.'

'Thank you.' Tatya took the crutches which leaned against her dressing-table and made her slow, halting way down to the small breakfast parlour on the ground floor. The house was a large one, in keeping with the other great houses of St Petersburg, built by Tatya and Lev's grandfather some fifty years before, in the 1770s. It was a fine example of Russian Baroque, with a magnificent entrance hall and staircase leading up to the grand reception rooms on the first floor, but Grandfather Sergei had liked his comforts too, and the private family part of the house was well-planned and pleasant to live in, with a suite of rooms on the garden side of the ground floor, connected to the upper floors by their own staircase, which Tatya now descended.

Going up or down stairs was even more difficult for her than moving on the level, and the servants tactfully kept out of her way as much as possible. It was only as she reached the breakfast-room door that Pavel, the major-domo, suddenly appeared from an alcove to open the door for her.

Her brother Lev and his wife were already at breakfast, and Irina, as she ate, was looking through the small pile of letters which had been delivered in anticipation of their arrival from Ryazan the night before. She rose to exchange a good morning kiss with her sister-in-law, while Lev, who was serving himself at a side-table, came to assist her to a chair.

'I'm glad you've abandoned that silly cap,' he commented as he propped her crutches carefully against the table. 'It's about time you stopped playing the elderly widow living in seclusion and came back to real life. You're still a young and attractive female, you know, yet ever since that damned accident you've hidden away at Ryazan as if you're the family skeleton!'

'Don't scold, Lev,' Irina said softly. 'You know how hard it is for Tatya to go about. You should be pleased that she's come to Petersburg with us this time.'

'I am pleased,' Lev replied, sitting down to a light breakfast of cutlets, ham, cheese and bread. 'I don't mean to nag you, pet.' He smiled at his sister. 'And I hope you enjoy this visit enough to want to come again for the winter Season. It should be great fun this summer, what with the wedding and our reunion.'

'Well, the wedding, yes,' Irina put in. 'But your reunion—old soldiers refighting old battles! Why on earth is it a reunion, in any case? You've all seen each other dozens of times since 1812. Why is this time so particular?'

'Oh, didn't I tell you?' Lev chased an elusive piece of

ham across his plate. 'It was when we were at Vilna for the Christmas of 1812, just after we'd chased the French back over the border. There was Vladimir Karachev and his brother Vassily, and young Boris Kalinsky, Tatya's nephew, and me. Nikolai Volkhov wasn't with us because he hadn't recovered from the wound he got at Borodino. Vassily and I were leaving the Army, but Vladimir and Boris were staying in, and somebody said something about where would we all be in seven years— I can't remember who it was now—anyway, we all agreed we'd make a special effort to meet in the summer of 1820, so here we all are. At least, I hope we are. Vladimir's here, because his regiment is on garrison duty at the Peter-Paul Fortress, and Boris is in attendance on the Emperor, and Nikolai's here because it's his wedding. I don't know about Vassily. Come to think of it, no-one ever does know about Vassily!'

'Surely he'll come for the wedding, even if he's forgotten about the reunion,' Irina said. 'I hope so. I like Vassily—he's so amusing. You haven't met him, have you, Tatya?'

'Oddly enough, no. The only time he came to Ryazan was when I was away, but I've heard so much about him that I feel as if I know him. Do you think he'll come, Lev?'

Lev shrugged. 'I hope so, but he's such an elusive character . . . He's no patience with romance and weddings, and he goes off abroad so often. He may be out of Russia now, for all I know.'

'He travels a great deal,' Irina said a little enviously. She had always wanted to travel, but five children in seven years . . .

'He does things for the Foreign Ministry,' Lev said vaguely. 'He has a gift for languages. I hope he does come . . . It'll do him good to see Nikolai happy at last.'

'It will do us all good,' Tatya said. 'Poor Nikolai . . . all those dreadful, wretched years when he was married to Anna, and then when she died and he was so lost and unable to respond to anyone . . . It's wonderful to know that he's found someone to make him happy at last.' There was nothing in her voice but pleasure in her old friend's new-found contentment, but both Lev and Irina gave her an anxious glance, remembering that at one time she had been very fond of Prince Nikolai herself.

There was a few minutes' silence while they all continued with their breakfast, and then Lev said, 'You seem to have a good deal of correspondence there, Sparrow. I didn't think there'd be anyone much in Petersburg at the end of May.'

'They're mostly from people who are here for the wedding,' Irina replied. 'There's a note from Maria Kirova asking us to dine this evening to meet Nikolai's bride, and another from Borovikovsky about our portrait.' (Lev had declared his intention of having a double portrait of himself and Irina painted while they were in St Petersburg, and had chosen the most fashionable painter for the commission.) 'He would like us to sit for him for an hour or so in the afternoon two or three times a week. I suppose that's all right?'

'It's a good thing we left the children in the country,' Lev commented. Irina looked a little sad at recalling that she was so far from her three little boys and twin girls, but made no reply.

'I could have looked after them while you went for your sittings,' Tatya said.

'That's precisely why we left them at home!' Lev replied with a grin. 'You need to rest a little in the afternoon, not be driven demented by those imps! Besides, you'll be coming with us on those expeditions Boris has planned.'

Tatya smiled in reply, but she wondered privately what likelihood there was of her being able to go on any of those expeditions. It was so difficult to get in and out of a carriage, and her wheelchair was such a heavy, clumsy thing. It didn't seem to have occurred to the others that she would not even be able to go to the wedding service. If only Lev could carry her, but his left arm was almost useless after two severe wounds, and the servants were always infected by her own nervousness when they tried to lift her.

Presently, Irina went off to consult Pavel about some domestic matters, and Lev finished his tea and repaired to the stables, saying something about one of the horses seeming a trifle lame when they arrived last night. Tatya sat on in the parlour, eating a croissant in an absent-minded fashion, having nothing in particular to do, but when the clock in the corner chimed ten, she realised that the servants would be waiting to clear the table, and reached for her crutches. Lev had put them a little too far away from her, and they slipped as she touched them and fell to the floor with a clatter, half under the table and both quite out of reach.

She looked at them helplessly, and stretched out her sound left leg, but it was inches short of the nearer crutch. Perhaps if she got down on the floor . . . Carefully, she eased herself off the chair and down on to her left knee, then reached out for the crutches, but they were both out of reach. She stretched further and touched one, but her hand slipped on the polished floor, knocked both even further away, and she fell almost full-length.

'Oh dear!' she exclaimed, at a loss what to do. Without one of the crutches, she was unable to get up again, unless somehow she could pull herself up by the chair. Before she could try, the door behind her opened and, thinking one of the servants had entered, she said in Russian, 'Please help me!' her voice raw with embarrassment.

'I thought . . .' a strange voice began in French. 'Yes, of course,' and she was seized by the waist and lifted bodily, set on her left foot, and then the newcomer slipped an arm about her waist and held her propped against his own body. She looked up and saw that he was a tall, slimly-built man with a thin, humorous face, green eyes, and the reddest hair she had ever seen.

'Vassily Karachev!' she exclaimed. 'You must be!'

He laughed. 'And you must be Tatya—no not Orlova—Kalinskaya, isn't it? Boris Mikhailovich's wicked uncle's widow? I suppose you recognised me by my hair.'

'Yes.' She found herself smiling back at him, and then realised that he was holding her in a close embrace and was made self-conscious by that and by the humiliation of the predicament in which he had found her, and said bitterly, 'I suppose you recognised me by my lameness.'

'No.' He looked surprised. 'By your eyes. You're very much like Lev, you know—or as much as a beautiful woman can be like a handsome man.'

She met his eyes, disconcerted by his self-possessed manner in such an odd situation, and found that they were twinkling with a mixture of interest and laughter. 'What were you trying to do?' he asked.

'I knocked my crutches down and they slid out of reach. I couldn't get up again.'

'Where were you intending to go?'

'To the garden room.'

Without any more ado, he picked her up like a child and carried her towards the door. She gripped his coat in a panic, stiffening in his arms, and he paused, saying gently, 'I won't drop you! I'm a great deal stronger than I look, and you don't weigh more than a feather! Just put your arm about my shoulders and relax, and you'll be perfectly safe.'

She obeyed nervously, and he carried her out of the room, along the wide corridor, and into the garden-room, obviously knowing his way about the house very well.

Tatya had always made the garden-room her head-quarters in this house. It was a very pleasant room, with half-open long glazed doors on the left-hand side as one entered, looking out on the formal garden a few steps below. The furniture was a scattering of shapely satin-wood chairs and tables and a sofa, upholstered in pale green velvet, and a matching, elegant daybed, which Lev had ordered specially for her. A white porcelain stove occupied the far right-hand corner, and there was a tall breakfront bookcase between it and the door. Vassily put her down carefully on the daybed, and then went to look at the books like a homing-pigeon.

'There's nothing very exciting there,' she said, remembering that he was a great bibliophile.

'I'm sorry—I can't resist books.' He turned back to her, drew a chair a little nearer to her, and, in response to her gesture of invitation, sat down. She noticed how naturally graceful all his movements were, without being in the least effeminate. He was informally dressed in a cream silk Russian tunic, high-necked and full-sleeved, close-fitting dark blue trousers and soft leather boots, and she looked him over covertly, having heard so much about him, and thinking how odd it was that no-one had thought to mention that he had such a beautifully-proportioned body.

After a few seconds, she realised that he was looking at her with equal interest, and as she met his eyes, he deliberately let them wander over her face with an admiration which at one time she would have accepted unthinkingly, for it had been an everyday occurrence. It was unmistakable, even after five years, and it gave her a little thrill of pleasure.

There was a small work-table beside her, with embroidery and books ready for her amusement, and he suddenly leaned forward and picked up the topmost volume, looked at the title-page and said, 'You read Russian, then? So many females of our class think it improper or something of the sort.'

'I know,' Tatya replied. 'Such a silly attitude, isn't it? One should be able to use the language of one's own country, even if French is more fashionable.'

He nodded agreement. 'I didn't know that Lev was bringing you to Petersburg. I'd heard that you seldom go anywhere now, but I'm glad to see that you haven't altogether lost your taste for worldly pleasures!'

She managed a strained smile. 'It's difficult, you see. I'd like to go about more, but Lev can't carry me because of his arm, and I'm so silly and nervous when the servants try. I have a wheel-chair, but it's an awkward thing, and someone has to push it. It's all very embarrassing for everyone, so it's easier to stay at home . . .' She stopped, surprised at how easily it had all slipped out.

'And the crutches?'

She looked away and pleated a small section of her skirt between her fingers. 'They're the worst of all. I hate anyone to see me . . . so grotesque . . .' A nervous gesture finished the sentence.

'I suppose you've come for Nikolai's wedding?' He changed the subject smoothly, so she was uncertain whether he had done so deliberately.

'Yes, but now I find that I can't even go to that,' she said flatly, hoping she did not sound too self-pitying or complaining.

'Can't, or don't wish to?' he asked casually.

'Of course I wish to!' she replied, disconcerted.

'You might have married him yourself at one time.' He sounded quite impersonal.

'Oh, years ago! That was a schoolgirl infatuation! We've both changed so much since then. I'm still fond of him, of course—he's such a fine man—but I wouldn't marry him now . . . I truly would like to go, but it's to be in the Cathedral of the Winter Palace . . .'

He made a comical grimace and said, 'Now, that could hardly be more inconsiderate! What is it—sixty steps in that staircase, at least? Crowds of people—guards of honour all over the place—half a mile of galleries . . . I see the difficulty! Never mind—I'll think of something.' He sounded quite serious and confident, and she was half-inclined to think that he meant it, but he immediately went off on quite another tack and said, 'It's a wonder that I'm here in time myself. Vladimir wrote to tell me about it, and the letter chased me the whole length of Norway. I'd meant to come to Petersburg this summer, of course, but the wedding was to have been just after Easter, and I thought I'd missed it. However, what with one thing and another and Alexander Pavlovich, it was postponed until the end of this month, and I'm here in time after all.'

Tatya was not sure what the Emperor Alexander had to do with the postponement, but she confined her reply to, 'It's as well that it had to be later, or half the guests would have been in difficulties coming to it during the Spring thaw. Norway, though? What were you doing there?'

'Oh, this and that . . .' he replied evasively. 'And then I had a sudden impulse to see a whale . . .' Before he could explain, the door was flung open and Lev irrupted into the room. Vassily stood up to greet him and was engulfed in a bear-like hug.

'Vassily! No-one seemed to know if you'd be here or not! I'm very glad to see you again! Irina!' in a loud bellow, 'Irina! Vassily Sergeivich is here!'

Irina came in, her face alight with pleasure, and Vassily kissed her hand and then her cheek with a great deal of elegant charm which Tatya, momentarily forgotten on her daybed, found very attractive to see. Lev suddenly recalled that she had never met Vassily before, and began to introduce him formally, then stopped and said rather lamely, 'But you've already presented yourself, I suppose.'

'Well, we couldn't sit about gazing politely at nothing in particular and waiting for someone to come in and set us free to speak, could we?' Vassily asked solemnly.

'Where are you staying?' Irina asked when the preliminary exchange of news had finished.

'At Nikolai's,' Vassily replied. 'Marisha Kirova and Boris' sister Olga are there too, as they're to attend the bride, and there isn't really room for Olga at the Kirovs' house. Er . . .' he hesitated, and then continued in a more serious tone, 'There's someone else there as well, and I've really come this morning as a sort of ambassador on his behalf.' He paused again, and there was naturally a little stir of interest. 'Nikolai would like to bring him to see you all this afternoon, but he's a little nervous about it as he's not sure if you know of his existence.'

'Ilya?' asked Lev.

Vassily nodded. Irina and Tatya exchanged a questioning glance, which Vassily intercepted and he said, 'Nikolai's son. You didn't know?'

'No,' replied Tatya. 'I'd no idea that Nikolai had a son . . . not Anna's child, surely?'

'No, it's more complicated than that. You recall, of course, that Nikolai left Anna—oh, when would it be? About 1810, I suppose—when her general unfaithfulness finally sickened him. He was very withdrawn after that, and when he was so badly wounded in 1812, his souls at White Gates were very worried about him—you know how the peasants on the country estates are about the master, especially if he happens to be a good one! For months, he had a very tenuous hold on life, spiritually, if not physically, and they were afraid that he'd just give up and die simply because he had nothing to live for. So they gave him a child.'

'That's all very well,' Lev said as Vassily paused again. 'I didn't know all this, because Nikolai's never talked about it, but the boy's obviously his get—he's just like him!'

'Oh, Nikolai's his father—no doubt about that! They were very clever really—amazing how resourceful these simple folk can be! They knew he was so drugged against the pain of his wound and so wretched that he hardly knew what he was doing sometimes, so they picked out a few healthy young virgins who waited their opportunity, and one of them managed to—er—seduce him, in a way . . . Very successfully! Ilya was born a few months after Anna's accident, when she broke her back and lost that love-child she was trying to foist on Nikolai.'

'But why . . .' Tatya began. 'I mean, why keep it a secret all this time—more than six years—and then suddenly bring the child to Petersburg now, just when he's going to be married again?'

'Because Tanya Kirova, bless her for a sensible female, has managed to piece together what actually happened and convince Nikolai that he needn't feel a great burden of guilt about the boy's existence, and now

Ilya's been legitimised by the Emperor, and can take his
place as Nikolai's son and heir.'

'You mean that Tanya is willing to let him come before
any children she may give him?' Irina exclaimed.

'Yes. It was her own suggestion! She's a remarkable
person!' Vassily replied with a faint note of something in
his voice which only Tatya noticed, and she looked at
him curiously. He was what . . . ? thirty-three or so?
Still a bachelor, supposedly much opposed to marriage
after some unfortunate love-affair in his youth. Perhaps
he wished it might be he who was to marry Tanya
Ivanovna Kirova in the Winter Palace on Thursday
instead of Nikolai. On the other hand, he'd only just met
her, and one mustn't let one's imagination run away with
one. Feeling that she should say something, she put in
quietly, 'After all, if Nikolai's first marriage had been a
happy one, and Ilya was the child of it, no-one would
think it strange that Tanya Ivanovna should accept
him—in fact, it would expected of her! It's strange to
think of Nikolai with a bastard, though—he's such a
moral man!'

'It's an unusual case,' Vassily pointed out. 'And besides, he isn't, if he's been legitimised. I'm sure you've
no objection to Nikolai bringing him here, have you?'

'Of course not!' Irina exclaimed. 'Surely Nikolai
didn't think we would?'

Vassily grinned fleetingly. 'He's had a very sore conscience about the boy for a long time. After all, he is a
very moral man, and he didn't understand that his souls
had intended the whole affair to happen just as it did!
His Rose had managed to enlighten him on that, but
there's still a certain shyness to be overcome.'

'He and his son will be very welcome in this house,'
said Irina firmly. 'Who is Rose, by the way?'

'Oh, that's what he calls Tanya, for some reason which
no-one has thought to explain to me! Everyone else
seems to have caught the habit from him, which is just as
well, or we'd have endless confusion between the two
Tatyanas—Tanya and Tatya!' at which Tatya smiled

ruefully, for her mother had been known as Tanya, and
she recalled the problems which had resulted from that.

Vassily left soon after, promising to return for a longer
call during the afternoon, and it was only after he had
gone that Tatya remembered her crutches, abandoned
under the breakfast-parlour table, and rang the little bell
on her work-table to summon a servant to fetch them.

'How did you manage to get here without them?'
asked Lev when they were safely in place on the floor by
her side. 'I left you in the breakfast-parlour, and I
assumed you'd used them to move to this room.'

'I knocked them on the floor, out of reach,' Tatya
said. 'I got down on the floor to try to get them, and
couldn't. Vassily came in while I was floundering about
. . . I suppose whoever opened the front door to him
thought you were still there, and he's so informal—he
just came in unannounced . . .' She realised that she was
whittering away foolishly in order to avoid the rest of the
tale. 'He picked me up and carried me in here,' she
finished firmly and thought how awful it sounded—Lev
would surely be annoyed that she'd let a stranger pick
her up and carry her . . .

'Oh, just what he would do!' was all Lev said. 'He's
extraordinarily strong for such a slight-looking fellow.
You should see him stripped—beautiful, like an antique
statue! Sinews like steel, though! And you should see
him dance—well, you will, of course—make sure you
save him a dance or two at the wedding ball—you won't
regret . . .' He broke off suddenly, appalled, as he
realised that Tatya would never dance again, with Vassily or anyone else. 'I—I'm sorry . . .' he stammered
awkwardly, and there was a tight little silence for a few
seconds as Tatya bit her lip and tried unsuccessfully to
smile, as if she, who had always loved to dance, really
didn't mind that it was no longer possible.

As the silence became agonising, Lev, casting around
for a means of ending it, caught sight of a large black cat
which had entered unobtrusively from the garden and
was regarding them placidly from a broad ledge on the

stove. 'What the devil are you doing in here?' he asked it, and it blinked pale peridot eyes at him in reply.

'That's Vron,' Irina said. 'You remember—he always sits in here when he's not working.'

'Working!' snorted Lev. 'Whoever heard of a cat working?'

Vron descended from the stove with a thump and made a dignified exit into the garden, his stiffly-held tail an acid comment on the ingratitude of persons who failed to appreciate the labour involved in controlling the rodent population of the stables, to which he now returned.

He had, however, provided an escape for the humans from an embarrassing moment, and Lev, after a brief hesitation, decided not to plunge them back into it by trying to explain that he had not really forgotten that his sister was crippled, and instead began to talk about the things he had noticed during his morning stroll about the gardens. Tatya picked up her embroidery and began to stitch the shaded petals of the rose she was working, and Irina fell into a quiet daydream about what her children might be doing.

After luncheon, they returned to the garden-room and awaited their expected callers. There was a very grand salon upstairs, of course, but they had no wish to involve Tatya in the business of getting there, and in any case, the garden room was much more pleasant for an informal summer occasion.

Vladimir Karachev was the first to arrive, and Tatya thought how odd it seemed that he and Vassily should be brothers, for Vladimir was a very tall, dark, taciturn man, with regular features marred by an almost total lack of expression, which she was sure that he cultivated purposely to hide his shyness. He was well-built, and looked magnificent in the dark green uniform of Lieutenant-Colonel of a Line regiment, quite unlike the quicksilver lightness of Vassily, who was, surprisingly, the elder by a year. His friends knew very well that his stiff, typical army officer manner covered a keen, intelligent mind and a strong character, but people who knew him less well were often misled by it.

He kissed the ladies' hands and received a friendly buffet from Lev, with whom he was soon engaged in military reminiscence, but when the next arrivals entered, he broke off in mid-sentence and went to greet them with unexpected eagerness, and Tatya, watching with interest, saw that the attraction was Olga Kalinskaya, who had come with her brother Boris.

Boris Kalinsky was much as he had always been, a slim, good-looking young man with smooth dark hair and large, expressive, almost black eyes, which he used to devastating effect on impressionable females. He had a strong affection for Tatya, which she believed was largely due to a sympathetic but unspoken understanding of how wretchedly unhappy she had been during her brief marriage to his uncle. It was a comfort to know that someone perhaps knew a little about it, but a relief that he never attempted to talk to it.

After greeting the others, he gravitated to Tatya's side and murmured a few sentences about his pleasure at seeing her again in Petersburg after so long, but she noticed that he glanced with some anxiety at his sister.

Olga bore a strong resemblance to Boris, with a slender figure and a captivating heart-shaped face, dominated by her big dark eyes. Tatya remembered her as a very shy girl, who had hardly been into Society, but now, at nineteen, she seemed to have changed a great deal, and certainly not for the better, for she flashed her eyes provocatively at Lev and turned her back on Vladimir with a silly little flounce which set her bunched curls bobbing and made him look blanker than ever and chew the edge of his heavy black moustache—a sure sign of anxiety.

Irina rang for tea, and under cover of the entry of the samovar and various loaded trays, Tatya leaned towards Boris, who had taken a chair beside her, and asked softly. 'What's happened to Olga?'

Boris grimaced. 'She was as sweet and natural as ever

when she came here in the winter, but she's attracted a deal of attention, and it's turned her head, I'm afraid. I could shake her, but she won't take any notice of anything I say to her. There are half a dozen young idiots dangling after her, and she flirts and rolls her eyes at them in the silliest fashion—just look at her!'

'And Vladimir?' Tatya asked. The Colonel was standing between Olga and the window, half-turned away, absent-mindedly stroking the black cat, who had crept in to lie on the sunny window-sill. He was listening to Olga's affected chatter with a marked lack of expression.

'He's very patient with her, but I just hope she doesn't lose him through her silliness. She will keep flaunting her conquests at him, as if she wants to make him jealous, and of course, he just puts up the shutters. You know how reserved he is.'

'But he's really interested?'

Boris gave a mischievous smile. 'When she arrived, he hadn't seen her for two or three years—he took one look, and—well, pole-axed is the term, I believe! He's never been a great ladies' man, except for—well, there was someone, but that was—oh, six years ago. I don't think he knows how to flirt.'

Vladimir turned his head and looked at Tatya, then walked across in a purposeful manner and flicked his eyebrows at Boris, who promptly excused himself and went to hand teacups, while the Colonel seated himself squarely in the vacated chair and said, 'It's good to see you again, Tatya Petrovna,' with a momentary gleam of very white, even teeth under the moustache. He had a deep, pleasant voice and spoke with a simple and unmistakable genuineness.

Tatya smiled at him and replied in kind, and then plunged in boldly, 'Boris has just been telling me how silly Olga is being. It must be very trying for you.'

Vladimir made a sound between a snort and a sigh. 'I'm tempted to put her across my knee and spank her, but one can't—wouldn't be proper. Besides, I've no formal claim on her. I suppose it's to be expected. She's had a very dull life, buried in the country, and Society's all been a bit too much for her. She's discovered the pleasures of *flirting*, that's the trouble. I'm no hand at it myself, so she thinks I'm dull.'

'That's all it is, though?'

'Oh, yes. On her side, at least,' he hesitated. 'You remember Sergei Dmitriev?'

'Only too well!' Tatya exclaimed with the sensation of distaste which Prince Nikolai's dissolute brother-in-law always aroused in her. 'Oh dear! Is he one of her flirts?'

Vladimir nodded. 'Afraid so. Trouble is, I think he means marriage. Her fortune, of course. Up to his ears in debt, as usual, and his father won't bail him out any more.'

'Ah, so that's it!' Tatya exclaimed. 'He came to Ryazan during Lent, visiting his cousins, and took the trouble to call on us "to renew old attachments" as he put it!'

'You?' Vladimir's eyebrows rose.

'Yes. Apparently my fortune is still desirable.' She could not help a note of bitterness creeping into her voice, but Vladimir failed to notice it as he was diverted by the entrance of his brother Vassily, who paused fractionally in the doorway and looked around the room, a smile on his thin face, before greeting Irina. He exchanged a few words with Lev in passing and kissed Olga's hand. She gazed up at him with a languishing look which banished his smile and made him look quite stern for a moment, and then he made a laughing comment on the elaboration of Boris' cravat, waved a casual hand to his brother, and made his bow to Tatya, kissing her fingers with his eyes on her face.

He had changed into a dark green coat and waistcoat with buff trousers and mirror-bright hessians, and was so exquisitely tailored that he made even Boris look provincial. He exchanged a straight, serious look with his brother, who rose, bowed to Tatya and returned to Olga's vicinity, and Vassily settled into his chair, crossed one leg over the other, and, with perfect timing, directed

Tatya's attention to the door with a gesture of one
elegant hand just as Prince Nikolai entered, hand-in-
hand with a small boy.

The transformation in the Prince was remarkable. He
had completely lost the bleak, lifeless look which he had
worn for so long, and now appeared younger than his
thirty-odd years, smiling with self-conscious pride as he
led his son into the room and began to take him round to
make his bow to the adults. Tatya watched with interest,
seeing the resemblance between the two, for Ilya was a
miniature copy of the Prince, with the same brown hair
and vivid blue eyes, even the same way of carrying his
head. Something made her glance at Vassily, who was
watching too, with an odd half-smile on his face.

Under his father's guidance, Ilya made a creditable
bow to each of the adults, reaching Tatya and Vassily
last. She gave him her hand with the gentle, radiant
smile which she had never seen in her mirror, and, after
a glance at his father for reassurance, he gingerly took it
in the tips of his fingers and kissed it, then, overcome
with the novelty of meeting all these tall grown-up
people, he felt a sudden need to take refuge and went,
not to the Prince, but to Vassily, butting his head into
that gentleman's waistcoat in a fit of shyness. Vassily put
one arm round his shoulders and looked at Tatya as if
daring her to laugh at the child.

'He's a charming boy!' Tatya said to Prince Nikolai.
'How old is he?'

'Six,' the Prince replied. 'I'm delighted to be able to
present him to you, Tatya Petrovna, and more than
delighted to see you in Petersburg again after so long.'

She smiled up at him. 'I'm pleased to see you so well
and happy. I had to come and see you married.'

The Prince laughed. 'Such a business! We meant to be
married very quietly, immediately after Easter, but the
Emperor declared that he must hold the crown for me,
and began to arrange all kinds of things. Of course, it
was eventually pointed out to him that it would be my
second marriage, so there couldn't be a full ceremony,

and he started a campaign to have my marriage to Anna declared void! The Holy Synod wouldn't agree to that, of course, but they conceded that there was some doubt about whether Anna ever intended to keep her marriage vows, so they've agreed to allow us the full rites.'

'Sounds like simony or nepotism or something,' Boris commented.

Prince Nikolai laughed. 'Alexander Pavlovich isn't my uncle!' he protested.

'Judging by your father's resemblance to Peter the Great, more likely your third cousin,' Vassily said sardonically. Prince Nikolai looked a trifle taken aback at that, but smiled and replied, 'Whatever he is, he's delayed my wedding quite appallingly, for by the time he'd settled the matter of the ceremony, the thaw had started, and we had to wait for the roads to be fit for our guests to travel, and then his erysipelas flared up again . . . However, on Thursday it will be, God willing!'

CHAPTER
TWO

TATYA was surprised to hear how easily the Prince, who had always seemed unable to speak of his troubles with Anna, now mentioned her blatant and continual unfaithfulness quite casually, as if it no longer mattered in the least, and she wondered if she would ever be able to refer to her own disastrous marriage so easily.

'There's a great improvement, isn't there?' Vassily's light, ironic voice said, almost in her ear. 'You'll understand why when you meet his Rose.'

Prince Nikolai had moved away to talk to Irina, leaving Ilya still standing in the circle of Vassily's arm, but he was now peering out sideways, curiosity overcoming his shyness.

'Can you hear my watch ticking?' Vassily asked him. He shook his head.

Vassily drew out the watch and held it so that Tatya could see it as well, and the three heads drew close over it as they looked at the wreath of olive and laurel engraved on the case.

'The Emperor gave it to me at the end of the war,' Vassily said. 'The first end, that is, in 1814. There's laurel for victory and olive for peace, you see.' He touched the button which opened the case and revealed the dial. In the centre, behind the elaborately-cut hands, was a crowned A in tiny rubies, surrounded by a circle of little flying doves enamelled white on a sky-blue background. Another little button set the repeater mechanism playing a faint, sweet chime.

'It's very beautiful,' Ilya said in a small gruff voice.

'*Belle*.' Vassily remarked impersonally, correcting the child's French. '*La montre*—neuter in Russian, but feminine in French—silly, isn't it! Your French is very good, Ilya.'

'My father says,' Ilya replied earnestly, with a touching emphasis on the first two words, 'that a gentleman should speak French as if it were his own language and ride a horse as if he could ride before he could walk.'

'Very true,' Vassily agreed.

'My father says,' Ilya continued inexorably, 'that you can stand on your head.' His bright blue eyes were fixed on Vassily's face with hopeful expectancy.

Vassily removed his watch and chain and handed them to Tatya for safe-keeping, then, with a quiet, 'Excuse me,' he stood up, took off his coat and moved a little way across the room to give himself more space. Then he bent over, placed his hands on the floor and stood on his head without any visible effort, perfectly steady, his lithe, slim body quite straight.

Ilya and Tatya watched entranced, and the others, who had been talking in a group round the tea-table, turned to watch.

'Mountebank!' said Boris jocularly.

'Only by request,' Vassily replied imperturbably. After a few seconds, he returned to an upright position, looking a little more flushed than usual as he resumed his coat and his seat.

'Time to go now, Ilya,' said Prince Nikolai. 'Make your adieux.'

Obediently, the child shook hands with Vassily and thanked him politely, bowed to Tatya, who impulsively drew him to her and kissed his cheek, which he didn't seem to mind. He crossed over to Vladimir, who was again standing by the window, and smiled up at him. Vladimir returned the smile, and suddenly looked remarkably handsome.

'I shall be a soldier,' Ilya said confidingly. 'Goodbye Vladim' Sergeivich. Goodbye cat,' to Vron, who yawned indifferently. He went round the rest of the company, much more confidently now, and Tatya was pleased to see that Olga forgot her affectations long enough to smile and give him her hand in a very pleasant manner.

Prince Nikolai also made his bows, and when he and the boy had gone, Tatya turned back to Vassily, gave him his watch, and said, 'Did you say the Emperor gave it you?'

'Yes. I was slightly involved in the peace negotiations.'

'In Paris?'

'Yes.'

'You travel a great deal, I believe?'

'Not as much as I used to. The Foreign Ministry occasionally finds a use for me, and sometimes I feel an urge to go and look at something or other.'

'A whale, for instance?'

He laughed. 'Yes, and a fine fool I made of myself over that! I went all the way to the far north of Norway, right into the Arctic, meaning to go to Spitzbergen, and didn't think to mention to anyone what I was after until I reached Tromsø, which is practically Ultima Thule, and only there did I discover that the whaling season is in the summer, not the winter at all. Whales are like swallows—they migrate!' His hands sketched the movement of wings, conjuring up an absurd image of a flying whale. 'Still, it was an interesting journey, and no worse than winter travelling at home.'

'Do they have towns there? I've never heard of any, except Christiana, of course.'

He began to describe some of the towns he had visited in Norway, and Tatya listened with deep interest, for he had a gift of painting a scene in words, a lively, humorous manner, and a fund of interesting anecdotes. When Boris came to take leave, Tatya realised with something of a shock that she had been listening to Vassily for nearly an hour, quite oblivious of the others.

Apparently Vladimir had been at least temporarily restored to Olga's favour, for she was now talking to him, her hand resting on his sleeve, with very little of her former coquettish manner. The tall soldier sat beside her

with his head bent, listening with full attention, and
Tatya, who was fond of him, said a little prayer for him
inside her head.

Vassily, recalled to a sense of the proprieties, also
took his leave. 'You'll be at the Kirovs' tomorrow night,'
he said, more as a confirmation than a question.

Tatya's face clouded. 'I'm afraid not,' she said sadly.
'All their reception rooms are on the first floor, and I
can't manage the stairs, you see.'

'No problem,' he replied lightly. 'Come and enjoy
yourself.' He kissed her hand and left with the others
after a few more minutes of conversation with Lev and
Irina.

Before she fell asleep that night, Tatya wondered how
seriously she might take Vassily's 'no problem' about
visiting the Kirovs', and his promise to think of a way of
enabling her to attend the wedding, if it was a promise.
'Just a casual remark, I suppose,' she thought with a
sigh. 'I'd like to go so much, but I can't face it . . . He's
very kind—how interesting that Ilya went to him like
that.'

She half-hoped that there might be a message of some
sort from him or from the Kirovs next day, but there was
nothing, and when Irina and Lev returned from Borovikovsky's studio and went to change for the dinner-party,
she said, 'You'll make my excuses, won't you?'

'But you're coming!' Lev protested.

'How can I?' She twisted her fingers together in a
manner only too familiar to her brother, who recognised
it as a signal that she was unable to face the matter under
discussion, 'I can't drag myself up their stairs with all the
guests and servants watching.'

Lev sighed. 'I'm sorry, pet. If only I had two good
arms . . .'

Tatya smiled and pretended that it didn't matter, but
when they had gone, she lay on the green daybed and
cried quietly for a time.

'Oh, it's no use, Vron,' she said to the cat, which
mewed enquiringly in reply. 'I shouldn't have come. The

journey was dreadful, with all the getting in and out of the carriage and people staring at the inns, and I might just as well have stayed in Ryazan, because I can't go anywhere.' She wiped her eyes and tried to concentrate on one of the new French novels which had arrived that morning from Belizard's, while the clock ticked louder and louder and Vron purred on the window-sill.

Suddenly, the garden door opened, and Vassily entered, closing the door behind him and smiling at her surprised expression. He was in evening dress, dark green, with a rich brocade waistcoat, his hair blazing as it caught the early evening sun.

'I expected to meet you at the Kirovs',' he said. 'I was poised in the entrance, all ready for you, and you didn't come.'

'I couldn't,' she replied. 'I didn't think you were serious.'

'I'm always serious!' he protested, looking anything but. 'You must come or the dinner will be ruined.'

'But I'm not dressed.'

He surveyed her thoughtfully. She was wearing an afternoon dress of lilac shot silk with a lace-trimmed cape and frilled sleeves to the elbow. 'You seem very adequately dressed to me,' he observed. 'It's quite informal—just a few friends. There's Maria and Alexei, of course, Fedor and a pretty blonde creature, Boris and Marisha.' He was counting them off on his fingers. 'Volodya and Olga, Lev and Irina, Nikolai and his Rose, and myself.' He paused significantly, holding up his fingers, and after a moment, Tatya realised what he meant.

'Thirteen!' she exclaimed. 'Oh, dear!'

'So you must come, you see. Besides, I've no-one to talk to.'

'Well . . .' she began, and without more ado, he picked her up and made for the door. 'But I'm not . . . I haven't a shawl . . . my reticule . . . !' He swept her round in a circle, paused long enough for her to snatch her shawl from the end of the daybed and her reticule from the work-table, and then made off with her through the garden to the stableyard, where his carriage was waiting. He seemed to slide into it sideways, still holding her and without the slightest difficulty, so that she found herself sitting in one corner before she realised what was happening. He called to the driver to go, and sank down beside her, laughing.

'There—expert abduction!' he said. 'Simple, wasn't it?'

'Y-yes,' she replied uncertainly, wondering what would happen at the Kirovs', but it was just as simple there. When the carriage drew up before the little house in Troitskaya Street, he carried her into the house and up the stairs to the salon, and everyone was so pleased to see her that she quite forgot to think about her dress or her unconventional mode of arrival, and thoroughly enjoyed the evening.

Alexei Kirov and his wife, Maria, were old friends, related to both Prince Nikolai and to Boris, and 'Rose' Kirova, whom Tatya had not met before, was Alexei's cousin. She was a tall, slender female, older than Tatya expected, with a wide, pleasantly-smiling mouth, large brown eyes flecked with little gold lights, and a warm, lively interest in everything. It was happily obvious that she adored Nikolai, who could hardly take his eyes off her for a moment. She greeted Tatya with a very genuine warmth, and they both soon felt that they were firm friends.

The 'pretty little blonde' was Dorya Tutaeva, the daughter of a neighbour, who said little, but occupied all the attention of Fedor, Alexei's only son, a brash young fellow of twenty-one. Marisha Kirova, the elder daughter of the family, was now seventeen, a quiet, self-possessed, pretty girl, who had just become betrothed to Boris Kalinsky, much to the relief of everyone, for they had been waiting two years for Alexei to decide that she was old enough.

Olga Kalinskaya had dropped most of her silly, affected manner as no-one here was likely to be impressed by it, and was absorbed in listening to Vladimir telling her some amusing incident in his routine duties at the fortress.

'You see how much I needed you,' Vassily murmured to Tatya as he carried her in to dinner. 'They're all so wrapped up in each other that they hardly think to throw me a word!' This was not in the least true, for the two married couples talked to him quite a lot, and the others were too well-mannered not to join in the general conversation, but after dinner, Tatya found herself somehow a little apart from the main group, seated with him on a sofa while he made low-voiced comments which were amusing without being unkind.

'Extraordinary about Boris and Marisha,' he said. 'She decided to marry him when she was about ten, you know, but he always had a strong predilection for little porcelain blondes—that one Fedor is showing off to would have suited him very well. I didn't think he'd finally succumb to a brunette!'

'He seems to have stopped flirting, too,' Tatya commented.

'Well, of course! It was only ever a minor pastime, not his life's work! I've no doubt he'll make a model husband.' Vassily sounded a trifle sardonic. 'Volodya intends to do the same, I'm afraid.'

'No-one calls him Volodya!' Tatya exclaimed.

'I do—it annoys him,' Vassily had a wicked twinkle in his eyes, but it disappeared as he said more soberly, 'I could strangle that silly little Olga, you know! She's playing games, and he'll wait patiently until she's finished. If he wasn't so revoltingly gentlemanly, I'd tell him to carry her off and knock some sense into her, but he treats her as if she's spun glass, and of course, she thinks he's dull.'

'Is he dull?' Tatya asked cautiously. She knew very well that in conversation among friends he was not at all dull, but that was not quite what she meant.

'I have it on the best possible authority that he's an excellent lover,' Vassily replied solemnly, but with that little gleam of amusement in his eyes. 'But of course, the idiot won't make love to an innocent girl, I shall have to take him in hand, I suppose.'

Tatya wondered how he proposed to do this, but before she could ask, Prince Nikolai came over to them, drew up a chair, and said, 'Tatya, my dear, we're wondering how best to get you to the ceremony tomorrow.'

'That's all arranged,' Vassily said casually. 'I'll drive with her from Lev's house and carry her as I did this evening. Perfectly simple.'

'If that would suit both of you, it does seem the simplest solution,' Prince Nikolai sounded a trifle disconcerted. 'To tell the truth, we've discussed all kinds of much more complicated methods, and narrowed it down to two large strong guardsmen, and either a ramp or rope and pulley to get your wheelchair up to the first floor, or Vladimir had offered to carry you—he's very strong, you know.'

'No stronger than I am,' Vassily's voice was the merest trifle acid. 'Anyway, he'd go red in the face and drop her!'

Prince Nikolai laughed, having heard similiar remarks several times before. 'Yes, Vassily, you may be right, but I'm concerned for Tatya's sake, not yours, and it might be as well to have your brother in reserve, in case you find the distances involved too much. Will you trust Vassily to carry you safely?' he asked Tatya seriously.

'Yes,' she replied, realising that, after the first few seconds in the breakfast-parlour, she had felt perfectly safe when Vassily carried her. 'Thank you, Vassily. I'd be very happy with your arrangement.'

'My pleasure,' Vassily made an elegant little seated bow.

Naturally enough, Tatya had some qualms about the arrangement before the time arrived to put it to the test, but these were mainly about people staring, and what might be said, so she told herself severely that she really wished to attend the wedding, and this was the least fussy way of doing so, and as Vassily was prepared to be so very obliging, she should be thankful and make the best of it.

The wedding ceremony was to take place in the late afternoon, followed by a dinner and a ball, and there was plenty of time to get ready for it. Nevertheless, the Orlov house was filled with a great scurrying all morning, and luncheon was a very hurried affair. Irina had spent an uncomfortable night in curl-papers, but her heavy, soft hair would never take a crisp curl, particularly in the slightly damp and salty atmosphere of St Petersburg, so she was forced to abandon the ringlets she had planned and return to her usual smooth coronet of plaits. There was a frenzied search through her jewel cases to find a tiara which would both suit the style and go with her new crimson satin gown.

Tatya had a lavender-grey velvet trimmed with a deep flounce of silver lace, and a falling collar of the same framing the deep décolleté. Once she had it on, she sat contemplating the result in the mirror with rather a solemn expression for several minutes. It looked well enough, and her shoulders and bosom were still very smooth and white. The high waistline showed off her slim, shapely figure very becomingly, and the Madonna hairstyle, parted in the centre and drawn smoothly to the sides, then cascading to the tips of her ears in little ringlets, with the back swept up in a raised puff on the crown, suited her oval face. A small tiara and a necklace of rubies gave the necessary touch of colour, but she felt that something more was needed.

While she was trying to think what it might be, one of the footmen provided the answer by knocking on the door and handing in a florist's box. When Elena re-moved the lid, she found inside a beautiful trail of little rosebuds, deep red, matching the rubies, and the perfect finishing touch when they were pinned carefully across her belled skirt. There was a card in the box, but all it had on it was a single letter B, and Tatya puzzled over it for some time. Who would send her flowers? In earlier days, she might have received a dozen or more such tributes from her admirers—Tatya's beaux, as her friends called them—but those days had ended five years ago. Who? Surely not Boris? He was most kind and attentive, more so than one would expect from a nephew-by-marriage, but six years her junior, and betrothed to Marisha Alexeievna. In any case, he would never send red roses! He was far too experienced to overlook the implied meaning!

She looked at the card again. The letter was a printed capital, not script. A small echo in her mind said, 'You read Russian, then?' Of course, in the Russian alphabet, B stood for V—Vassily? A little joke, something to divert and puzzle her? It seemed in character, both with his odd sense of humour, and also with his reputation as an accomplished, if evasive, flirt!

When they were ready at last, Irina, Tatya and Lev met together in the garden-room and surveyed the results of their labours with interest. Lev, of course, had simply stood still and let Josef, his valet, dress him up in his best Court dress, and very fine he looked in the well-cut coat and knee-breeches of wine-coloured cloth, a few shades darker than his wife's gown, with his red ribbon and star of the Order of Alexander Nevsky, and his little cross of St George nestling in the crisp folds of his cravat. The two ladies nodded approvingly at each other, and then Pavel announced Count Karachev, and Vassily came in with his quick, light step.

'Very charming!' he said. 'The belles of the ball, I'm convinced—especially you, Lev!'

'Oh, you'll put us all in the shade!' Lev replied, surveying him enviously. He was also in Court dress, in black doeskin with gold buttons set with emeralds. 'Who the devil is your tailor? Your breeches fit like a second skin. I suppose you can sit down?' with a sudden doubt.

'There'll be a decapitated tailor tomorrow if I can't!' Vassily observed. He carried Tatya out to his carriage, with Lev and Irina giving a great deal of unnecessary help and advice, and she was quite relieved when the vehicle drew away from the portico and turned north into the Gorokhavaya for the short drive to the Palace, leaving Irina and Lev to follow in their own carriage.

'Thank you for sending the flowers,' she said hesitantly.

He laughed. 'I wondered if you'd guess. I thought the puzzle might amuse you, and if you guessed wrong, the result could be entertaining! How fortunate that they're the right colour!' He had, of course, tipped one of the Orlovs' servants to find out what colour to order.

She touched one of the perfect little blooms. 'You're a very kind man.'

'You sound surprised.'

'One understands that you don't like females.' She darted a glance at his face, wondering if he was offended. He gave her a twisted little smile.

'I *like* them well enough, but I don't trust them. I take my pleasure where it's readily available and give the same in return, but nothing more. No involvement.' It was said gently, as if he were trying to explain something.

'Do you find that's enough?' Tatya asked, feeling obscurely sorry for him.

He looked away, out of the window. There was a slightly overlong pause, and then he replied reluctantly, 'No.'

Tatya didn't know what to say. She looked at him with her clear grey eyes serious with concern, and he met her gaze without the slightest trace of his usual smile, and she realised for the first time that his face was melancholy and almost haggard without it.

'You're in much the same case, I imagine,' he said. 'At least, you can't bring yourself to trust a man, can you? Boris has told me some things about your late and unlamented husband, his uncle—did you know that when Boris was a child, the man used to twist his arms and pinch his ears, pretending it was a game, but really to hurt him? It's not difficult to guess how a man like that might treat his wife!'

Tatya said nothing, but she looked away, twisting her hands together and turning pale at the memories which pushed into her mind.

'He wasn't normal, you know,' Vassily continued conversationally. 'I don't say you'd never meet another man like it, but they're not all that common. It's a kind of disease—the inability to feel pleasure except through another person's pain. I expect you haven't married again for fear that you'd have the same experience, but it's extremely unlikely. If you've anyone in mind, anyone you think you might marry if you could be sure, you've only to tell me, and I'll find out for you if you'd be safe with him.' He spoke in the casual tones of one offering to look out for a good horse or match a ribbon for her.

'Thank you,' she replied with a strong sense of unreality about the whole conversation. 'But there isn't anyone. Not now.'

'There was once, then?'

'Oh, more than once.' Suddenly, the strange conversation seemed quite natural. 'It's fifteen years since he died.'

'What a waste,' he murmured, as if to himself.

'And you?' Tatya was bold enough to ask.

'No-one,' he replied. 'It's easier for a man.'

The carriage turned out of Admiralty Square and passed along the river front of the Winter Palace, and he said, 'Nikolai's had a wheelchair provided for you as well, in case I get tired or sprain a wrist, I suppose, but you'll know it's readily available if you feel it would be more convenient. No doubt you'll wish to retire with the other ladies before the ball begins, and you mustn't mind telling me when you prefer it to being carried, or vice-versa. I'm always delighted to have a beautiful female in my arms!' His usual light, ironic mode of speech had returned, put on like the mask which she now knew it to be, and the humorous tone made her smile as the carriage mounted the ramp and drew up at the porte-cochère of the Palace.

A large crowd had collected on Palace Quay, largely composed of the idlers and strollers out enjoying the third consecutive day of early summer sunshine before the inevitable mist and rain returned. Tatya was painfully aware that if it had been necessary to rely on servants to lift her from the carriage and her crutches to enable her to drag herself up the great Jordan staircase, she would never have found the courage to go on, but Vassily managed it so easily and quickly that they were inside, through the vestibule and mounting the stairs almost before she realised that they had arrived.

Progress was slow, for Prince Nikolai had a very wide acquaintance, and it seemed that they had all stayed in or returned to St Petersburg at this unfashionable season to attend his wedding. Vassily carried her as if she was composed of feathers, unobtrusively resting a little of her weight on the balustrade when they were forced to a halt by the slowly-moving throng. She had plenty of time to look about her at the soldiers of Prince Nikolai's old regiment (now commanded by Vladimir) lining the staircase and standing as motionless as the great marble caryatids, the gleaming white plaster decorations, the gold baluster-pillars, and the six huge pink marble columns at the head of the double curve of Rastrelli's Baroque masterpiece.

Several people looked curiously at them as they passed through the long gallery above the central courtyard of the Palace, but Tatya decided that there was no sense in being self-conscious and spoiling the occasion for herself by wondering what they might think, when everyone had been to so much trouble to allow her to enjoy herself. This was much the most comfortable way of going about that she had tried since her accident, and if anyone thought it peculiar or shocking, well, let them think!

The Cathedral was not so named in the western sense, but in the Russian sense of a great church, and was the chapel of the Palace. It was ornately decorated with gilded cascades of plaster flowers, festoons, flying cher-

ubs and the cypher of the Empress Elisaveta. Soaring
tiers of candles supplemented the daylight, rendering
the atmosphere even more oppressive than it had
already been made by the throng of people and the
mingled smell of incense and perfumes. The iconostasis
towered up to a crucifix high in the lantern dome,
supported by tier upon tier of pillars, angels and cher-
ubs, the transparent icons, painted on glass, glowing
with light and impressing the fashionably-dressed guests
to a suitably reverent quietness.

A chair had been placed for Tatya quite near the
beautiful silver screen, very close, it appeared later, to
where the ladies of the Imperial family were to stand.
Vassily lowered her into it carefully and arranged her
skirts to show his roses to advantage in an impersonal
manner, then stood beside and a little behind her instead
of crossing to the men's side, positioning himself so that
no-one was likely to push past him to stand in front of her
and spoil her view.

Tatya said her prayers, then discreetly looked about
her, listening to the soft singing of the choir, smiling at
her friends, and observing the fashions, serenely aware
that her own gown was copied from the very latest Paris
fashion-plate by an excellent dressmaker, and as becoming to her as anything could be to a female past thirty.
'Two years past thirty' she told herself to check any
tendency to vanity, and set her mind to more suitable
thoughts for the place and the occasion.

The choir broke into a joyful anthem, and all heads
turned towards the door as the Imperial family entered,
informally as this was the bridal couple's grand occasion.
Alexander Pavlovich, leading the Empress Elisaveta by
the hand, was followed by his two younger brothers,
Nikolai with his wife, the Grand Duchess Alexandra,
and Mikhail, still unmarried and showing no inclination
to change his state, squiring the Empress Dowager,
Maria Fedorovna. Tatya was sorry to see how much the
Emperor had aged since she last saw him. His hair had
receded, his magnificent six-foot figure grown stout, and

he limped quite badly on his lame leg, but at least today he had cast aside his growing melancholia and was beaming happily about him as he acknowledged the bows and curtseys of the assembled guests.

There was a short silence, and then the choir again burst into song as the bridal procession entered and slowly advanced across the patterned wooden floor. Rose was in white, a beautiful figured silk with swansdown edging the skirt and the modest décolleté. Tatya had expected her to wear the magnificent Volkhov emeralds, but she had only a single strand of diamonds round her throat, and a ruby and emerald brooch in the shape of a rose pinned to her bodice. Her hair was arranged in a simple chignon and curls, with a wreath of little white flowers. A long velvet train was fastened to her shoulders with diamond clasps and stretched behind her for several feet along the floor. White kid slippers with little diamond buckles showed below her belled skirt.

Prince Nikolai was in dark blue Court dress, his remarkably blue eyes even brighter than his ribbon of the Order of St Andrei, the star of which was his only ornament. He looked calm and very happy.

The bride was attended by Ilya, dressed in the same dark blue as his father and looking so much like him that there was a little ripple of whispering among the guests, many of whom had not known of his existence. He looked very serious about his responsibility for Rose's train, but was obviously going to be helped (against his will, if necessary) by his cousin Irina Kirova, a self-confident young lady of seven with doll-like fair hair and blue eyes, enchanting in a white lace gown.

Behind the children came Marisha Kirova and Olga Kalinskaya, much alike in colouring and dressed alike in a soft rose-pink wild silk which flattered their dark hair and eyes, and each carrying a posy of matching roses.

The ceremony began in the centre of the Cathedral with the Invocation, and then Prince Nikolai took his Rose's right hand in his own and led her forward, following the gorgeously robed Metropolitan to the great lectern. Acolytes brought the flower-wreathed bridal candles, the Bishop blessed the bride and groom, his fingers resting lightly on their bowed heads, and handed each a lighted candle. Prince Nikolai's candle-flame flickered a little, then steadied, and the two grave, silent figures knelt side by side as the Bishop intoned the prayers for blessing, for peace, for salvation, for the Holy synod, for the Emperor, and finally, for the bride and groom, 'the servants of God, Nikolai and Tatyana. Vouchsafe to them love made perfect, peace and help, oh Lord, we beseech Thee.' Tatya, her head bent in prayer, pressed a minute handkerchief to her eyes in as unobtrusive a fashion as she could, remembering the same prayer at her own wedding, and how the weeks following had made a bitter mockery of it.

The blessing and exchanging of the rings followed, and the solemn benediction of the couple, and then the acolytes brought a fine silk carpet and spread it before the bride and groom. Nikolai and Rose stood up and he took her hand again. They exchanged a look, then stepped on to the carpet together, obviously remember-ing the superstition that whichever stepped first on the carpet would rule the household. The Bishop asked them each in turn if they consented to the marriage, and both replied firmly and clearly, then knelt again for the prayers for continence and fruitfulness. Now the Bishop lifted each of the wedding crowns in turn and crowned them. As they stood again, Alexander stepped forward to hold Nikolai's crown above his head, while Alexei did the same for Rose. They continued to hold them while the Deacon went to the lectern to read the Epistle, then Vladimir and Vassily took their places, Vladimir with Rose's crown and Vassily with Nikolai's.

After the couple had received the wine, Boris and Lev took over the crowns and followed as the Bishop led bride and groom in the little procession symbolic of the journey of life, while the choir chanted the Gloria. Then the Bishop received back the crowns and handed them to the acolytes, the final prayers were said and the candles extinguished, to be kept safely until Rose bore her first child; and the bride and groom turned to face one another, and Tatya, who was close enough to see the expression on Rose's face, knew that she had never felt for any man what Rose felt for Nikolai. The groom bent his head to kiss his bride, and the ceremony was over.

CHAPTER
THREE

THE BRIDAL procession left the Cathedral, followed by the Imperial family, and then the guests filed out, all of them going to one of the great salons, which was soon alive with the outburst of chattering which followed the solemnity of the religious service. Rose's train was removed, and she and Nikolai began to move together among their guests, receiving their congratulations and good wishes.

Vassily carried Tatya to a sofa by one of the long windows and opened the small central panel which allowed a little fresh air to pass through the double glass, before sitting down beside her. 'It was devilish hot in there,' he commented quietly.

'Yes.' Tatya smoothed her long kid gloves at the wrists and wished she didn't feel so inclined to cry. Of course, it was usual to feel emotional at a wedding, but the thoughts which brought the lump to her throat and the prickling to her eyes were bitter. If she had been allowed to marry Nikolai all those years ago, perhaps they might both have been spared a great deal of misery, but her father had decreed otherwise and arranged her marriage to the General, just as Nikolai's equally strong-minded and dictatorial father had decided that Nikolai should marry Anna. Both marriages had been desperately unhappy, and although her schoolgirl attachment to Nikolai had died with the passing of time, there had been a bond of sorts between them. Now Nikolai had broken the evil spell of his first marriage and found happiness, while Tatya . . .

To distract herself from her own thoughts, Tatya looked round the great gallery, which was so huge that the two hundred or so guests had plenty of room to move about. Little Irina and Ilya were sitting side by side on a nearby sofa, their short legs sticking out in front of them and their small faces wide-eyed and solemn as they stared about them.

Ilya whispered in Irina's ear, then hitched himself off the sofa and went towards his father and Rose. Tatya and Vassily watched anxiously, seeing him slow down appreciably as he neared them and then stop by Rose's side.

He waited until she had finished speaking to a guest and was about to move on, and then put a tentative hand on her arm. 'Mamma?' he said, his childish treble carrying clearly through the babble of adult voices.

Rose turned to him, dropped to her knees and took him in her arms in one swift, graceful movement. 'Ilyusha!' she said, and kissed him. The child's anxious face dissolved in a radiant smile as he put his arms round her neck and hugged her.

'Thank God for that!' Vassily said softly, letting out his breath in a long sigh. 'He's always addressed her as Tatyana Ivanovna, or Madame before! Ah, time for dinner, I think,' as the double doors at the end of the gallery were opened and an impressive major-domo entered. 'I'm ravenous—all that incense and emotion!'

'I wouldn't have thought that a wedding would make you emotional!' Tatya said, falling into his own light manner.

'Why ever not? Seeing one of my dearest friends put his head into the noose, and for the second time at that! It was a very disturbing experience, I may tell you!' He picked her up as he spoke and started to join the flow of guests towards the dining-room, but encountered Rose and Prince Nikolai on the way and stopped to greet them. There was an exchange of kisses between the four of them, which, as Vassily remarked, only required a large serpent to make an interesting variation on the Laocoön.

Ilya, firmly holding Rose's hand, tilted back his head to look up at Vassily. 'What's a Laocoön?' he asked.

'It's a statue of three people tied up in knots with each other and a big snake,' Vassily replied succinctly.

Tatya smiled down at Ilya, and Prince Nikolai said quietly, 'That's enough for now, Ilya. Pyotr is waiting to take you home. Say goodnight.'

Obediently, Ilya recited, 'Goodnight Tatya Petrovna, goodnight Vassily Sergeivich, goodnight Mamma, goodnight Father,' then looked round at all the other people with a worried expression, obviously wondering if he had to speak to all of them in turn, but Prince Nikolai's valet, a stalwart, moon-faced man, picked him up, held him while his father and Rose kissed him, and then carried him away, listening with interest to his chatter, while the adults took their places in the procession forming up to go in to dinner.

The meal was served in the State Dining-room, with the guests seated at round tables, each of which had a large orange tree growing through its centre, filling the air with the sweet scent of blossom. The great chandeliers, which had unusual lustres of blue glass, blazed with the light of thousands of candles, as bright as the daylight outside. The bride and groom shared a table with the Imperial family, and Tatya and Vassily were seated at the second table, with the two older bridesmaids, Maria and Alexei Kirov, Boris and Vladimir.

'No disasters, then,' Vassily commented cheerfully.

'Did you expect any?' Vladimir enquired dourly.

'Well, you never know. Sometimes the bride runs off with someone else,' Vassily spoke lightly, but with an undercurrent of bitterness which Tatya noticed made Vladimir shoot an anxious look at him.

'Not likely in this case,' he said abruptly.

'No, of course not.'

'Your gown is quite beautiful,' Marisha said to Tatya. 'It looks like silver in the candlelight, and how clever to match your flowers to your jewels!'

'Your own gown is very charming and becoming,'

Tatya replied. 'Did Rose choose the colour?'

Marisha nodded. 'I like it, but Olga wanted something more adult. She thinks that pink is a young girl's colour.'

Tatya looked across at Olga, who was not joining in the conversation with the others, but looking across at the next table. As Tatya watched, she smiled and tossed her curls, then glanced sidelong, still in the same direction, in a coquettish fashion.

Unhurriedly, Tatya turned her head, letting her eyes roam casually over the other tables until she reached the one which was holding Olga's attention. A dark-haired man with a sulkily handsome face was ogling Olga under drooping eyelids. Tatya recognised him only too well—Prince Sergei Dmitriev, Prince Nikolai's brother-in-law.

As she turned back to her own table, she met Vladimir's gaze. His face was calm and near expressionless, but he gave a sudden, unexpected little grimace which made her wonder how much longer his patience would last.

'What a fool she is!' she thought. 'He's such a kind, good man, and she could very well lose him . . .' She gave him a sympathetic smile and got a twitch of his moustache in reply.

The dinner was a long affair of many courses, perfectly cooked and exquisitely presented on gold plates and dishes. Champagne circulated freely, and there was a great deal of lively chatter, and some speeches, varying from the Emperor's sentimental toast to the bride and groom to Vassily's brief and witty tribute, which set everyone laughing. At length, the diners filtered away from the great room, most of the ladies going to the apartments set aside for them to rest and freshen their toilettes for the ball, while the men gathered in little groups, smoking, talking and strolling about.

At a signal from Vassily, a footman brought the wheelchair which Prince Nikolai had thoughtfully provided, and Vassily lifted Tatya into it and took her to the rooms where the other ladies had gathered, where her maid took charge of her, and she was glad of the chance to bathe her face and hands in the warm scented water provided, and sit quietly for a while, talking to Irina.

Vassily strolled back to the long gallery near the Cathedral, where he encountered Lev, who drew him aside into a window alcove and said, 'I'd like a word with you, Vassily Sergeivich.'

There was a tenseness in his voice, and his black brows were drawn together in a scowl which actually conveyed nothing more than an intention to speak seriously. Vassily flicked his eyebrows enquiringly and perched on the narrow window-sill.

'I—er,' Lev cleared his throat and started again. 'What are you playing at, Vassily?'

Vassily tilted his head and looked puzzled.

Lev made another fresh start. 'It's very kind of you to look after Tatya, and I'm grateful for it, because she'd have a very dull time otherwise, but what's your motive?'

Vassily looked straight into his anxious grey eyes and said, 'What do you think?'

'I don't know,' Lev replied. 'I can't fathom what you're up to.'

Vassily looked out of the window at the courtyard below. A couple of Palace guardsmen were pacing backwards and forwards, and he watched them meet and turn before he replied quietly, 'I don't know that I'm "up to" anything. I'm sorry for her, I suppose. She's not happy.'

'Yes, I know. We try to keep her amused, and she never complains, but there's not a great deal for her to do, really, and she seems to be afraid of the problems of going about and meeting people. If only she'd married again . . .'

'Do you know why she didn't?'

Lev shrugged. 'It wasn't for lack of offers! I think she's afraid. She never speaks about her husband, but something she once said to Irina . . . We think he ill-treated her, and she's afraid it might happen again.'

Vassily nodded. 'She needs a lover, Lev. Someone who can show her what it should be like.'

'Is that what you intend?' Lev asked.

Vassily looked at him thoughtfully. 'I don't think you'd have much difficulty in breaking my neck, even with one hand,' he said evenly. 'And I imagine that's what you'd do to any man who seduced your sister.'

Lev considered the matter, scowling more than ever, and then said, 'Not necessarily. Anyway, I don't know that you'd need to go as far as that.'

'I've no intention of marrying,' Vassily said flatly, still watching his friend's face. 'I doubt if I could seduce her, in any case—she's not that sort of female. I might manage something less drastic.'

Lev ran his hand over his thick, springy hair. 'The trouble is, she might fall in love with you, and then where are we?'

Vassily laughed. 'I doubt it! I'm not a lovable fellow, you know! Too cynical and selfish. I'll see what I can do, Lev, but you'll have to trust me. I can't have you breathing heavily in my ear all the time.'

Lev nodded. 'Oh, I trust you—I always have. You're an odd fellow, Vassily, and I'm not at all sure that you really are cynical or selfish—I've caught you being kind and self-sacrificing too many times! Do what you can for her, and good luck!' He held out his hand, and Vassily shook it with a wry smile, and then they went to find Boris and Vladimir, tracking them down eventually to the half-finished 1812 Gallery, among the portraits of the generals who commanded in the Great Patriotic War against Bonaparte, arguing happily about the battle of Maloyaroslavets.

Shortly before the ball was to start, Vassily went to fetch Tatya and carried her to the great ballroom, passing along that same long gallery, past the dozens of impassive guards and footmen who stood like statues along the walls. On each of the previous occasions when he had carried her, Tatya had been preoccupied by something else—fear that he might drop her, anxiety about what people might think—but this time she felt secure with him, and everyone now seemed to accept that he was only deputising for her brother, whose war injuries prevented him from using his damaged arm, so this time she suddenly became acutely conscious of him as a man.

It happened as they passed across the head of the Jordan staircase to enter the vestibule of the ballroom. He had been telling her some trivial, amusing anecdote, but they both happened to fall silent, and for a few moments she was vividly aware of the steel and whipcord strength of his arm about her waist, the pressure of his other arm supporting her legs, and the warm hard vitality of his body. It was very disturbing, and she wondered if he felt anything of it—if he was equally aware of her.

She stole a glance at his face, but he was nodding and smiling in greeting to an acquaintance, and she had time to collect herself before they entered the ballroom, unaware that the odd experience had left a becoming touch of colour in her cheeks.

As he set her down on a gilt sofa halfway down one side of the room, he said softly, 'You look positively ravishing, and there's nothing at all to worry about. I'll be within call all the evening if you need me.' He glanced round to see if he had chosen a good position for her. It seemed satisfactory. Behind her and a little to her left, a pair of doors opened into a wide corridor, but they were closed and there was no draught. She was facing across the room to the windows on the river front of the Palace, where the sky was bright blue and the sun gleamed on the gilt spire of the Peter-Paul Cathedral across the river, for the season of 'white nights' was fast approaching. Overhead, the five vast chandeliers were dazzling, a thousand candles in each making the lustres blaze like diamonds.

Tatya smiled at him. 'You mustn't concern yourself about me' she said. 'I'll be very comfortable here, and I

know you're fond of dancing. I'll enjoy watching you.'
Something of her longing to be able to dance herself
gave her voice a touch of sadness, and Vassily said
reassuringly, 'You won't be left alone.'

At that moment, the orchestra struck up the first
waltz, and Rose and Prince Nikolai opened the ball,
circling the vast patterned floor while their friends
looked on, smiling benignly on their happiness. Alexander watched with them, keeping to his own insistence
that he was to be only one of their throng of guests
tonight, and not to be treated with the usual formality
due to the Emperor.

Vassily sat down beside Tatya to watch, and remained
with her until the orchestra passed on to a set of polo-
naises, when Boris came over and asked leave to 'sit out
with his aunt' as he put it, and Vassily went off with a
smiling bow to choose a partner. Tatya soon saw that he
was, as Lev had said, a superb dancer.

Her eyes followed him as he moved round the ballroom, his face alight with merriment and all his attention
on his partner, a pretty young lady with bewitching
dimples and large blue eyes. Tatya wondered who she
was and how well Vassily knew her, and tried to attend
to the easy flow of conversation with which Boris was
endeavouring to entertain her.

Presently Boris too went away to dance with Marisha
in a mazurka, and Vladimir took his place, asking her
permission to sit beside her in a formal manner. He was a
fine figure in his full-dress uniform with his cross of St
George and his four campaign medals. After a few
conversational remarks about the gaiety of the scene and
the splendour of the ballroom, he fell silent, and Tatya,
glancing sideways at him, saw that he was watching
Olga, now dancing with Vassily and laughing up at him
as if he had just made a joke.

'She's a very pretty girl,' Tatya observed.

'Yes. She needs time to enjoy herself before she
settles down. I don't mind waiting,' Vladimir replied,
then turned to face Tatya, cleared his throat and asked

gruffly, 'D'you think I'm too old for her? Twelve years is a big difference.'

'I don't think so. You want to marry her, don't you?'

Vladimir brushed his moustache with one finger and said, 'Yes,' rather abruptly, then added, 'Not just for the sake of being married, either. Everyone knows that Vassily isn't likely to marry, so it falls to me to provide an heir to the estates, but that's not why . . . I really do . . .'

'Love her,' Tatya prompted as he seemed unable to say it.

He ran a finger round his stiff leather stock as if it had become too tight and said, 'Yes.'

'Have you told her so?'

'Yes. I thought I sounded rather silly, blurting it out, but she seemed to like it. We get on very well when there's no-one for her to flirt with.'

At that moment, an equerry arrived discreetly before them and murmured to Vladimir that His Imperial Majesty would appreciate a few words with Colonel Karachev if he would be so kind, and Vladimir perforce excused himself to Tatya and went away with the equerry, leaving her alone.

She sat watching as a gavotte was followed by another waltz, and found her eyes repeatedly seeking out Vassily's gracefully athletic figure as he moved among the dancers, always with his entire attention on his partner, always with someone young and pretty and light of foot. It became increasingly difficult to look alert and interested, and she felt the muscles of her face becoming tighter and tighter, her smile more fixed and unreal. Her head began to hurt, the blood throbbing in her temples, and an aching sensation began to constrict her throat.

The door a little way to her left opened and closed again, and she glanced in that direction to see Sergei Dmitriev standing before it with one of his cronies. His eyes surveyed the dancers in a bored, sullen way, and passed over Tatya without a flicker of recognition.

'The truth is, Misha,' he drawled to his companion,

'I'm completely at a loss, and I don't think the old fellow will stump up this time—he said last year that it was the last, and I think he meant it.'

'You'd better find an heiress, then,' his companion replied in a similar affected drawl. 'I thought that was what you were after in Ryazan. The Widow Kalinskaya, wasn't it?'

Sergei's eyes slid towards Tatya, who looked away unseeingly across the room, the dancers and the flashing lustres blurring in her vision as she prayed that her colour hadn't risen. She gripped her fan tightly with both hands and felt the fragile ivory sticks snap as he raised his voice a little and said, 'Oh, that frigid prude! No, she's quite lost her looks and aged incredibly since she was crippled. I couldn't face that, not while there are younger and prettier alternatives!'

Tatya choked back a gasp and her eyes filled with tears, but suddenly Vassily was beside her, his voice an urgent whisper in her ear. 'Tatya! Give me leave to deal with him! I'll thrash him insensible for that!'

Tatya was startled by his vehemence and jerked back into control of herself. 'No!' she whispered. 'Ignore it! I didn't hear what he said . . . *please* Vassily!' She looked anxiously at his tense face, very close to hers, his green eyes blazing with fury. Suddenly, his lids drooped a little and his usual smile returned as he said easily, 'As you wish. You look a little unwell. May I get you anything?'

He gently and unobtrusively removed the broken fan from her gloved hands and dropped it into his pocket.

'My head aches a little,' she confessed. The constriction in her throat was becoming intolerable. 'I'd like to go home, Vassily.'

'I'll take you.'

'If you would just carry me down to the carriage—I'll be all right then.'

'I'll take you home,' he repeated, picking her up and carrying her swiftly out through the nearby doorway, brushing Sergei Dmitriev aside without so much as a glance as he did so.

The door opened on to a corridor, thickly carpeted and hung with a long row of portraits on one side, facing the windows which looked out on a courtyard. Two of the Emperor's giant Nubians stood at the far end, staring impassively into space, but otherwise the corridor was deserted.

'If you'll just take me to the carriage,' Tatya said again, feeling that she would not be able to hold back her tears very much longer.

'I said I shall take you home, and if you try to argue the point, I shall set you down here in the middle of the floor and leave you!' he replied firmly. 'Now, find your hartshorn, or your vinaigrette, or whatever you use, and we'll be off.'

Tatya found her little gold vinaigrette in her reticule and sniffed cautiously at the aromatic spirit. It made her eyes prick more than ever, so she closed them and let her head droop to hide her face a little from the guards on the staircase as Vassily carried her down, sending a footman running ahead to summon his carriage.

They had to wait a few moments in the vestibule, and he bent his head a trifle, his lips brushing her cheek as if by accident as he said softly, 'Not long now, *dushenka*. Just a few more minutes,' in a gentle, caressing tone quite unlike his usual dry, slightly sardonic mode of speech. The endearment (little soul) was unexpected and surprising, more suitable for a wife or a fiancée than the sister of a friend, and it diverted her from her unhappiness long enough to prevent her dissolving into tears in front of the servants as the carriage mounted the ramp and stopped at the door, and then there was a brief bustling as a footman lowered the carriage step and steadied Vassily as he climbed in with her, setting her down carefully on the seat. He put his head out to give instructions to the driver, then sat down beside her as the step was put up and the door closed, and handed her his large clean handkerchief as the horses negotiated the ramp and the carriage drew away along Palace Quay.

Tatya would very much have liked to cry her eyes out, but it would only take a few minutes to reach home, and, although Vassily was looking out of the window as if he had never seen the Winter Palace before, she felt too embarrassed by his presence to let the tears flow. Instead, she twisted his handkerchief round her fingers and sat in silence for the whole of the short drive, staring out of the window on her side, but not seeing the pearl-grey sky with little puffs of cloud stained pink by the sunset, or the groups of people strolling about in the summer twilight.

The carriage turned in at the gate of the Orlov house at last and went straight round to the stableyard without stopping. Vassily gathered her up and got out, saying something to the driver, then carried her into the house by way of the garden, entering through the glass doors of the garden-room.

Two candles burned in silver sticks by the door, shedding a soft glow on the light wood of the furniture. The stove gleamed a ghostly white in the corner, and the room was very still and quiet, only the cat moving, uncurling himself in the middle of Tatya's daybed to stretch and yawn, then composing himself to sleep as Vassily took Tatya to the sofa and sat down beside her.

'Come, *dushenka*,' he said softly. 'let it go. You'll feel better when it's over.' He carefully unfastened her tiara and put it down on the sofa table, leaning across her to do so, which brought him so close to her that she had only to move the slightest distance towards him to lay her head on his shoulder before she dissolved into tears. He put both arms round her and held her silently until she had finished crying.

When her sobs subsided, she raised her head and drew away from him a little. He took his handkerchief from her and wiped her cheeks and dried her eyes with concerned concentration, then said, 'There, that's better. I wish you'd let me thump the fellow about a little—it would give me the greatest pleasure.'

'I wouldn't give him the satisfaction of knowing that

he hurt me,' Tatya replied unsteadily. 'Besides, it would create a scandal.'

'What, two men fighting over you?' Vassily smiled. 'Yes, I suppose it would. The fellow's a fool and a damned liar, though. It's only sour grapes, you know.'

She shook her head and looked away. 'What he said was true enough.'

'For Heaven's sake! You're a beautiful woman, despite your advanced age—why, you must be nearly as old as I am, I suppose, and I'm almost senile!'

'I'm past thirty,' Tatya admitted wretchedly.

'You've plenty of time before you need despair, then. A few more years to marry and have half a dozen children.'

She shook her head again, still looking away from him, but he put two fingers under her chin, turned her face towards him, and inspected it at very close range.

'Your complexion is perfect,' he said. 'Your mouth droops a little, and your eyes are sad, but that's because you're lonely and unhappy. If you had something to interest you and make you laugh, you'd be as lovely as ever. You need a lover, my dear.'

'I've never . . . !' she faltered.

'Oh, nothing immoral! Just a good, old-fashioned *cavaliere servente*—someone to visit you, bring you flowers and little gifts, to talk with, to give you interest and a touch of excitement, perhaps kiss you and caress you a little.'

It sounded very attractive. Tatya looked at him uncertainly, wondering if he was joking. He looked quite serious.

'Will you take me for your lover, Tatya?' His voice was so soft and gentle. Her lips parted, but nothing came out, and she had no idea what she wanted to say.

He leaned forward and kissed her lips. It was a very gentle, lingering kiss, but nothing alarming.

'Shall I be your lover, Tatya?'

'But you don't love me . . .' It was not even a sensible

reply, but the response of her body to his kiss had surprised her, and she was confused.

'Pretend I do. Just a game, Tatya! An amusement for all those hours when Lev and Irina are sitting for Borovikovsky. It shan't go an inch further than you want it to, I promise. Anything at all, from light conversation to lovemaking, but as you dictate, and it shall end whenever you wish.'

She hesitated, torn between an almost overpowering longing to accept the offer, and a numbing fear of becoming involved in something which might lead her back into the nightmares of the past. The question of propriety hardly entered her mind.

'I won't hurt you. There's nothing to be afraid of.' He kissed her again, harder and deeper this time, his tongue sliding caressingly between her parted lips. She flinched a little and put her hands on his shoulders to push him away, but instead they slid over the smooth cloth of his coat and her arms went round his neck as his own embrace tightened round her and the kiss became a shade more passionate.

When it finally ended, she was almost suffocating. Vassily's face lit up with amusement as she gasped for breath, and he said lightly, 'You're allowed to breathe, you know! It doesn't have to be a competition to see who can hold a breath the longest!' and then, more seriously, and a trifle puzzled, 'Haven't you been kissed before?'

'N-not like that,' she whispered, staring at him wide-eyed, amazed at the turmoil of feeling inside her.

'Didn't your husband . . . ?'

She shook her head. 'He never kissed me.' Her voice held a poignant note of misery, and she added reluctantly, 'I wouldn't have wanted him to.'

'No, of course not,' thoughtfully, then, more lightly, 'Shall I be your lover, then?'

She managed a faint smile. 'It . . . it wouldn't be wrong?'

'How could it be, *dushenka*? We'd not be harming anyone, would we? It would only be an amusement, a secret game. You can tell Lev about it if you wish. I don't mind, and he knows I'll not harm you. I think he'll approve, if it lifts you out of that pit of depression you've fallen into.'

She smiled more certainly this time, and said, 'Yes, then,' with sudden resolution.

'You won't regret it,' he promised, his eyes twinkling. 'We'll both enjoy the game a great deal, I'm sure, and you can end it whenever you wish, remember, without any ill-feeling.'

She sat in the circle of his arm, and gradually relaxed against him, her head resting on his shoulder, fingering the emerald buttons on his waistcoat and watching them sparkle in the candle-light, surprised to find how contented and safe she felt. She could feel the warmth of his body like the glow of a good fire, and his arm round her shoulders was protective and comforting. She sighed without knowing that she had done so, and Vassily looked across at Vron, who gazed sleepily from the middle of the daybed, his eyes a lighter shade than the green velvet. The man winked at the cat, and the cat yawned widely, all pink gums and white teeth, then curled up, twitched the end of its tail over its nose, and returned to a mouseful dream, and there was a long, peaceful silence.

It was broken eventually by a sound from inside the house. Vassily stirred and raised his head to listen. 'Lev and Irina, I think,' he said, dropped a light kiss on Tatya's lips as she raised her head from his shoulder, and then unhurriedly removed himself to a chair. By the time Irina came in, followed by Lev and two servants with a samovar and tea-tray, he was lounging elegantly with his legs crossed, his elbows on the arms of the chair and his finger-tips lightly together in front of his chin, saying carelessly 'It's a pity young Pushkin has become involved with the Union of Welfare. Politics and poetry don't mix very well, I'm afraid, and I hear he's been exiled for it.' He rose to his feet to greet Irina, and said, 'Has the ball ended already?'

'No. I think most of them mean to go on all night,' Irina replied. 'How are you, Tatya?'

'Quite well, thank you,' Tatya replied, smiling. 'I was a little tired after all the excitement, and my head ached with the heat, so Vassily kindly brought me home. You didn't leave early because of me, I hope?' She was unaware that her eyes had an unaccustomed sparkle and her cheeks were slightly flushed, but Lev noticed the change in her and looked at Vassily, who winked fractionally, and went to hand tea-glasses for Irina as she sat down and began to pour, saying, 'No, I was tired myself.'

The servants withdrew, and Lev, informal in his own home, took off his coat and sat down in his shirt-sleeves. 'Why the devil they have all those candles, I can't imagine!' he complained. 'I slipped on the grease a dozen times. It gets so hot, and the light is quite painfully bright.'

'Besides, it's much more amusing to dance in the dark,' Vassily said, carrying a glass of tea across to Tatya, who suddenly found that she was very thirsty. 'I take it that the bride and groom don't intend to dance all night?'

Lev guffawed, then turned it into a cough at a reproving glance from Irina. 'No,' he said. 'They left soon after the second waltz.'

Vassily quirked his eyebrows and raised his tea-glass in the general direction of the Volkhovsky Palace in a silent toast, and then sat down.

Lev leaned across and picked up one of the books on Tatya's work-table and looked at the title. 'Oh, *that* Pushkin,' he said. 'The *Ruslan i Lyudmila* fellow. Funny idea, writing poetry in Russian.'

'Why not?' asked Vassily. 'It's a more melodious language than German.'

'But no-one ever does,' Lev put the book back on the table. 'Russian poetry's always in French.'

'Everything's always in French,' Vassily complained. 'Bad French, usually! Why on earth should we four

Russians be sitting here conversing in a foreign language?'

'Well, everyone speaks French, don't they?' Irina said. 'I mean abroad, in other countries . . . people in our class of Society all speak French. It's the . . . the *lingua franca*!'

CHAPTER
FOUR

WHEN Vassily rose to take his leave, he said, 'Oh, I'll just take you upstairs before I go, Tatya,' as if it was the most natural and old-established of customs, and he was halfway upstairs with her before she had recovered from the surprise enough to protest, and by then there was obviously no point.

'Which room?' he asked as he reached the second floor, and she indicated the door opposite the head of the stairs. Elena, who had been sitting by the window, rose as they entered, and looked quite taken aback to see a man carrying her mistress into her bedroom.

'You've left your tiara in the garden-room!' Vassily exclaimed. 'Perhaps your maid should run down and fetch it, for it's in full view of the window . . .'

Elena exclaimed, 'Oh, madame!' reproachfully at such carelessness, and whisked out through the door, while Vassily advanced into the centre of the room, still carrying Tatya, and turned slowly round in a full circle, looking about him with great interest.

Tatya also looked at her familiar room, and it was much like seeing it for the first time. It was, of course, a large room, for nothing in the Orlov house was small or cramped. The walls were covered with a delicate Chinese brocade of stiff little figures walking about among lakes and pagodas, seen as if in the distance between branches of flowering prunus. The dressing-table and other furniture were made of pale Karelian birch, beautifully figured, with ormolu fittings, except for two large gold-lacquered cabinets for small articles of clothing and accessories. The porcelain set on the wash-stand continued the Chinese theme in *famille rose*, and the same brocade curtained the windows and covered the bed, which had white muslin curtains. The inlaid floor of polished wood was scattered with soft silk rugs.

Vassily set her down carefully on the bed and sat down beside her, still with his arms round her, and showered her face with a dozen light kisses.

'There!' he said mischievously. 'I've shared your bed for a few seconds, at least!'

'Elena will come back . . .' Tatya began nervously, but he kissed her mouth before she could close her lips against him.

'Goodnight, *dushenka*. I'll dream of you in your Chinese fairyland!' and then he was gone, and Tatya heard him bid Elena goodnight as he met her on the stairs.

Elena helped Tatya to undress, slipping her fine embroidered silk nightshift over her head, then supporting her across to the bed, making sure that her crutches were within reach on the floor beside it. The sheets were cool and pleasant to the touch, and Tatya suddenly felt extremely tired, what with the emotion and missing her usual afternoon rest. Her eyes closed and she drifted off to sleep, half-listening to Elena moving about as she tidied away the discarded clothes and put the wilted rosebuds in water.

'He's so kind and so entertaining,' she thought. 'I wonder if he'll come to see me tomorrow . . .'

She wondered the same thing almost as soon as she woke in the morning. It was a dull day, with a thick mist drifting in from the Gulf of Finland to shroud the city in a grey pall. When she was dressed, she went out on to the little balcony outside her window for a moment to look out at the garden, but the mist had robbed it of colour, and the wall of the water-garden was invisible. Even the sundial could hardly be seen, and the mist touched her face clammily, making her shiver and pull her shawl closer round her neck and shoulders. The sun was a flat silver disc, already high in the sky, and she felt guiltily that she should have been downstairs long ago.

'Your cap, madame?' Elena enquired, holding out one of her lace widow's caps.

'No, thank you, Elena. I shan't wear them any more. You may get rid of them.' The maid looked surprised, and then her comfortable, plump face creased in a smile, but she was too well-trained to make a comment, and went to see if the corridor and staircase were clear of servants.

Tatya went downstairs with an unaccustomed feeling of anticipation. For so long, her days had been empty of interest, with only trivialities to occupy her, and now there was something to look forward to, even if that, too, was only a pastime. Then she remembered Vassily's kisses, and went into the breakfast parlour with a very becoming touch of colour in her cheeks.

Lev looked up from his croissants and coffee. 'You're looking well, pet! I thought you'd be exhausted after yesterday.' He rose to kiss her and help her to her seat. Irina came in soon after, and they chatted happily about the wedding for some time.

After luncheon, Irina and Lev set out for Borovikov-sky's studio, having agreed to sit for the artist on which-ever afternoons he was able to fit in among his many commissions.

'Are you sure you don't mind?' Lev asked Tatya. 'It seems unkind to leave you alone so much, but perhaps you'll have some callers. I don't think Boris is in waiting today.'

'It doesn't matter in the least,' Tatya replied, smiling. 'I'm supposed to rest in the afternoon, and I've plenty of books to read, and my embroidery.' She was tempted to tell Lev about Vassily's extraordinary offer, but was unsure of his reaction to the idea of such an unconventional amusement.

When they had gone, she settled back against the cushions on the daybed and picked up the novel she had started earlier in the week. It seemed a very silly story, and the characters were unnatural and over-sentimental.

'Please let him come!' she thought, and then wondered what she would say to him if he did. It had been
great fun in the old days to flirt with the handsome young
men in Society, like a game with a set pattern of rules,
unwritten, but known to all the players and strictly
adhered to . . . well, not quite all of them—sometimes
people had real *affaires*—but in Tatya's set, people
behaved according to the rules and only flirted. Vassily
was so different. He composed his own rules in life, she
already knew, and his 'game' might move in any direction. None of her former flirts had ever kissed her
lips—only kissing the hand or wrist was permissible—
but Vassily . . . the thought was a little alarming, and yet
she felt that she could trust him . . .

The garden door opened quietly and he came in,
closed it behind him and stood smiling at her wide eyes
and parted lips.

'Did I startle you? I'm sorry.'

'I didn't think you would come in that way.'

He was wearing green again, but without a waistcoat,
and his shirt had a soft turn-down collar with a dark silk
cravat tied loosely in a bow. 'You look like Lord Byron,'
she said.

He leaned against the door and looked at her thoughtfully. 'You read English too?'

'A little. Someone sent me the first canto of *Childe
Harold's Pilgrimage*. There was an engraving of the poet
in it.'

'You'd *shake the sainthood of an anchorite*,' he quoted
and then translated it into French when she looked
puzzled. She flushed and nervously smoothed the skirt
of her afternoon gown.

He crossed the room and sat on the edge of her
daybed, twisting to face her, and put his hands on the
high curved end of it, on either side of her head. It
brought him very close to her, and she caught her breath
nervously.

'I'm not in the least like Byron,' he said. 'He's a
dissolute, arrogant, unpleasant fellow, not at all roman-

tic really. You'll be safe with me, Tatya, as safe as *you* wish to be.' He kissed her. 'Trust me,' and kissed her again.

She put her arms round him, inside his unbuttoned coat, and smoothed the lean hard strength of his back through the fine linen of his shirt, and closed her eyes and let him kiss her ardently, pressing her back against the cushions, caressing her neck with one hand while the other arm went round her waist.

After some time, he raised his head and said smilingly, 'I've a great deal to teach you, I see! Making love isn't only something a man does to a female!'

'Isn't it? I thought . . .'

'No, *dushenka*. It's something they do together, to give each other pleasure. You just lie there and let me kiss you, but you're doing nothing yourself.'

'I didn't know I was supposed to do anything,' Tatya said, troubled. 'What should I do?'

'What do you feel like doing?'

She bit her lip, perplexed, and he laughed, but quite kindly. 'I'm going too fast for you. Never mind. Next time, perhaps,' and he went to sit in the nearest chair and continued the conversation of three days before as if there had been no interval, so that Tatya soon lost her feeling of awkwardness and embarrassment as he talked, and sat listening with shining eyes and an eager expression to his easy, fluent description of Norway.

'You must have spent a great deal of your life travelling!' she remarked enviously. 'Do you always go alone?'

'Usually. I find that a bought woman rarely makes a good travelling companion.' He spoke in a dry, ironic tone, and watched her face as he said it. 'Does it offend you that I speak of such a person?'

Tatya, who had not been thinking of a female companion, considered her answer, then replied, 'It depends. I mean, if someone refers to—to fornication in a salacious manner, then yes, I find it offensive, but when it's a matter of fact—well, I know that such things happen, of course, and they can't really be ignored . . . like—like bad weather!'

He smiled at her simile. 'I'd like to think we could talk about anything at all to each other,' he said seriously. 'Lovers and friends should be able to, I believe.'

'Yes,' Tatya said a little doubtfully, and then, after a moment's thought, 'yes,' far more definitely.

'Good. Then I'll confess to you that I have, in the past, kept a succession of mistresses and led an immoral and dissolute life, but for the last six years or so, I've been a comparatively reformed character. I've never raped or seduced anyone.'

'Oh.' Tatya had no idea what to say. He had spoken in much the same tone that he might have employed to tell her that he had once had the measles or bitten his tutor, and although he sounded brisk and business-like, his smile lurked in his eyes and at the corners of his mouth. Suddenly, she smiled and replied, 'I've led a much duller life, though I was considered a flirt in my younger days, I believe. Would you like some tea?'

He said that he would, and she rang her little gold bell to summon the footman on duty. While they were drinking tea from the delicate porcelain cups, she said hesitantly, 'Someone—I think it was Boris—told me that you nearly married once . . .'

He looked at her consideringly. 'I'll tell you about it myself next time I come, if you'll tell me something in exchange.'

She put a tremulous hand to her throat, feeling that she had been suitably paid back for her temerity, and asked fearfully, 'W-what must I tell you?'

'Nothing too difficult to begin with. Don't be afraid, Tatya. I know how hard it is to speak of—of some things. I'm offering to tell you my most difficult thing to start with—it's something I've never spoken of to anyone, not even Volodya, although he was there when it happened—so don't think it will be any easier for me than some things will be for you. Are you coming to Nikolai's tomorrow?'

'I'd like to.' Prince Nikolai had invited them to spend the afternoon and evening at his house to plan the programme for their reunion.

'Shall I come for you, or can you get yourself into the carriage?'

'I can get in quite well. It's getting out that is difficult.'

'I'll be there to help you when you arrive.' He glanced at the clock and set down his teacup. 'I'm to dine with my brother at the fortress, so I must go now. I've no doubt that he'll put me in his deepest and most rat-infested dungeon if I'm late.' He sat on the edge of the daybed again and put his hands on her shoulders. 'Shall I kiss you goodbye?'

'Please.' It was not much more than a shy whisper, but when he kissed her, she remembered what he had said earlier—'What do you feel like doing?'—and responded so well that he looked at her with raised eyebrows afterwards and remarked, 'You learn quickly!'

As he stood up, he felt in his pocket and said, 'I'm afraid I made off with your fan last night,' and produced a long, flat package, which he dropped in her lap, then left with a last, 'Tomorrow . . .' and a smile from the door.

Tatya looked at the parcel with very mixed feelings. Why, when he had been so kind and given her such a pleasant and interesting afternoon, had he spoiled it all by reminding her of last night's humiliation? And why had he gone to the trouble of returning her broken fan, let alone wrapping it in white tissue paper and tying it with a blue ribbon? She picked it up and realised that it didn't feel broken at all, so she untied the ribbon and unwrapped the paper. It contained a fan, but not her own little ivory one of grey silk to match her gown. This one also had ivory sticks, but they were inlaid with gold in a design of lover's knots. The body was of silk brocade, a deeper shade of ivory, figured with roses and more lover's knots in pale pastel colours, cleverly woven so that the colours changed as the light moved across the surface. The leading guard was set with tiny brilliants in

a flowing cursive T. It was quite the prettiest fan she had
ever seen, but with a quiet, subtle beauty which required
a close inspection for appreciation.

'I can't possibly accept it,' she thought. 'It's very kind
of him, but it's much too expensive!' She had been
strictly brought up with the maxim that a lady should
never accept a valuable gift from a gentleman—flowers
or gloves, yes, but jewels, anything costing more than a
few roubles, never! She reluctantly wrapped it up again,
then felt that she must have just one more look . . .

She was still looking at it when Lev and Irina came
home. She slipped it into the pocket of her skirt as they
entered the room, and somehow thought no more about
how she could return it to Vassily without offending him.

'How are you, pet?' Lev asked, dropping a vague kiss
on her hair. He didn't ask if she had received any callers,
and Tatya assumed that it was simply because he didn't
think of it, especially as he went on to give an amusing
account of their afternoon with Borovikovsky. It
appeared that the artist was a temperamental fellow with
a strong preference for female sitters, and he had been
quite difficult about including Lev in the painting at all.
Halfway through the tale, Tatya caught sight of Vassily's
cup and dish on the edge of her work-table, and waited
nervously for Lev to finish his story and notice that there
were two cups, her own being with the other tea things,
but fresh tea was brought while he was still in full flow,
and the footman took the evidence away as he left the
room.

During the evening, a dozen or so callers dropped in
after dinner to talk about the wedding and exchange
news and gossip. When the last of them left Tatya began
her slow and painful progress up to bed, Lev gave her a
steadying arm up the stairs and said anxiously, 'Are you
finding all these visitors and going about too tiring?'

'No,' she assured him. 'I'm quite well in myself, you
know—it's only getting from one place to another that
tires me.'

'Glad you came to Petersburg?'

'Yes, very glad. I wondered at first if people would stare—oh, you know—but everyone's so kind . . .'

'Oh, good,' Lev said rather lamely.

Tatya lay awake for some time wondering again what she should do about the fan. It seemed inconsistent to return it when she had allowed Vassily to kiss her, and she began to worry about the whole idea again. Perhaps she should tell him that she didn't wish to play his game after all, that on consideration she found it . . . what? Improper? It was so pleasant to have something to look forward to . . . how quickly the afternoon had passed . . . surely there was no harm in a few kisses . . . after all, nothing very terrible could happen . . . there were always servants within call. In any case, she was not really afraid of anything Vassily might do, for it was impossible to imagine him forcing her into anything she didn't wish for—not like . . . He had even suggested that she tell Lev about the game, and with that thought, her problem seemed to solve itself, and she slept very well indeed.

She woke to another misty morning which Lev gloomily said would probably turn to rain. 'Can't imagine why Peter ever thought of building a city here,' he grumbled. 'Damp, marshy, always foggy or raining, winter lasts half the year. Can't even have a cellar under the house, the ground's so water-logged . . .'

'Don't exaggerate!' said Irina. 'The Venice of the North,' she added slily, knowing what he would say, and he did.

'Venice! Dirty, stinking place, canals full of dead dogs and everyone speaking Italian!'

Nevertheless, the sun broke through during the morning, and they arrived at the Volkhovsky Palace in one of those perfect Petersburg summer days, when the river sparkled and the gilded spires and domes swam in a clear azure sky, and the creamy stone buildings on Vassilievsky Island looked like a classical dream.

When the carriage drew up before the impressive portico, Vassily came sprinting round the corner of the house with Ilya in pursuit, trying desperately to keep up with the man's long legs, but being left further and further behind. It would have been understandable in so young a child if he had protested, or even cried, but his sturdy little legs pounded away across the gravel, and his round face was set in an expression of fierce concentration until he arrived at the carriage door.

By then, Irina and Lev had descended, and Vassily had got in and lifted Tatya from her seat, surreptitiously kissing her ear, and she tugged his hair gently in reply, smiling as she exclaimed, 'How fast you can run! Poor Ilya! Look, he's puffing like a little steam engine!'

'I've seen a steam engine!' Ilya informed her proudly, then recalled his manners and bowed to the visitors. Vassily carried Tatya through the house to the terrace at the back, with Ilya marching along beside them, chattering happily about the kite which Vassily Sergeivich was making and how they were going to fly it when it was finished.

The Volkhovsky Palace was even larger than Lev's house, and had an extensive garden running down to the river, for the palace turned its back on the centre of the city across the Neva and faced on to the Bolshoi Prospect. A very fine balustraded terrace ran across almost the whole width of the house at the back, between the winter garden projecting on the right and the stables and carriage-house on the left. In the centre, a large room opened on to this terrace by means of a dozen double glazed doors, which enabled the terrace to become almost a part of the room. It had been shut up for years, but Nikolai had opened it up and had it redecorated for Rose to use as her sitting-room for informal occasions, rather than the state rooms on the first floor.

As Rose had hoped, the decoration of the room drew expressions of admiration from these first guests, who were delighted with the panels of silk tapestry woven with soft-coloured flowers, which had been mounted in white frames on the walls. Between them were areas of misty green, where white consoles carried vases of real flowers. The stoves were tiled in white with occasional sprays of flowers, the white furniture was upholstered with the same flowered tapestry, and the floor was of light-coloured polished wood. Rose had already added her own personal touches with a few books, some pretty pieces of china and some embroidered cushions. The garden doors were open, framing the view across the terrace to lawn, and beyond lay a formal garden running down to the river, with the distant prospect of the city in the background.

The ladies sat out on the terrace after luncheon, enjoying the warm sun and ostensibly stitching their embroidery, though most of their attention was on their conversation. Vassily and Ilya had their heads together over the long tail of the large kite which Vassily had constructed out of strips of bamboo and a piece of gaily-coloured silk. Lev and Prince Nikolai had disappeared in the direction of the stables, and Boris, Vladimir and Marisha were not expected until later, as Boris was in attendance on the Emperor, Vladimir on duty at the fortress, and Marisha, who had returned home, was out shopping with her mother.

'That's the tail finished,' Vassily said presently, stretching it out along the terrace steps, where he had been sitting. 'Now, where's the ball of twine?'

'I'll fetch it.' Ilya ran into the house, and while he was gone, Vassily looked up and met Tatya's eyes. A few days ago, she would have looked away, having grown used to seeing indifference or even pity in the gaze of other people, but now she coloured a little and gave him a grateful smile for the open admiration with which he let his eyes slide over her face.

Ilya returned with a large ball of twine, and watched closely while one end was secured to the kite, and then man and boy walked out into the middle of the lawn, Vassily carrying the kite while Ilya importantly supported the tail.

'Oh dear!' said Rose. 'I hope to goodness that it flies, or he'll be so disappointed!'

'*They*'ll be disappointed, you mean!' Irina corrected.

'Vassily's so good with him,' Rose was watching with an anticipatory smile curving her mouth. 'We were worried when Nikolai brought him here that he might not take very kindly to us being married, and he looked so anxious when I met him, and he wouldn't look at me or speak, but Vassily said, "Come on, old fellow. I'll tell you a story," and took him off somewhere. They were gone for some time, but when they returned, Ilya came straight to me and said, "Vassily Sergeivich says you are going to be my mamma, and I'm glad, because everyone else has a mamma, and I've only had a father," and everything was all right after that.'

There had been a short conference between the kite-fliers, but now Ilya took the kite and held it above his head, standing on tiptoe and watching Vassily closely, the tip of his tongue sticking out with anxiety, as Vassily walked away, paying out the twine. Then he called 'Now!' and broke into a run. Ilya let go, the kite rose, dipped almost to the ground, then rose again, swooping from side to side, steadied, and soared up into the sky. Ilya gave a shriek of triumph which brought his father and Lev hurrying round the corner from the stables, and in a matter of minutes there were four enthusiastic kite-fliers on the lawn.

Presently, Vassily wandered over to the terrace and perched on the balustrade near the ladies, twisting half round to watch the progress of the kite. He remained there when Ilya came running over to invite the ladies to come and take a turn at holding the string. Rose allowed him to take her hand and tow her across the lawn, Olga and Irina following to join in the fun. Vassily and Tatya were left alone together.

'I don't know how to thank you for the fan,' she said quietly. 'It's such a beautiful thing . . .'

'. . . that you can't bear to give it back and tell me you can't accept it,' he finished for her. It was not what she had intended to say, for she was a female who kept to a decision once she had made up her mind, but his words so closely echoed her thoughts of the previous night that she was startled.

He laughed at her surprised expression and went on, 'You'll agree, I hope, that your accredited lover may be allowed a little more licence than any other man? After all, it's only a fan, not a diamond parure.'

'But a very expensive one!' she protested, smiling.

'I'll not embarrass you with anything too extravagant. After all, the game is intended to amuse you, not cause you anxiety.'

There was a sudden cry of alarm from the group on the lawn, and they both turned to look. The kite, inexpertly handled by Olga, had somehow become entangled in the upper branches of a large oak tree on the far side of the grass, and they were all looking up at it in consternation. Ilya turned away and came back to the house, head down and feet dragging. He stopped just below the terrace and raised a woebegone face to look up at Vassily, his blue eyes swimming with tears, which began to trickle down his cheeks.

'Don't cry, old fellow,' Vassily said gently. 'I'll get it down for you.'

'But it's right at the top of that great huge tree!' Ilya hiccuped.

'Well, let's see. If it's too badly stuck, we'll make another.' Vassily swung his legs over the balustrade, dropped lightly to the lawn and walked across to the tree. After looking up for a moment, he crouched, poised on his toes, then jumped for the lowest branch. Tatya saw his legs wave about for a moment, and then he disappeared into the foliage, his progress up the tree marked by an agitation among the young reddish-green leaves and an occasional glimpse of his light-coloured tunic.

'Good afternoon,' Vladimir's voice said from behind her, and she glanced round to reply as he came out of the house and kissed her hand in greeting. Then he surveyed the scene before him, looked up at the kite, and said drily, 'I suppose that's Vassily playing the monkey?'

'He's trying to rescue Ilya's kite,' Tatya replied, with a stronger note of reproof in her voice than she had intended. She was surprised when the Colonel gave her a friendly grin and said, 'We've been sparring all our lives, you know. It don't signify anything.'

Tatya gave a gasp as Vassily appeared at the top of the tree, standing on a branch which bent ominously under him, and reached for the kite with both hands.

'He won't fall,' Vladimir said reassuringly. 'If the branch breaks, he'll catch hold of another on the way down.' His faith was not put to the test as it was the kite which fluttered to the ground, and Vassily descended in a more leisurely fashion. By the time he was down, Vladimir had joined the others and was inspecting the kite. It was undamaged, and he had it in the air again very quickly, then gave the string to Olga and took the opportunity to instruct her in the proper way to handle it, which of course required that he put one of his own hands over both of hers to see that she kept the right amount of tension on the string.

Vassily returned to his perch on the balustrade, wiping his hands on the sides of his trousers, and stayed talking to Tatya until it was time to change for dinner.

After the meal, they all returned to Rose's sitting-room, and Boris arrived soon after, full of plans for a number of picnics and outings in which the ladies could join, for, as he said, 'I know it's supposed to be a reunion, but we don't really want to mull over old battles all the time, do we?'

Vassily had carried Tatya up to dinner and down again, and had seated himself beside her on a sofa by the window. When the conversation broke up into more general topics, she said to him, 'What did you mean the other evening when you said that Pushkin had joined the Union of Welfare? It sounds like a charity of some sort.'

'It's a secret society,' Vassily replied. 'Nikolai can tell you more about it than I can.'

'What's that?' the Prince asked, catching the sound of his own name.

'Tatya was just asking about Alexander Pushkin's Union of Welfare.' Vassily replied. 'It's one of the secret societies, isn't it?'

'Don't get yourself mixed up with those lunatics!' Prince Nikolai exclaimed.

'I don't know anything about them,' Tatya said. 'What are the secret societies?'

'Political organisations.' Prince Nikolai moved nearer and began to expound. 'Some of them are known to the Emperor and have his unofficial interest—one might even say his approval. The main one is the Society of Salvation, which was founded a couple of years ago by Prince Trubetskoy, the Colonel of the Preobrajenskys. They prepare reports on various things—suggested reforms of some of our institutions, mostly—in the hope of persuading Alexander Pavlovich to deal with what they consider our problems. They're interested in the emancipation of the serfs and a more constitutional government, and most of their ideas are quite sensible, but some of the other societies are much less moderate than Trubetskoy's friends, and want actual revolution!'

'Like the French?' Tatya was horrified. 'But what good would that do?'

'Some of them quite seriously talk of exterminating the Romanovs and setting up a republican government on democratic lines. They don't just want to liberate the serfs, but give them complete equality!'

'Sheer lunacy!' Vassily commented. 'The Autocracy suits Russia very well. Given an able, well-intentioned Emperor with a sound set of advisers, you'd hardly find a better form of government for an empire of this size. What's the use of giving equality to ignorant, illiterate peasants? They have to be educated first, so that they know how to think and make decisions, otherwise they'd be like sheep without a shepherd!'

'Autocracy's all very well if the Autocrat's the right kind of man,' put in Boris. 'But what if he isn't? What about the last Emperor?'

'He was dealt with easily enough!' replied Vassily sardonically. There was a moment's uneasy silence. Even among friends, it was not altogether wise to refer openly to the rumours that the half-mad Pavel I had been murdered, and not simply died of an apoplexy as the official account said.

'What about the serfs, then?' Boris hastily changed the subject a little. 'I don't believe it's right for anyone to own people—human souls.'

'Have you freed yours, then?' Vassily asked, knowing the answer already. Boris wanted the family serfs to be freed, but his father, a conservative with an eighteenth-century outlook, would not hear of it.

'I shall,' Boris replied firmly, 'when I can. Nikolai has, and Lev and Tatya.'

Vassily looked surprised. 'I knew Nikolai had, but . . . hmmm.' He dropped out of the conversation and appeared very thoughtful for some time, while the others went on to discuss the best method of providing education for the peasants.

CHAPTER
FIVE

On Sunday, Lev and Irina attended morning service in the Kazan Cathedral, and in the afternoon Boris and Vassily arrived on horseback and suggested a ride in the country. Lev agreed readily, and Irina said she would like to go too, but only if she might ride in the carriage as she was not a good horsewoman.

Vassily looked at Tatya. He didn't say anything, but she replied to the unspoken question by saying 'I'll come with you, Irina,' in a nervous tone. Irina looked quite startled, and so did Lev, for Tatya had not suggested going for a drive for years.

She enjoyed the afternoon, and began to look forward to the next day's planned excursion to Pavlovsk. If only the weather would stay fine!

Fortunately, it did, and they set out quite early in the morning, the ladies in Prince Nikolai's large berline and the men on horseback. Vladimir appeared in civilian dress, much to everyone's surprise, and Vassily commented, 'Good Heavens, Volodya! I didn't know you had any ordinary clothes! In fact, I thought your uniform grew on you, like a second skin.'

'Don't call me Volodya,' Vladimir replied repressively. 'I like to give the moths an airing occasionally, and it serves to remind some of you that I'm not just a clockwork soldier—there is actually a man inside the uniform.' He spoke quite lightly and kept his eyes on Vassily as he spoke, but Tatya, glancing covertly at Olga, was pleased to see that the shaft went home and the girl was at least looking thoughtful.

A second carriage brought up the rear of the party, carrying some of Prince Nikolai's servants and all the equipment and food for an al fresco luncheon, which they took in a pleasant spot near the Apollo Colonnade, looking across the lake to the simple Palladian central block of the Palace, which the Empress Ekaterina had given to her son Pavel.

After luncheon, Boris said that he had the permission of the Emperor to take them inside to view the State apartments, and there was a little confusion as most of them wished to go, but no-one was quite sure whether Tatya would want to go with them or not. Vassily, guessing correctly that she had no great wish to do so, said, 'I'll stay out here in the sun, I think. Will you stay with me, Tatya?'

Her acceptance solved the problem, and the others went with Boris to stroll along the lakeside to the bridge and so across to the Palace, leaving the servants to clear away the remains of the picnic and eat their own food. Vassily stretched out on the grass, his hands clasped behind his head, contemplating the sky above him.

Tatya, sitting on some cushions a few feet away from him, took the opportunity to look at him. He was an attractive man, she thought. Not handsome—not with that outrageous hair, and his face was too thin—but his body was lithe and slim, wide shoulders tapering to narrow hips and long, well-shaped legs, set off by the close-fitting clothes which he favoured.

'I'd be happy to carry you around if you'd prefer to go inside,' he said suddenly.

'I'd rather stay out here,' Tatya replied. 'It's not my most favourite of palaces, by any means.' She looked up at the Apollo Colonnade, and went on, 'That's odd! Last time I was here, the colonnade was a complete circle, but now it's half ruined. It looks more romantic like that.'

'It fell down one afternoon after some very heavy rain.' Vassily rolled over on his stomach, propped his chin on his hands and contemplated it. 'Yes, I suppose a ruin is more romantic, but it needs some ivy and an owl or two. Classic Doric columns are—well, classical, not romantic.'

'Yet another copy of the Apollo Belvedere,' Tatya gestured towards the statue in the centre.

'Yes. I saw the original in Paris.' Vassily gave a reminiscent laugh. 'Part of Bonaparte's loot. I expect he's gone home again by now. Someone said I looked like him. Do you see any resemblance?'

Tatya strained her eyes to see the statue's face. 'I shouldn't think so—I don't believe your features are at all Greek.'

Vassily laughed again. 'I don't imagine that was what she meant! I was—er—dressed in the same way at the time, except that I lacked a cloak.'

Tatya looked at the nude statue and thought that she would like to see Vassily like that, and then flushed. He saw her colour, and for once misinterpreted her thoughts.

'I'm sorry. I'm a shocking fellow, I'm afraid. I tend to say whatever comes into my head when I'm at ease with someone, and I'm very much at ease with you. I don't mean to be offensive.'

'You're not,' she replied. 'You speak of things quite naturally, with no unpleasant overtones, so they're not offensive.'

He studied her face for a few moments, and then said, 'Tatya. Is it true what Boris said—that you've freed your serfs?'

'Yes. I inherited my—the General's estates, and I freed them then.'

'I'm afraid I've not thought much about it. I've provided mine with schools and hospitals, and I've started a few manufactories so that they can earn money if they choose. I try to treat them fairly, and I think they're quite happy. Would you like me to free them?'

'It's not for me to say,' Tatya replied, disconcerted. 'I mean—what difference can my opinion make? It's a very important matter, something you must decide for yourself.'

'But something a lover might do to please his sweetheart.'

Tatya was really shaken by that. 'But you're not . . . You wouldn't do such a thing just in support of a game?'

He looked at her quizzically, then became quite serious and said, 'I'll offer you a bargain. When you tell me that you've spent a night in bed with a man, I'll free half my serfs. When you tell me you're with child, I'll free the rest.'

Tatya's first reaction was to look to see if any of the servants could have heard, but they had gone some way away to eat their meal. Then she looked at Vassily, wide-eyed and shocked. 'But that's . . .'

'Blackmail,' he supplied. 'It's not as bad as it sounds, *dushenka*. I don't suggest that the man should be me, and it could as well be in wedlock as out of it. In fact, that's what I mean. You want a husband and some children, don't you? Oh, don't look so surprised—it's easy enough to see! I've only to watch your face when you look at Ilya! That brute frightened you so much that you're torn in half between longing and fear! I'm just offering you a little extra incentive to help you overcome your fear, find your man, marry him and be happy.'

Tatya's eyes filled with tears, and he moved closer and took her hands in his, saying, 'Don't cry, Tatya. I'm not trying to force you into anything. I want to help, that's all. I can't stand by and see someone as gentle and sweet as you waste her life in loneliness and heartache for want of a little encouragement. I'll show you a little of the pleasure you could find in love-making, but I'll not trespass on the rights of the man you'll marry. Don't be afraid of me, *dushenka*.'

'I'm not afraid of you,' she replied quite calmly. 'In fact, I think that one day I might be able to tell you . . . Not yet, though, but if you'll be patient with me . . . You've helped me a great deal in these past few days, and I feel so much better already. I think I was moping myself into old age, too wrapped up in self-pity to make the effort to do anything. You've made me see that there's still a life to be lived, and perhaps I can still hope to find someone . . . someone I could love and trust.'

'Yes.' He gave a wry smile. 'I thought we shared much the same problem. Love and trust. Perhaps you'll help me as much as I help you. Shall we take a ride round the park?'

The change of subject was abrupt, but it served to release the tension. Tatya replied, 'The drivers are still eating.'

'We'll go on horseback, then.' He went to fetch his horse, and lifted her on to it, then mounted behind her and set the animal to a gentle amble along the neat pathways of the park. Tatya leaned against him, enjoying the fresh air, the fine trees and the flowers as they rode along by the lake and the river which fed it, crossing over to see the cascades and the Temple of the Graces, and then back again to the carriages. The others had returned and it was time to drink the lemonade which had been kept cool by plunging the bottles in the lake.

A little later, they set out on the drive back to St Petersburg, where they all dined at the Orlov house and spent a merry evening talking and amusing themselves with music and singing. Tatya went to bed tired out, but feeling happier than she had been for a very long time.

The next afternoon, Irina and Lev had arranged another sitting with Borovikovsky, and set off after luncheon, leaving Tatya in the garden-room with her hair becomingly arranged, and dressed in a very pretty sprigged muslin gown, for the fine weather persisted and it was very warm. She told herself firmly that none of this was intended for Vassily's benefit, but was only a necessary effort to make the best of herself, for there was no need to be dowdy just because one was past thirty and crippled. After all, Vassily might not come . . .

But he did. He came strolling across the garden from the stableyard, whistling a tune from a Haydn concerto, wearing his Byronic shirt and soft cravat, and carrying his coat, which he dropped carelessly across a chair before taking Tatya in his arms. He had such an air of

merriment and vitality that she greeted him with a
responsive smile and entered into his kiss in a far more
positive way than she had done before.

'You're the fairest flower in the garden, Tatya,' he
said, appreciatively, surveying the pretty gown and the
shining hair. 'So why are you indoors?'

'Because I can't go far into the garden. There are too
many steps for my chair.'

He picked her up and carried her outside, carefully
stepping over Vron, who was sunning himself on the
steps. The cat got up and stalked after them, tail erect, as
they passed between the beds of rose-bushes, already
showing flower-buds, and the newly-planted pansies. At
the far end they descended a few steps, passed under an
arch in the high brick wall, and entered the water-
garden.

'Oh!' Tatya exclaimed. 'I'd forgotten what it's like!
It's so long since I was here!'

The garden was worthy of her delighted exclamation.
The large pond occupying the centre was a perfect oval,
and a tiny rocky islet had been constructed on its golden
section, with a willow tree growing on it, its branches
sweeping down to meet their own reflection in the clear
water. Round the pond was a broad band of brick paving
with clumps of aromatic herbs growing here and there,
their sharp scent heavy in the sunshine, attracting drowsy
bees to their pale flowers. Between the paving and the
walls of the enclosed garden there were informal beds of
summer flowers, with little mossy paths running among
them. The whole garden had an air of peace and tran-
quillity, warm and sheltered inside its old walls in the
afternoon sun, and looked much larger than it really
was.

At the far end of the pond, the paving curved back
into the flowers and another willow tree formed a little
arbour over a rustic seat. Vassily took Tatya to it,
brushing through the thin pale branches with their bright
new leaves, and sat down with her on the seat. He
watched her face as she gazed about her at the pleasant

scene. Vron had followed close behind, and he now sniffed dubiously at Vassily's soft leather boots, decided that he was probably harmless, and wandered away to sit hunched on the edge of the pond like an elderly fisherman, with much the same intention towards the golden carp swimming lazily in the green water.

'*Dushenka!*' Vassily's arms slid round Tatya, and he began to kiss her neck, nuzzling his face into her curls and caressing her back and shoulders with gentle hands. It gave her a delightful sensation which was exciting without being in the least alarming, and made her give a little gasping laugh and exclaim, 'Oh, Vasya!'

He was suddenly quite still, his whole body rigid, and she said in concern, 'What is it?' He relaxed, moving a little away from her, and stared at her with a drawn, painful expression on his face.

'It's a long time since anyone called me that,' he said quietly.

Tatya had a flash of understanding. 'Is that what *she* called you?'

He nodded.

'I'm sorry. I won't say it again.'

'But I'd like you to call me Vasya,' he replied with an uncertain smile. 'I said I'd tell you about it, so perhaps I'd better get it over, if it won't bore you.'

'Of course it won't.' Tatya took one of his hands between both her own and held it while he talked, his eyes set on some invisible point across the garden and his voice quiet and carefully controlled.

'I was twenty. She was our neighbour's daughter, Natalya Stepanovna. A sweet, pretty little thing, merry and good-natured, or so I thought. Two of us loved her. The other was a dissolute fellow—a gambler and a drunkard—and her parents favoured my suit. She said she loved me, over and over again, and I believed her—trusted her. We were betrothed and the wedding day set. Everything was arranged, then, just a few days before the wedding was to have been, she ran off with my rival. She left a letter for her father, saying she'd

meant to marry the other fellow all the time and she'd
only pretended to love me to disarm suspicion, but she
didn't leave any message at all for me. If she'd only been
honest with me . . . It destroyed something in me. I've
never been able to trust a female since.'

The short, painful sentences came to an end and he
was silent. Tatya put up one hand to his head and drew it
down, and he slid to his knees beside her, his face
pressed against her breast, and they were very still for
some time.

At length, he raised his head and said, 'There's a little
more to it. I saw her again last year, in Karlsbad. She was
taking the waters with her husband and a couple of
spotty children. She'd grown enormously fat, with a
shrewish face and an ill-tempered voice. Her husband
and I got very drunk together one night, and he told me
what a lucky escape I'd had!' He gave a laugh which
broke in the middle and sounded more like a sob.
'Ironic, isn't it? I let her spoil my life because she left me,
but she'd probably have spoiled it equally if she'd stayed
and married me!'

'Dear Vasya,' Tatya whispered. 'I'm so sorry.' It
seemed an inadequate response to his story, and she
wished she could think of something more to say. She
stroked his bright hair, and then ventured, 'It's not that
she didn't love you that hurts so much, I suppose. It's the
feeling that you've been used—treated as a thing, not a
person with feelings of your own that matter.' Her eyes
filled with tears, and she made no attempt to stop them
trickling down her cheeks.

'Yes,' Vassily's voice was muffled, his face against her
breast again. 'That's it exactly. Being used. If only she'd
told me the truth . . .' He raised his head to look up at
her face and broke off when he saw that she was crying.
In a moment, he was sitting beside her again, taking her
almost violently in his arms, his eyes intense with concern. 'Oh, my sweet girl! You mustn't cry for me! Tatya,
dushenka! Don't cry!'

He kissed her cheeks and eyes, and then her mouth,

and for a second she was frightened, for his kiss was wildly passionate, beyond anything she had ever imagined, but the fear passed almost before she realised what it was, and she felt just as though something inside her snapped.

The kiss went on for a long time, crushing her lips against her teeth until she was sure they were bruised, but that was of no importance at all. The only thing that mattered was the extraordinary feeling that her whole body was melting, blending with Vassily's into a new entity. She felt oddly disappointed when he suddenly broke away and said, 'I'm sorry,' in a curiously unsteady and abrupt voice.

'It's not really the pain at all,' she said in the tones of one making a momentous discovery. 'It's the feeling of being used. The humiliation of knowing that you don't matter as a person at all.'

'I'm not . . .' Vassily began, then realised that she was not talking about the way he had kissed her. He nodded slowly. 'Yes. You've learned something from that kiss. Perhaps you'll forgive me for it after all. Nevertheless, I'm sorry, my dear. I promised I wouldn't hurt or frighten you.'

'You didn't,' she replied softly. 'I'd no idea it was like that.'

'Then imagine what it's like when two people love one another,' he said, smiling. 'Thank you for listening to me, Tatya. Will you talk to me now?'

'What shall I tell you?' she asked nervously.

'About your accident.'

She was so relieved that he had not said her marriage that it seemed quite easy to talk about the lesser bitter memory, although she had not found it so before.

'It was nearly five years ago, late in August. We were at Ryazan for the summer, and we were invited to a christening at the home of some friends in the town, about six miles away. Irina was carrying the twins, and it was near her time, so she decided not to go as the roads were not very good. Lev didn't wish to leave her, so I went alone, with just my maid and the coachman. I stayed rather later than I had intended, and it was dark when we set out to go home. I think the coachman had probably had too much to drink, for he was driving much too fast for the state of the road. I called to him to slow down, and I think he reined in the horses, but there was a sharp bend in the road and we were still going too fast. The carriage came off the road and overturned. Dolly, my maid, and I were trapped inside, and the coachman was flung against a tree and broke his neck.'

She was silent for a moment, gazing into space and remembering the horror of that night. Then she reluctantly continued, 'The glass in the windows had smashed and cut Dolly very badly, and . . . and she died during the night. I couldn't do anything to help her. I couldn't move, and I could feel the terrible pain in my leg, but I didn't know what had happened to it. Lev assumed I'd stayed the night with our friends, so no-one came until a farmer passed along the road in the morning, going to town.' She stopped again and there was a short silence, then Vassily asked, 'What had happened to your leg?'

'It was crushed. The bones were smashed from the knee to the ankle. The surgeons wanted to amputate it, but Lev wouldn't let them. It healed in the end, but it's no use at all. It won't take any weight, so I can't use it, even to stand, let alone walk. It's very ugly.'

Vassily held her in a comforting embrace, and after a time, he said, 'There's nothing one can say, is there? I'm sorry it happened, but what use is it to say that? There's only one thing worse than pity, and that's self-pity.'

'I try not to,' she said sadly.

'Not to what?'

'Wallow in self-pity.'

'I hadn't thought you did. There's a great difference between feeling lonely and depressed, and merely feeling sorry for yourself.'

'There are many people much worse off than I am. I'm perfectly healthy, with a loving brother and sister-in-law to look after me, and they try so hard to keep me amused and happy. I've their children to love. I'm so wealthy that I can have anything I want that money can buy. I've servants to fetch and carry for me, and it doesn't really matter that I can't walk. Many people are blind or deaf or diseased, starving, alone, cruelly treated. I've no reason to feel sorry for myself.'

'All very true, but it's no comfort, is it?' Vassily said gently. 'If you're healthy, you want to run about and dance. However much Irina and Lev love you and care for you, you've still no-one of your own. Money can't buy the things you really want.'

'And you?' Tatya asked, looking him straight in the eyes.

He looked disconcerted for a moment, then replied, 'I'm still trying to find out what I want. Let's concentrate on you for the moment.'

'What more is there to say? I want a husband and children, but I don't think anyone would want me now I'm crippled, and I'm so afraid of being used and humiliated again.'

'The first of your fears is nonsense,' he said firmly. 'If a man loves you, he won't refrain from marrying you because you can't walk. It certainly wouldn't stop him from falling in love with you in the first place. As for the other—I don't know exactly what General Kalinsky did to you, but I hope that you'll trust me enough to tell me before long, because I think you'd lose a great deal of the bitterness and fear if you could talk about it. Whatever it was, the odds are heavily against the same thing happening again with another man. If you really love someone, you'll find you can trust him. It's a matter of having faith in him, and I'm afraid I can't help you very much there, as I'm in the same case. If you find the secret of how to learn to trust someone, I'd be grateful if you'd tell me, because I've lost it too. Does your leg hurt very much?'

'No, only when I'm tired or the weather is cold or damp.'

'Perhaps Petersburg isn't the best place for it, then. It

does tend to be damp here . . . What on earth is that cat doing?'

Vron had suddenly risen to his feet and was stretching out as far as he could reach with one paw, dabbing at something in the water, apparently torn between desire for whatever it was and a dislike of getting his foot wet.

'I think he's trying to catch a fish,' Tatya began. Vron made a particularly hard jab at the water, over-reached himself completely, and fell in with a great splash. Vassily jumped up and was halfway to the rescue when the animal fairly leapt out of the water with a shrill yowl of fury and ran off into the flowerbeds, dripping a trail of water and rich green weed behind him.

'I think a fish caught him!' Vassily returned to Tatya's side laughing.

'Will he be all right?' Tatya asked anxiously. 'He won't take cold, will he?'

'He'll lick the worst off and dry in the sun. I should think he'll have worse adventures than that in his nine lives!' Vassily went on to talk of other things, and once more his talent for description and anecdote held Tatya fascinated, oblivious of time, until the distant chime of the bells of the Petropavlovsky Cathedral reminded them that it was time for Vassily to go.

He carried her back to her daybed and kissed her goodbye, saying, 'We're all to come here again tomorrow. Will you mind if we bring Ilya? He'll like to see the fish.'

'Yes, do bring him, if Nikolai will allow it. He's such a good child!'

He picked up his coat and took a small, round object from the pocket, which he gave to her. 'This will puzzle you. See if you can open it.' Then he kissed her again and went away, turning to wave before he vanished through the stableyard arch.

Tatya sat looking after him for quite a long time, trying to come to terms with the emotional experiences of that afternoon. There was so much to think about, and how strangely different she felt about so many things

. . . and what had happened when he kissed her? . . . it was all very confusing.

She turned her attention to the object which he had put into her hand. It was a little larger than an egg, but quite spherical, and made of metal. The whole surface was covered with enamel—little trails of ivy in natural colours on a very pale blue ground. In the spaces between the leaves were little insects—lady-birds, a butterfly, a greeny-blue beetle, and one tiny scarlet heart, which was slightly raised. She studied it carefully, entranced by the delicate workmanship, and presently saw that a fine line ran round it among the ivy trails. It did not twist nor pull apart, but when she pressed the little raised heart, it sprang open on a concealed hinge and spring.

Inside was something soft which pulled out and unfolded into a very, very fine pale green silk scarf which shimmered in the sunlight like a spider's web, and, indeed, was not much thicker than one. Tatya held it against her face, where it felt like a dragonfly's wing, and then stretched it out across her lap and admired it with delight.

She was still looking at it when Lev and Irina came in, catching her unawares by entering through the open garden door.

'Hallo!' exclaimed Lev. 'What's that? It looks like a puff of wind!'

'Oh, how lovely!' Irina stretched out a hand to touch it. 'Wherever did it come from?'

'It was inside this.' Tatya showed them the enamelled ball, fitting the two halves together again. They looked at it with interest and admiration, but had to be shown how it opened, and then Irina asked again, 'Where did it come from?'

'Vassily brought it,' Tatya replied, and waited for the inevitable questions.

'I wonder where he found it. In the Gostinny Dvor, I suppose,' Lev said, referring to the warren of tiny shops in a building in the Nevsky Prospect, famous for the pretty trifles, toys, bibelots, gloves and jewels sold

there. 'We must go and find some little gifts for the
children there before we go home.' He went on to talk
about the various interesting things he had seen on his
own visits to the little shops, and somehow there was no
question about why or when Vassily had given Tatya the
ball. She slipped it into her reticule and laid the fine silk
scarf round her shoulders, enjoying the cool softness
against her neck and joining in Lev's reminiscences
about the many Christmas and name-day gifts they had
given or received which had come from the Gostinny
Dvor.

During the evening, Olga and Boris called. They sat
talking for some time, and then Boris went with Lev to
his study to look at the plans of a sawmill which Lev
proposed to build on one of his estates, Irina went to
dose a sick servant, and Olga stayed chatting with Tatya
in the garden-room, discussing the visit to Pavlovsk,
which Olga had never visited before.

'In fact, I've hardly been anywhere,' she said wistful-
ly. 'I just pray every morning that there won't be a letter
from my mother telling me I must go home.'

'But I thought you were to stay with Rose and Nikolai
until they go to Poland with the Emperor at the end of
July.'

'That is the plan,' Olga replied. 'But plans are always
being changed. Every time I've planned to go anywhere
before, it's fallen through because Mamma wanted me
at home. I was supposed to have my come-out nearly
three years ago, when I was seventeen. My aunt brought
me to Petersburg, and I had dozens of gowns and
bonnets all ready. I went to one ball at the Palace and
was Presented, and the very next day I had a letter to say
that Mamma was ill again, and I had to go straight
home.'

'Does she become very ill?'

Olga hesitated. 'I don't really know. She had several
babies, but they were all born dead except for Boris and
me, and I believe it's something to do with that. She lies
on a daybed all the time, and the slightest thing gives her

the headache or palpitations, and if I'm not there to bathe her head or give her hartshorn, she cries and says that no-one cares about her. She promised I should come here for this last Season, but I didn't actually get here until just two weeks before Lent began, and nearly everything was over by then. I don't mean to be wicked or ungrateful, but I do wish she would try to do without me a little more. It's so dull at home, and I never meet anyone there, for we don't entertain at all—it tires Mamma too much.'

'I hear you were very shy when you came,' Tatya began cautiously. 'It must have been quite an ordeal to meet so many people when you weren't used to it.'

'I was *terrified*!' Olga replied candidly. 'I thought everyone was staring and criticising me all the time! Vladimir Sergeivich helped me, though. He was so kind and gentle, and do you know—he told me that he's shy himself! I was a little afraid of him too before he told me that!'

'But you're not afraid of him now?'

Olga laughed. 'Oh, no! He's a wonderful, good, kind man! The only thing is . . .' she sobered and hesitated. 'He's . . . well . . . just a bit . . .'

'Dull,' Tatya supplied.

Olga looked at her wide-eyed. 'Do you think so too?'

'No. I'm quite sure he's not. He's very shy, and he's also very correct. You see, he's never had much time to spend in the society of ladies, for he's so taken up with his military duties. He's a very good officer, not one of those frippery young fellows who just want to lounge about in a smart uniform. You'll meet any number of men who'll flirt with you, or worse, and seem exciting, but all of them together wouldn't be worth exchanging for Vladimir.'

'Yes, I know that really,' Olga said sadly. 'I do really care for him, and I know that when I marry him, I'll be very safe and happy, but I've never had any real *fun*, Tatya! I just want a little excitement and enjoyment before I settle down. There's nothing wrong with that, is there?'

Tatya smiled sympathetically. 'No dear, not really. It's only natural, and I think Vladimir realises that's all it is, but don't try his patience too far. If you really care for him, it would be a great pity to lose him through going on too long with your flirting and enjoying yourself. I think you'll find that Vladimir isn't at all dull once you're betrothed and he has the right to kiss you, and show you a little more of his feelings.'

'I don't want to hurt him,' Olga said anxiously. 'It's so exciting to be liked and admired! I've never known it before, you see.'

'Don't let it go to your head,' Tatya said kindly. 'Some men seem very much attached to you and pay you compliments, but most of it doesn't really mean very much, and some of them are quite dangerous.'

'I suppose you mean Sergei Dmitriev?' Olga sounded defensive. 'He said you'd all try to turn me against him, just because his sister made poor Nikolai so unhappy.'

'That has nothing to do with it,' Tatya said firmly. 'Sergei Mikhailovich is a weak, dissolute, selfish fellow, and he's ruined three or four innocent, silly girls who let him turn their heads. A girl I knew at school drowned herself because he seduced her and wouldn't marry her. He drinks too much and gambles as well—he's so much in debt that he's trying to find a rich heiress to marry just to get himself out of trouble. He came to Ryazan during Lent, dangling after me, so you can imagine how desperate he is!' She made it a little joke against herself.

Olga looked very serious and thoughtful. 'Yes, I believe you're right. I don't really like him very much. He's nothing like Vladimir.'

CHAPTER
SIX

PRINCE Nikolai did bring Ilya the next day, and the child
spent a couple of happy hours watching the fish in the
water-garden and sailing the little boats which Vassily
made for him out of chips of wood with twig masts. Lev
fetched a large model schooner from the house, the
property of his own children, but Ilya seemed to prefer
the simpler boats which he could watch being made, and
it was Prince Nikolai, Boris and Lev who amused themselves trying different methods of setting the sails on the
big expensive toy.

'It's very much like my yacht,' Prince Nikolai
observed. 'I wonder . . . do you think we might make
our visit to Oranienbaum in her? We could sail along the
coast and put in to the harbour there, spend as long as we
like at the Palace, and then dine and sleep on board, and
perhaps sail in the Gulf of Finland the next day and call
at Peterhof on the way back.'

'That's a first-class idea!' Lev exclaimed. 'Will there
be room for all of us, though?'

Prince Nikolai counted on his fingers. 'You, Irina,
Tatya, Rose, Marisha, Olga, Boris, Vladimir, Vassily
and myself—ten. If the ladies could manage in the two
cabins, I'm sure we men could make ourselves comfortable in the day cabin for one night—it's very large. What
do you all think?'

The plan was greeted with enthusiasm, even by Boris,
who was a notoriously poor sailor, despite having an
Admiral for a Godfather. None of the ladies had ever
been to sea, and they were all quite excited at the
prospect.

Ilya studied their faces as they talked with large,

watchful eyes, then went to his father and said hopefully, 'May I sail in your big boat?'

The Prince smiled, 'If you're a good boy and do exactly as Pyotr tells you.'

'Perhaps little Irina Alexeievna would like to come as well,' Rose suggested. 'Would you ask your mother if she may, Marisha?'

The outing to Oranienbaum had been planned for the end of the following week, and there were several other visits arranged for the intervening days. They all dined one evening with Vladimir in the Petropavlovsky Fortress, a grim, rather frightening place, Tatya thought, but she was interested to see the Cathedral again, taking some flowers to lay on the tomb of Peter the Great. The Cathedral was inside the walls of the Fortress, and its bells chimed out across the city every quarter of an hour. Here were the tombs of all but one of the Romanov Czars since Peter and their Czarinas, and Boris remarked that it must give Alexander Pavlovich the shivers to look across from the Winter Palace and see his ultimate resting-place waiting for him just over the river.

Vassily commented, 'It would be just like our revered Emperor to have himself deposited somewhere else, if only to be as far as possible from his father!' Vladimir cast an anxious glance around the Cathedral and hastily changed the subject.

Lev had worked out a way to take Tatya's wheelchair with them in a small britzka which followed behind their carriages, and it was possible for her to sit in it and be pushed about on some of their visits, but wherever there were stairs or even steps, it was much easier and caused less fuss if she was carried by Vassily, and he seemed quite happy to do so, keeping her amused by his witty comments and sharing her pleasure in the fine things of the city. In this way, they visited Peter's Kunstkamera, his little cottage and Summer Palace and Garden, and the Engineers' Castle (all with tickets of entry obtained for them by Boris) and several of the great churches. Boris could not always accompany them, for he had his duties in attendance on the Emperor at Czarskoe Selo, and Prince Nikolai also had to go to Court several times in connection with the planning for the Emperor's forthcoming visit to open the new session of the Polish Diet in Varsava.

The afternoon before the visit to Oranienbaum, Lev and Irina went for another sitting to the artist's studio, and left Tatya at home reading Pushkin. The fine weather had broken, and after a couple of unsettled days, had now decided to be thoroughly wet, and the rain was falling in a steady downpour. The stove in the garden-room had been lit against the chilly damp, and Vron had come in from the stables to take advantage of it.

Tatya lay on her daybed trying to concentrate on the adventures of Ruslan, glancing occasionally at the dismal prospect outside and wishing that Vassily might come. It was a week since she had been alone with him, and although the time had been far from dull, filled with interesting visits and conversation, she felt a strong wish to have him to herself again for a little while. Her leg ached naggingly, and she felt depressed.

'He won't come, Vron,' she said sadly. 'Not in this wretched weather.' The cat purred at the sound of its own name and industriously washed itself behind the ears. Tatya laid her book aside and watched the rain for a few minutes. It was a very melancholy sight, and presently she turned her face against the cushion and indulged in a few tears.

Vassily came in through the house and opened the door so quietly that only the cat heard him and stopped washing for a moment to look at him as he crossed the room, put the parcel he was carrying on the worktable, and took Tatya in his arms.

'Crying, *dushenka*? What's wrong?'

'Oh, Vasya! I didn't think you'd come!' She put her arms round his neck and kissed him, too pleased and surprised to see him to be shy about it, and he dried her eyes and kissed her in his most gentle and lingering manner.

'You didn't think a few drops of rain would keep me away? Is your leg paining you?'

'It aches,' she admitted. 'It makes me feel low and sorry for myself, and I didn't think you'd want to come out in this weather.'

'Now, that's a fine thing!' he said, laughing. 'I'd be a poor sort of lover not to battle to your side through tempest and blizzard, not to mention hurricane and flood! Besides, it's such a horrible day that I need a little comforting myself! I hope it clears for tomorrow. Boris has arranged for the Sliding Hill at Oranienbaum to be put in order for our use, and we'll all slide to our hearts' content. It's for the children really, but I shall certainly take a turn or two. Shall you come with me?'

'Oh, I'd love to! I haven't done it for years! Is that the one where the sledges run on greased rails? The old Empress had it built, didn't she?'

'I can't imagine any of the Romanovs but Ekaterina bothering with such a harmless and pleasant amusement! All the others were too busy plotting, scheming and playing soldiers to bother with so much as an ice-mountain in winter, let alone a permanent, all-the-year-round one!'

'Vasya!'

'Oh, I've nothing against them really!' he said, amused by her shocked expression. 'I'm a loyal supporter of the Autocracy—you've no need to report me to the police for subversion. In fact, I have the greatest admiration for Alexander Pavlovich, but he is a little on the serious side! See what I've brought you today.'

He got up and carried Tatya over to the sofa, then arranged a small table of convenient height, unwrapped the parcel he had brought with him, and laid a large leather-bound portfolio where they could sit together and look through its contents.

Tatya lingered first over the cover. It was bound in dark red morocco, tooled with gold in a pattern of arabesques forming a border, with flourishing loveknots at the corners. Within the border it was dotted with tiny stars, and in the centre was an oval cartouche with her initials, TPK in Kyrillic script.

'Vasya, it's very beautiful, but you shouldn't . . .'

'Don't you like it?'

'Yes, of course, but . . .'

'No buts, then. Say "Thank you, Vasya", and take as much pleasure in possessing it as I did in choosing it.'

'Thank you, Vasya,' she said obediently, and turned in his arms to give and receive a kiss.

Several minutes later, he opened the portfolio and together they looked through the assortment of prints inside. There were about three dozen of them, and they covered a variety of subjects. Some were delicately hand-coloured flower-studies, including two or three of Redouté's lilacs and roses, but most were views of towns and buildings in various parts of Europe.

'I just picked out a few which I thought you would like,' he explained. 'They make rather a curious assortment, I suppose. Look, here's the geyser at Karlsbad, where I encountered my lost love again.' He spoke lightly, but with an underlying bitterness which made Tatya say, 'Don't, Vasya!'

'Don't what?'

'Pretend it's a joke.'

'The habit of long years. No, it's not really funny, my dear. Or perhaps it is, but I'm the butt of the joke. Seeing her again like that gave the whole business an element of farce.'

He looked at the print again, then suddenly ripped it across again and again, and crossed the room to stuff the remains into the stove.

'That's done with it—over and forgotten!' he said briskly, sitting down again and picking up the next print, which portrayed a very romantic-looking castle perched on an improbable crag above the Rhine.

'Ah, now! How about that? Just the place to carry you off to, and hold you victim to my wicked will until some handsome knight-errant comes to rescue you from my evil clutches!'

Tatya laughed. 'I didn't know you were cast as the villain!'

'What did you take me for, then?'

'The handsome hero.'

'With this hair?'

Tatya, thinking of the lithe, masculine grace of his body, said softly, 'I think you're beautiful.'

He laughed. 'Do you mean *krasivy* (beautiful) or *krasny* (red)?' he asked in Russian.

He was answered by a loud cry from Vron, who had risen from his comfortable place by the stove and was now standing by the door to the garden demanding to be let out. Vassily went to oblige him, and said, 'I do believe the rain's stopped, and the sun's trying to break through! Perhaps it will be fine tomorrow after all!'

The next day was, indeed, very fine, with a clear blue sky set off by little puffs of white cloud, and a brisk breeze which Lev said would be just the thing for sailing, though neither Irina nor Tatya could think how he knew, for twelve years in the Heavy Cavalry does not normally give a man much idea about sailing a schooner.

Prince Nikolai's yacht *Siryena* had been brought to the English Quay for his guests to embark, and Tatya waited in the carriage there with Irina while Lev went to consult Prince Nikolai about having her chair swung aboard. The quayside was a busy, bustling place, the air full of the smell of spices, timber, tar and tallow, which were all unloaded there, with the all-pervading tang of the sea to meld them together. The yacht seemed quite a large ship, Tatya thought, nearly as big as the naval frigate slipping down the river behind it ('her' she corrected herself). The decks were very white, like a well-scrubbed kitchen table, and the hull was painted blue with a quantity of ornamental gilding and pipe-clayed ropes and fenders.

Vassily appeared on the deck, clad in an open-necked shirt and blue trousers, and came down the gang-plank to greet them. He looked them over smilingly and said, 'You both look very charming. 'I'm glad to see you've

Accept 'Give Us Forever' and 'Cloud Over Paradise' **FREE** as your introduction to **HARLEQUIN** SuperRomance.

Here's your chance to be among the first to enjoy two brilliant and sensuous new novels – absolutely FREE! They're your introduction to a brand new romance collection from Harlequin – America's leading Romance Publisher – and they offer more spellbinding involvement than you ever thought possible.

Turn the page and discover how 'Give Us Forever' and 'Cloud Over Paradise' can be yours FREE!

These blockbuster novels have taken America by storm – millions of copies have already been sold!

These two free books are our gift to you, to introduce this fabulous new collection.

If you enjoy your first Free parcel of books, we will send you the four latest SuperRomances every month for just R5.25 (plus GST) each, postage and packing free.

If you decide you no longer wish to subscribe, just let us know and we will close your subscription. There's no commitment, and *the first two books are yours to keep, whatever you decide.*

It's an opportunity too good to miss!

'Cloud Over Paradise' and 'Give Us Forever' are the first novels in a major new series — enthralling and exciting stories of love and life that will leave you breathless.

Send for yours today — accept this offer by filling in the card below and POST TODAY!

Harlequin Reader Service, IBS Group of Book Clubs, Post Bag X3010, RANDBURG 2125, 5th Floor Metro Centre, RANDBURG

Enjoy over 380 pages of sensuous excitement in each book!

- - - - - - - - - - - - - - - - ✂ - - - - - -

Yes, please send me 'Cloud Over Paradise' and 'Give Us Forever' absolutely FREE. Thereafter, please send me the four latest SuperRomances each month, which I may buy for just R5.25 (plus GST) each, postage and packing free. If I decide to close my subscription I shall write to you within 10 days of receiving my monthly parcel of books. The first two books are mine to keep, whatever I decide. I am over 18 years of age.

Please write in BLOCK CAPITALS

Name _____

Address _____

_____

Signature _____

Orders returned without a signature will not be accepted. One offer per household.

Please enclose Postage and Packing R1.00

dressed yourselves for a life afloat. Olga Mikhailovna's arrived in a silk gown, all frills and lace, and a large bonnet which will go sailing off to Sweden at the first puff of wind.'

Tatya and Irina were sensibly clad in plain fine wool gowns, Tatya's dark blue with a white braid trimming and a small white bonnet, Irina's brown with little gold buttons on the bodice and cuffs, and a plain straw bonnet. Both outfits were the result of considerable thought and consultation between the two ladies.

Marisha and Rose, who were standing on the deck with the younger Irina, were also plainly dressed, Marisha in white and Rose in a dark wine colour. They waved to their friends, and Vassily handed Irina down from the carriage, and instructed Josef, Lev's valet, who was to accompany them on the voyage, to see her safely on board. Josef gave him a faint, frosty smile, and looked about him at the nautical scene with every appearance of disapproval.

'Josef actually smiled at you!' Tatya remarked as Vassily lifted her from the carriage seat.

'Oh, we're old friends. I think he approves of my tailor,' he replied as he carried her aboard to where a chair had been bolted to the deck so that she could sit safely and watch the passing coastline in comfort.

When they were all aboard, *Siryena* slipped down the river and passed into the Gulf of Finland. The breeze was 'just right' as Lev had predicted, and beyond a few lurches as they reached the more open water beyond the river-mouth, their progress was quite smooth. Even Boris, who had looked decidedly apprehensive as they left the wide granite quay, presently relaxed and began to enjoy himself. The land receded to the north until it was lost in the haze, and fell away into the distance to the south.

'How far is it?' Tatya asked.

'To Oranienbaum? About fourteen miles, as the seagull flies,' Vassily replied.

'Which seagull?' asked Ilya, who had, as usual, firmly

attached himself to his red-haired hero. (Literally so on this occasion, as he was holding on to Vassily's shirt-sleeve, apparently in case the ship suddenly sank under them).

'That one,' Vassily replied, pointing to a handsome black-headed bird which was gliding on a parallel course almost level with the deck. 'He's the official distance-measuring seagull for the Gulf of Finland, as far as the other end of Kronstadt. Another one takes over then.'

Ilya watched the bird for a few seconds, then looked up at Vassily with his slow, sunny smile, and said, 'You are funny, Vassily Sergeivich! What's Kronstadt?'

'An island,' Vassily replied. 'There's a big fortress built on it to protect the entrance to the river.'

'Like Vladim' Sergeivich's fortress?'

Tatya wondered, more or less simultaneously, why the boy had difficulty saying 'Vladimir', but not 'Sergeivich', which she would have thought much harder, and what the Emperor would think if he heard that the Petropavlovsky had passed into new ownership. She looked along the deck to where Vladimir was pointing out a passing ship to Olga, and noticed that he had put his arm round her waist to steady her against the slight rolling of the yacht, and was bending his head so that his moustache was very close to her dark curls. She had taken off her impracticable bonnet, and her hair shone in the bright sunshine.

There were many other ships on the sea, of all kinds and sizes. Other pleasure craft were taking advantage of the good weather, fat, heavily-laden merchantmen were toiling into the Neva with goods from the coasts of Europe, and others were cutting through the dark sea westwards with furs and softwood in return, and two naval ships were heading out under new sails and rigging towards their normal station at Kronstadt after refitting in the Admiralty dockyard.

After some time, *Siryena* turned a little south of the main shipping lane and approached nearer to the coast, and they could see the great palace at Peterhof, which was now uninhabited and rarely used, and soon the fortress and harbour on Kronstadt came into view to the north-west, with a forest of masts showing that the greater part of the Russian Baltic fleet was there, and then the schooner headed inshore towards the harbour of Oranienbaum.

It was approached by a canal which passed between avenues of trees to a large square of enclosed water with deeply recessed bays at either end, surrounded by an ornamental quay lined with poplar trees, the whole large enough to accommodate half a dozen ships the size of *Siryena*. Inland, more poplars lined a long terrace, and on higher ground above it could be seen the huge formal garden of the Great Palace, which was raised on a yet higher terrace, and formed a long, shallow curve, with a central pavilion and two side pavilions, each crowned by a dome.

The destination of the party was not, however, the Great Palace, but the much smaller Chinese Palace on the far side of the park. It was quite a long walk across the romantically landscaped grounds with their little hills and valleys, woods and open spaces, many with artificial ponds contrived in them, and Tatya went in her wheelchair, which Vassily pushed, with Ilya and Irina Kirova walking on either side of him, asking questions most of the time, which he answered apparently un-tiringly, frequently with absurdities which set them laughing and skipping with delight.

The Chinese Palace, built for the Empress Ekaterina II, was a small building by Romanov standards, painted a pretty pale pink, its garlanded columns picked out in white. It was not the least Chinese in appearance, although parts of the light Rococo interior had a vaguely oriental look. The only really Chinese features were the abundant pottery tea-barrels in the formal garden, a few large porcelain vases, and the silk panels in one of the smaller rooms.

Prince Nikolai had sent some of his servants ahead by road to prepare luncheon, and this was served in the larger of the 'Chinese' rooms, which had a few oriental motifs. Tatya wondered why they did not use the actual dining-room, and mentioned this to Vassily, who replied, 'Some of the wall-paintings in there are mildly obscene, and might put us off our food!'

After the meal, they wandered about the little palace for a while, and Vassily carried Tatya to one room which he said she would particularly like, and, indeed, she gasped with delight when she saw it, for its main decoration was twelve large panels of strange birds among exotic trees and flowers, embroidered in thick silks. The magic of the room lay in the backgrounds of these panels, for they were covered with little glass beads, and the whole room had a milky moonlit effect as they shimmered with ever-changing shades of the palest pastel colours.

'Isn't it a romantic room?' Vassily said. 'If this place were mine, I'd have this for my bedroom, and have my own private supply of moonlight.'

'It's very beautiful,' Tatya agreed, and caught herself wondering what it would be like to share it with him, and then realised that the idea aroused neither fear nor revulsion, and hastily concentrated on something else.

Presently, they all strolled back across the park to the Sliding Hill, which was built on to a very pretty blue and white pavilion of an odd triangular plan, topped by a dome shaped like a sugar-loaf. They entered by means of a curving double flight of steps to the first floor, and then up an inside staircase to a large circular hall painted in delicate colours, with very large windows all round, from which they could go out on to the terrace where the slide began, and the attendants were waiting for them.

Vladimir went first, embarking on one of the sledges with Ilya sitting in front of him, firmly held between the Colonel's knees. Their sledge went off down the long ramp, gathering speed on the first steep descent, rising over the 'hill' in the middle, then swooping down the slope beyond to the accompaniment of a wild shriek of excitement from the boy, to the foot of the slide, where an attendant pushed it round to the side and hooked it to the rope to be winched up one of the rising lanes on either side of the central slide.

Boris was already preparing to follow as soon as Vladimir's sledge reached the bottom. He had little Irina with him, and was telling her reassuringly that he would hold her very tightly, oblivious of the fact that the child was almost bouncing with impatience to be off and not showing the least sign of nervousness. She started to laugh as the sledge was launched, and shrieked with merriment all the way down.

Prince Nikolai and Rose went next, then Lev and the older Irina, although she said that it was rather undignified for elderly married ladies, but was obviously not going to miss the fun for all that. Vassily, who had found a seat for Tatya on the low balustrade of the terrace, bent over her to ask if she would take a turn with him, and she replied, 'I should very much like to. I used to enjoy an Ice Mountain when I was young.'

'Were they invented then?' asked Vassily as he carried her to the next sledge and settled her in it. 'I don't recall—it was so long ago!'

'Then you must be even older than you pretend,' Tatya replied in the same vein as the attendant gave her a length of silk cord. She wrapped her skirts firmly round her legs and secured them with the cord to prevent them blowing up or hanging over the side, recalling that some friends had once been thrown off an ice mountain by a coat-tail catching under the sledge-runner.

Vassily was laughing at her quick retort as he slipped into position behind her with a leg on either side, his thighs gripping her tightly, clasped her round the waist, and said, 'You're quite safe. This is far less dangerous than an Ice Mountain. All right?'

'Yes,' she replied, smiling in anticipation as she recalled the childhood thrill of rushing down the slope. She gave the word to the attendant, who loosed the sledge and gave it a hard shove. It shot forward, tilted at the top edge of the incline, then roared down the rails at ever-increasing speed, the air rushing past in a gale, and the dip and rise coming to meet them at an incredible rate.

Tatya gasped as they reached the bottom of the dip and shot up the other side, slowing perceptibly as they neared the top, hesitated, apparently on the point of flying off, and then began the final descent. Vassily's arms tightened round her and he gave a Cossack yell, a wild, exultant shout, as they swooped through the air, faster and faster, then slowed and came to rest safely at the foot of the ramp.

'Oh, it was *wonderful*!' Tatya exclaimed, her eyes sparkling and her cheeks flushed.

As the hauling rope took the strain and they began to glide up the righthand incline towards the terrace, Vassily murmured in her ear, 'It's one way of getting you to fly with me, I suppose. We're not really so very old, are we *dushenka*?'

'No,' she replied, catching her breath at the tumult of feeling inside her, which was by no means all due to the excitement of the slide. 'No. I've shed at least ten years on the way down!'

They were all as boisterous as children on the way back to the harbour after a couple of hours of sliding, laughing and joking, flushed with the excitement and exhilaration of the Sliding Hill, even Marisha, usually such a sedate young lady, showing a rare animation.

After dinner, they sat out on deck, where a number of folding canvas chairs had been set out, and there they stayed until far into the night, talking and singing. Boris had borrowed a couple of balalaikas from the sailors, and he and Vassily played them. Boris sang a few very sentimental ballads, his dark eyes gazing meaningfully at Marisha, and then Vladimir leaned across and took his instrument from him, cleared his throat a trifle self-consciously, and sang a German serenade in a rich, deep baritone, which made Olga sit up and stare at him with wide eyes and parted lips, turning away in momentary confusion when he looked straight at her and smiled at the end of it. After a second, she dimpled at him under her lashes, and Tatya thought to herself that Vladimir would have no rivals if he smiled more often. He was really very handsome behind that wooden exterior.

Later, when the sun had sunk behind the trees and the twilit 'white night' was already showing the pink tinge of dawn in the north-east, Vassily sang an Italian lovesong. He had a pleasant tenor voice, well-suited to the song, and Tatya listened to it with a strange, sad yearning. She did not understand the words, but the beauty of the melody brought a catch to the back of her throat, and she wished she could believe that he was really singing for her, but he sat half turned away from her, his eyes on the strings of the instrument, and his face was serious and melancholy in the half-light, apparently absorbed in his thoughts and the words of his song.

When it ended, they were all silent for a few moments, and then there was a murmur of applause which Vassily acknowledged with a slight bow. Prince Nikolai shifted a little in his chair, no doubt to ease the constant ache of his old wound, and said, 'When do you and Marisha plan to be married, Boris?'

'In the winter,' Boris replied. 'Marisha hasn't properly come out yet, so we thought we'd wait until about halfway through the Season, to give her a chance to meet a few more people, and perhaps change her mind.' He said it with the calmness of a man entirely confident that he could safely make such a joke, and Marisha's 'Boris!' was accompanied by a serene, happy smile.

'Perhaps it will be a double wedding,' Lev remarked with a glance at Vladimir, who cleared his throat, tugged his moustache and said nothing, while Olga looked down at her hands clasped in her lap and probably blushed in the twilight.

'Why has the conversation taken this morbid turn?' Vassily asked lightly. 'Weddings and funerals!'

'No-one mentioned funerals!' Boris exclaimed.

'What's the difference? A wedding is the funeral of a man's freedom!'

'Vassily!' Prince Nikolai protested. 'I just hope, for

your sake, that someone manages to enlighten you before it's too late!'

'Ah, but I'm probably past redemption,' Vassily replied, then added with a tinge of bitterness under the lightness of his tone, 'I can't imagine that anyone would wish to be bothered with me, in any case.'

'I would,' thought Tatya, so clearly in her own mind that for a moment she feared that she might have spoken aloud. The two words were so unequivocal that they shocked her, and she felt immediately that, even in her own thoughts, she must qualify them with all kinds of additions—'I mean, I'm sorry that he was so let down, that he's lonely and bitter,' and a number of other confused and incoherent excuses, shying away from the memory of all those strange, tremulous feelings which had been troubling her since she met him, and telling herself severely, 'It's only because he's kind to me, and I wish him happy in return. It's only a game—I mustn't take it seriously—only a game . . .'

When he carried her down to the cabin she was to share with Irina and Rose, she murmured, 'Your song was so beautiful and so sad.'

'It was meant to be happy,' he replied with unusual seriousness. 'If you felt the sadness, it was mine, not in the words or the music.'

She lay awake for a long time, listening to the lap of water against the hull and the gentle breathing of Irina and Rose and trying not to think of anything in particular, but sleep eluded her, and she was filled with an oddly melancholy, aching sensation, as if she wanted something very much, but without knowing what it might be.

CHAPTER
SEVEN

IN THE morning, a brisk easterly breeze made it necessary for *Siryena* to tack back to Peterhof, accomplishing the short distance in two legs, the first of which took her purposely very close to Kronstadt to give the passengers a good view of the great granite walls of the fortress and harbour. The sea was fairly choppy, sparkling in the sun, and the schooner surged along with a fine bow wave creaming away from either side of her hull. Boris watched it thoughtfully for a little while, and then retreated below deck and did not return until they were safely in harbour again.

Tatya enjoyed the sail. The motion was not unpleasant, she found, once she had become confident that her chair was securely fastened and could not throw her about. She sat watching the water, the birds and the passing ships with a feeling of exhilaration. The breeze was a trifle chilly, and she was just wondering if someone would fetch her shawl from the cabin when Vassily came up behind her and put it round her shoulders.

'You looked tired at breakfast,' he said. 'Didn't you manage to sleep?'

'Not very well. I expect it was the strange surroundings.' She caught his eye, and he gave her an enigmatic smile, which made her wonder if he guessed anything of her confused thoughts.

Ilya had brought some bread on deck to feed the gulls, and was holding a piece above his head, calling, 'Here, gull! Nice gull!' in a hopeful manner. Just at that moment, half a dozen gulls caught on to the idea and swooped on him, fighting and screaming in a mad whirl of black and white wings and stabbing yellow beaks.

Vassily ran like the wind, leaping nimbly over the coils of rope at the foot of the mast, and plunged into the mêlée to rescue the child, who was petrified with fright. Lev, leaning on the rail nearby, moved closer to his sister and commented, 'Did you ever see anyone move so fast? I was still thinking about going when he arrived! I don't wonder he was in the Light Cavalry—he could have kept up with a charge without the horse!'

'I can't imagine him as a soldier,' Tatya said thoughtfully.

Lev laughed. 'He wasn't really! They gave him a uniform, but he worked in the Marshal's office as an interpreter all through 1812. Mind you, he did his share of carrying messages under fire, and he saved Boris' life and his Regimental Colour once—that was at Maloyaroslavets. He's no coward, even if he wasn't very military! I think some of those mysterious errands he's carried out abroad for the Foreign Ministry have probably been more dangerous in their way than being in the Army.' He looked sidelong at Tatya and added, 'You like him, don't you?'

'He's very kind,' Tatya replied evasively.

'Yes,' Lev gazed out to sea and whistled a little tune, and then some of the others joined him and Tatya and there was no more chance of private conversation.

The harbour at Peterhof was in an odd position at the end of a stone jetty, and by the time Prince Nikolai's guests had reached the shore, most of his sailors were sitting along the edge of it with their fishing lines.

The contrast between Peterhof and Oranienbaum added a great deal to the interest of the visit. Each had originated as a small country house, but that at Oranienbaum had been enlarged until it became a sizeable palace, and the grounds were largely naturalistic and romantic in appearance, with the exquisite pavilion of the Sliding Hill as an eccentric toy.

Peterhof, on the other hand, had been built as an afterthought. Peter Alexeivich's little house of Monplaisir remained, and a vast complex of waterworks had

been constructed in the gardens to rival Versailles and
Marly. The palace had been built to go with them.

It was far too large for everything to be seen in one
visit, and as it was such a fine day, the visitors decided to
concentrate on the gardens, and leave the inside of the
palace for a later occasion. Ilya was anxious to visit the
fishpond, he confided to Tatya, showing her a large
spotted handkerchief full of bread which *Siryena*'s cook
had given him.

'They won't all jump on me like the birds did, will
they?' he asked.

'I don't expect so,' Tatya replied gravely. 'They're
much more quiet and timid.'

Prince Nikolai said rather sternly that Ilya was not to
make a nuisance of himself about the fishpond. 'Other
people may not wish to see it,' he said. 'It's some way
from the main cascades and fountains, and you must
wait and see if anyone else wants to go there.'

Ilya replied, 'Yes, Father,' with ready obedience—he
was obviously very fond of his father and anxious to
please him, but he cast a hopeful eye on Vassily, and said
to Tatya in his confiding half-whisper, 'You could have
some of my bread for the fishes, Tatya Petrovna. I've
lots and lots, and perhaps you'd like to feed them.'

'Indeed I would,' replied Tatya, 'but I can't go there
by myself, you see, and perhaps no-one else is interested, so there may not be anyone to push my chair.'

Vassily, who was pushing the chair during this conversation, remarked over their heads, 'If anyone wants
me to push this heavy thing all the way to the fishpond,
they'll have to pay me.'

'What with?' asked Ilya anxiously.

'Bread to feed the fish.'

Ilya gave a little skip and said, 'That's all right, then.
May Irina Alexeiena come too?'

Little Irina, however, preferred to walk sedately with
her sister and Boris (who did not appear over-
enthusiastic about having her company). Rose elected to
go with Ilya, and the party split up at the main bridge

across the canal, agreeing to meet for luncheon on the terrace of Monplaisir. Vassily pushed Tatya's chair along the righthand path, Rose walking on one side, twirling her parasol and looking about her with her usual lively interest, and Ilya skipping along on the other, keeping up a steady stream of questions.

'My father says that the Emperor Peter had the fishpond made so there'd always be fresh fish, but nobody is allowed to catch any of them. Why isn't anyone allowed to catch them, Vassily Sergeivich?'

'Because they'd stop being fresh if they were taken out of the water.'

'Ilya,' Rose put in gently after the twelfth question, 'no more questions until we get to the fishpond. You'll make Vassily Sergeivich tired.'

'Yes, Mamma.' The boy smiled at Rose with great affection, and did actually manage to keep quiet until they reached the Marly lake, which was a large square area of water with a path round the margin, but the trees seemed to press closely round it, as if only the path held them back, and the water had a green, mysterious look, with the unbroken reflection of the little square house called Marly stretching towards them from the other end.

'Is it a doll's house?' asked Ilya.

'In a way,' replied Vassily. 'Look at the fish!'

The sound of their approaching footsteps had brought a number of fat carp and perch to the surface, and many of them were tame enough to take crumbs from the boy's fingers. Rose kept close to him, not actually holding on to his clothing, but obviously poised for a quick grab if he showed signs of falling in.

Vassily sat on the grass beside Tatya's chair and said softly, 'You'd like a boy like that, wouldn't you?'

'Yes,' she replied, and then added, 'wouldn't you?' because somehow Vassily's easy, patient way with the child had struck her as being out of keeping with his avowed dislike of the idea of marriage and all it entailed.

He was silent for a full second, then sighed and said,

'Yes, I suppose I would. Perhaps next time I owe you a confession, I'll . . .' He broke off because Ilya, remembering that he had some debts to pay, came running to offer him and Tatya some of his bread.

'Will you give it to the fish for me, please?' Tatya asked with a smile, but Vassily went with him to kneel by the water and crumble the bread into the waiting mouths of the greedy fish.

When the bread had all gone, they wandered along the winding path among the trees to the fountain called the Golden Staircase, and then to the great Samson fountain at the foot of the cascade in front of the Palace, where they found Olga and Vladimir sitting by one of the smaller jets bordering the canal which ran from the foot of the cascade down to the sea. They did not appear to be talking, and Olga was looking towards the Palace, her head half turned away from the Colonel, and he was watching the water sparkling in the canal, but they were holding hands, so Tatya assumed that they were not dissatisfied with one another's company, and whispered to Vassily not to disturb them.

Obediently, he pushed her chair towards the Palace side of the Samson basin, and they remained for some time looking at the staircase cascade, the plumes and jets of water shooting in all directions, and Koslovsky's fine golden statue of Samson forcing open the mouth of a lion. Ilya found it all so awe-inspiring that he held Rose's hand and stared about him with eyes like saucers, not saying a word.

After a time, they saw some of the others crossing the bridge lower down the canal, and went to join them. Olga and Vladimir fell in behind them as they passed, and they all strolled in a leisurely fashion past some more fountains—the Adam, the Sun, and the 'joke' fountain of a wrought iron tree and flowers which suddenly spouted water all over anyone who sat on the seat beside them—and so to the terrace of the original house of Monplaisir, where the whole party met for luncheon under the trees, looking out to sea.

During the afternoon, Lev and Vassily took the two children down on the shore to hunt for shells and amber, finding a sufficient quantity of both to keep them happy, and Boris kindly offered to have the amber pieces polished and made into a little necklace for the younger Irina, which delighted her. Then, all too soon, it was time to return to *Siryena* for the short voyage back to St Petersburg.

Dinner was served on board, and then the whole party returned on deck as they entered the Neva, to make the most of this unaccustomed view of the city, with its golden spires and domes bright in the evening sunshine. Prince Nikolai, who knew the river well, pointed out the great sheds where warships were built under cover to enable work to continue on them in the winter. They passed the smaller Admiralty building, and could see the gardens of the Volkhovsky Palace opposite, on Vassi- lievsky Island, and the bridge of boats which joined the island to the main part of the city just by Falconet's statue of Peter the Great, and then the schooner turned in to the south bank and came neatly alongside the English Quay.

They all went to the Orlov house and stayed for a late supper, talking about their two days of sailing and sight-seeing, and Tatya was very tired when she even- tually stretched out luxuriously between the silk sheets in her pretty Chinese bedroom.

The nights were never dark in St Petersburg in June, and even now it was light enough to see the stiff little figures on the brocade wall-covering. They reminded her of the Chinese Palace at Oranienbaum, and her feelings in the 'moonlit' room there, and she fell asleep hoping that Vassily would come to see her tomorrow— no, today, for it was past midnight—while Irina and Lev were at Borovikovsky's.

It was another fine day, and she had the glass doors of the garden-room wide open, so she heard his lilting whistle as he came through the gate from the stableyard, and watched him come towards her across the garden, his red hair and white shirt bright in the sun, and his coat slung carelessly over his shoulder, and there was no denying the eagerness she felt for his kiss of greeting.

'Well, *dushenka*? Are you quite recovered from all those fountains? Shall we go into the garden?'

He carried her through the archway into the water-garden, then nodded his head towards the wrought iron gate in the opposite wall and asked, 'What's through there?'

'A little orchard,' she replied. 'At least, my grandfather called it that, but it's just a wild garden with a few old fruit trees.'

It was impossible for him to open the gate while he was carrying her, but she twisted in his arms and managed the stiff latch, and they went through into the walled enclosure beyond.

There were perhaps a dozen apple and pear trees, mostly left to grow as they pleased, protected from the winter frosts by straw wrappings and seldom bearing any fruit worth picking, for they were still bearing the last of their blooms in the late northern season. Their trunks and branches had an eerie green glow where the light caught the lichen which covered them. Roses grew in profusion among the trees, climbing among the branches and cascading down in a tumble of fragrant petals.

Vassily looked about him appreciatively, and said, 'I like your grandfather—he had the right ideas. This is much better than all that stiff formality at Peterhof. I prefer something wild and unpredictable, like myself. It must be my romantic disposition.'

'Are you romantic?'

He laughed, then replied quite seriously, 'In spite of everything, yes, I think I am.' He glanced aside at the grass, which looked as if it had recently been cut. 'I'd better fetch a rug for us to sit on, I think. Elderly folk like us shouldn't sit on damp grass. If I set you down here, by this tree, could you support yourself until I come back?'

'Yes, I think so.' He set her down carefully, waiting to

see that she was securely supported by a low, curving branch before running off, back the way they had come.

He returned in a few minutes, laden with a large carriage-rug and an armful of cushions. His light step was noiseless, and he paused in the gateway to watch Tatya for a few seconds. She was leaning against the branch, with the thick foliage setting off the light freshness of her sprigged silk gown, and a mass of pale pink roses hung diagonally behind her dark, glossy curls, making a charming picture. As he watched, she reached out and picked one of the fat, globular flowers with a graceful movement of her shapely arm. As she held the flower to her nose, she turned her head, saw Vassily and smiled at him, her clear grey eyes soft and vulnerable. She held out the rose to him, and he dropped his burden and went to take it, kissing it and her hand as he did so.

'*Let us crown ourselves with roses before they be withered,*' he quoted, kissing her lips, and then turned away to spread the rug on the grass and pile the cushions into a comfortable seat for her, laying his rose carefully aside on one corner of the rug. He carried Tatya to the cushions and dropped to his knees beside her, and it seemed the most natural thing in the world that she lifted her face and their lips met and clung and his arms tightened round her.

Suddenly, Tatya was seized with a return of her old fears, and she jerked her head away. Vassily's embrace immediately loosened, but he kept his arms round her.

'Don't be afraid,' he whispered. 'I won't hurt you. If you don't wish to be held and kissed, you must say so—I'll not be offended.'

She turned back to him smiled uncertainly. 'It's all right now—only, just for a moment, I was afraid again. I'm sorry.'

'No need to apologise. You haven't been quite so frightened lately, have you?'

'No. It's getting better.'

'Then you'll soon find yourself a gentle, loving fellow to marry, *dushenka*. There are any number of them, just looking for a lovely creature like you to cherish. Will you invite me to your wedding?'

'But you don't like weddings!'

'I shall like yours. I shall bring you a large bundle of freed serfs on a silver salver!'

She laughed. 'You bring me such interesting presents! You're very kind to me Vasya.'

'A lover should always be kind to his lady. May I kiss you again?'

She raised her face in silent invitation, and he kissed her with a mounting intensity which increased her longing to be closer to him, so that she pressed against him, and he returned the pressure until their bodies seemed almost moulded together.

Neither was aware that Boris had come through the water-garden, and at that moment stood with his hand on the latch of the iron gate, staring incredulously through its convolutions at the picture, framed between two curving tree-trunks and a tapestry of leaves and roses, of a pair of lovers lying in a close embrace amid a scatter of cushions and rose-petals. He swallowed a gasp of astonishment as he realised that it was Tatya in the arms of Vassily—no doubt about that red hair!—and then hastily fled back to the far side of the pond and called out 'Tatya! Where are you?' before walking slowly back to the orchard gate.

After a couple of seconds, Tatya's voice answered, 'Here, in the orchard!' and by the time he had unlatched the gate and walked through the arch, Tatya was sitting on the cushions and Vassily was lying on his stomach with his chin propped on his hands, quite five feet away from her.

'Hallo, young Boris!' he exclaimed. 'Are you paying a formal call?'

Compared with Vassily, Boris did look decidedly formal in his buckskin riding breeches, well-cut coat, stiff collar and cravat, pigskin gloves and curly-brimmed hat. He kissed the hand which Tatya held out to him, and sat down on the rug at her invitation.

'Not exactly,' he replied. 'I thought last night that Tatya looked a little done-up, and I came to see if she was all right. How are you?' he asked her.

'I'm very well,' she replied, and, indeed, she both looked and felt well. 'It was all that sea air and sunshine, and seeing so many fine things, that's all. I've had such a quiet life these past few years that I'm not used to so much excitement. How is Marisha?'

'I've not seen her today,' Boris replied. 'I've been out to Czarskoe Selo, but the Emperor has excused me from attendance for a few days, so I called here on my way home.'

He sat talking to Tatya, and Vassily joined in occasionally, but for most of the time he was content to lie in the sun and listen to the others. Neither of them noticed that he had picked up the rose Tatya had given him, wrapped it in his handkerchief, and stowed it away in the full sleeve of his shirt, no doubt to prevent Boris from seeing it.

Boris was always good company, but Tatya found herself wishing profoundly that he would go away. However, he showed no sign of doing so, but lounged comfortably, leaning back on one elbow, his hat balanced on his bent knee, talking in his usual pleasant way about this and that, and presently said, 'Thank you for talking some sense into my sister's pretty little empty head. She told me what you said to her, and it certainly seems to have done her good. To tell the truth, I've been worried about her—she seemed to be turning into such a flirt!'

Vassily gave a cough which began as a laugh at this from Boris, the recently reformed flirt, and commented, 'Olga's a dear girl, but I've felt much inclined to shake her lately. There's no harm in a female flirting when she knows what she's about, but Olga's such an innocent, I'm afraid she has no idea which men are safe to flirt with, and which are the Sergei Dmitrievs of this world!'

'She's not a complete fool!' Tatya protested. 'She'd already realised something of what he's like before I said anything about him. It's only because she's led such a dull life, and craves a little excitement. I think she genuinely cares for Vladimir, but he behaves so properly with her . . .'

'I've spoken to him about that,' said Vassily. 'I think he's taken notice—I saw him being decidedly less stiff several times during our voyage in *Siryena*!'

When it was time to leave, Boris gathered up the cushions and rug and followed Vassily as he carried Tatya back to her daybed. Tatya asked him to put them on the sofa, and while his back was turned, Vassily took a small packet from his coat pocket and put it on her work-table, half-hidden under her embroidery. Then he kissed her hand formally with a wicked grimace which made her laugh, and, when Boris had made his farewell, the two men went off together.

Tatya picked up the packet when they had gone and untied the crimson silk ribbon, unwrapped the pale green tissue paper, and found a leather case inside, tooled with her initials. It contained an enamelled étui, shaped like a book. The front cover had a picture of a schooner sailing on a very rough sea, with fish sporting in the waves and a couple of seagulls hovering over the masts. On the back were two dolphins with their tails intertwined and a border of bladder-wrack. Inside was a block of cedar-wood, grooved to hold the tiny silver pencil, knife, folding scissors, ivory slip for notes, thimble and needlecase. The whole thing was no larger than a playing-card, and was a delightful memento of the sea-trip.

She looked at it very closely, appreciating the fine workmanship of the enamel and the little tools. It was something far too fine and expensive for her acceptance within the confines of normal propriety, and yet she could well understand that anyone as fastidious and sensitive to beauty as Vassily could never be content with the second-rate. With him, everything must be of the first quality.

Of course, this probably extended to people as well as

things. His sympathetic nature obviously made him tolerant of defects of character, but it was impossible to imagine him as the lover of an ugly woman . . . 'or a crippled one.' she thought. 'He's playing this game out of compassion for me, but that's all,' and she picked up her embroidery and concentrated on it with all her attention, refusing to give way to the sadness which would keep welling up in her.

Meanwhile, Boris and Vassily had mounted their horses and were riding slowly along the Gorokhovaya, still discussing Olga.

'Has it really been necessary for her to stay at home so much?' Vassily asked.

Boris frowned. 'It's difficult to say. Mother is an invalid, and she seems worse if Olga is away from her.'

'Is she very ill?'

'Well, no—not really. She had several miscarriages both before and after Olga was born, and ever since the last, she's given up doing anything at all. She lies about all the time, sewing or reading, and expects Olga to be at hand to fetch and carry and find her spectacles, or her vinaigrette, or whatever. She never goes out or entertains.'

'It's very hard on Olga.'

'Yes. There's never been anything much I could do to help, for I've been away from home nearly all the time since I was six and went into the Cadets. I went from there into the Army, and then into attendance on the Emperor, and Mother regards me as practically a stranger! I suppose it's not surprising that poor Olga's lost her wits a little on suddenly finding herself in Society at last!'

They reached the Ekaterina Canal. Boris had an apartment on the banks of it, and said firmly, 'Will you come in for a few minutes? There's something I wish to discuss with you.'

'Well, I ought to . . .' Vassily began, then glanced at Boris and realised that he was looking troubled. 'Very well, then—just for a few minutes.'

Boris had a handsome bachelor apartment on the first floor. His valet opened the door, and Boris foolishly ushered Vassily into his study. He realised his mistake at once, for Vassily promptly made a bee-line for the nearest bookshelf, took down a finely-bound copy of Pascal's *Pensées* and showed every sign of becoming totally immersed in it. Boris took the book out of his hands, replaced it on the shelf, seized his arm and propelled him out of the study and into the dining-room.

Vassily looked mildly amused and suffered it meekly. He sat down on a convenient chair by the window, looking out across the narrow road to the canal, crossed his legs and composed his face to a suitable gravity, while Boris poured two glasses of wine and handed him one of them.

He tasted it, nodded approval, and said, 'Very good.' Boris drew up a chair and sat facing him, twiddling the stem of his glass between his fingers and staring frowningly at the carpet in front of his feet while he made up his mind what to say. Vassily held his glass in a beam of sunlight and admired the sparkling crystal and the clear gold of the wine.

'I—er—' Boris cleared his throat and started again. 'I think I should tell you that when I arrived at Lev's this afternoon, I got as far as the orchard gate, but what I saw through it made me go back and call out.'

'Oh, yes?' Vassily replied coolly. 'And what did you see?'

Boris sipped his wine nervously. 'Two people making love.'

Vassily's eyebrows twitched and he turned the glass in his hand a little to change the pattern of light on the facets.

'At least,' Boris was trying to be accurate, 'I thought . . . well, what I saw exactly was you and Tatya lying on the rug with your arms round each other, kissing, and you were half on top of her.'

'That sounds an accurate description,' Vassily said equably. He finished his wine and set the glass down on

the window-sill. 'Is that what you wanted to say to me?'
He looked as if he intended to get up and go.

'I wanted to ask—well—what's going on,' Boris said
unhappily. 'I suppose you'll say that it's none of my
business, but it worried me.'

'Oh? Why?'

Boris sighed. 'Tatya's my aunt, and I feel . . . My
uncle ill-treated her, I think, and I feel a sort of family
responsibility.'

'You were only a child when she married him,' Vassily
said gently. 'Besides, you're not to blame for what he
was, or what he did.'

'I know, but I can remember how wretched she looked
at the wedding. I didn't understand much about it then,
but I can guess what it might have been like for her from
some of the things he did to me. She's had more than her
share of unhappiness, and I don't want her to suffer any
more.' He was silent for a moment, and then asked
abruptly, 'What are you up to, Vassily?'

'What do you suspect?'

'I don't know. I've always found you kind and helpful,
but I know how you feel about the female sex . . . I just
don't know.' He sounded miserable.

'I see. You think I may be revenging myself on all
females in some way by hurting Tatya?'

'Not really, but I can't imagine Tatya letting any man
embrace her as you were doing without being very
deeply involved with him, and yet I know you've repeatedly said that you'll never marry.'

'And also, of course, you're a little jealous.' Vassily
sounded completely matter-of-fact.

Boris gave an exclamation of protest, but Vassily went
on, 'Yes, I know she's your aunt by marriage, but how
frequently you have to remind yourself of the fact!'
Also, she's six years older than you, but that's not a great
deal.'

Boris had appeared tongue-tied with shock at Vassily's sudden move to the offensive, but he managed to
stammer, 'I—I love Marisha! I'm going to marry her!'

Vassily's eyebrows rose a fraction. 'It's quite possible to be in love with one female and attracted by another at the same time, I believe.' He suddenly relented and smiled, his voice changing from the hard, brittle tone of the last few minutes to a more kindly mode. 'Your feelings towards Tatya are your own business, lad, and I'm sure they do neither of you any dishonour, but you see how things can be misinterpreted? I won't hurt her, I give you my word. Lev knows some part of what I'm doing, and it has his approval, so stop worrying unnecessarily, and try to trust me with your precious aunt!'

'Yes. I'm sorry.' Boris still looked wretched, but now for fear that he might have offended his friend. Vassily smiled. 'No need to apologise—your concern does you credit. Now, be easy about it, lad, and let me go—I'll be late for dinner.'

Boris shook hands with him and rather illogically thanked him with great sincerity. It was some time before he realised that he was, in fact, none the wiser about Vassily's intentions.

CHAPTER
EIGHT

A FEW days later, Irina and Lev went yet again to Borovikovsky's studio, where the portrait was not making very rapid progress, and Vassily came in their absence to visit Tatya again.

It was a dull, sultry day, with stormclouds building up on the horizon, and the sun had a hard, brassy look about it which boded ill for the weather prospects. Tatya's leg ached, and the heavy, oppressive atmosphere made her feel distinctly out of sorts, so Vassily's arrival was a welcome relief from the vague depression which pulled down her spirits.

He had brought more prints for her portfolio, and they spent a pleasant afternoon looking at them together and talking about the scenes they depicted, sitting together on the sofa, with Vron asleep between Vassily's feet, an awkward and inconvenient place which the animal seemed to think might afford protection against the approaching storm.

'Why do you travel abroad so much?' Tatya asked, for he seemed to have been to all the places shown in the prints.

'I pursue happiness,' he replied half-seriously, 'and lamentably fail to catch it.' As Tatya was not acquainted with the American Declaration of Independence, the allusion passed her by, but his meaning was clear enough, and she touched his hand in a graceful gesture of sympathy.

'There'll be thunder by tonight,' he observed. 'Is Irina still afraid of it?'

'Yes, she is.' Tatya was surprised. 'How did you know?'

He laughed. 'My romantic nature again! I remember
Lev telling me that he fell in love with her during a
thunder-storm. Does thunder worry you?'

'Not really. I don't like the lightning much, but I find
the worst part is this awful sultry heaviness beforehand.
Once the storm breaks, it's such a relief that I quite
enjoy it!'

He left her an hour or so later, saying, 'I shall see you
at Nikolai's this evening?'

'Yes. All three of us are coming.'

'I'll be there to carry you in.'

Tatya was looking forward to the evening at the
Volkhovsky Palace. It was not to be a formal entertainment of any kind, but just a gathering of the little circle
of friends who had already enjoyed so many hours
together, for the usual conversation and a light supper.
For Tatya, it was so much easier than visits to places of
interest or more formal dinners and dances, as it involved little moving about, and no hours of just sitting
and watching other people enjoying themselves.

She sat in the carriage during the drive to Vassilievsky
Island, her green gossamer scarf resting lightly on her
shoulders over a fine *mousseline de soie* evening gown of
darker green and daydreamed a little in anticipation of
interesting and amusing talk, and Vassily's green eyes
watching her, smiling and alert. She was quietly confident that she was looking her best, and there would be
genuine admiration in his glance, not just a kindly
pretence, for even Lev had noticed the improvement in
her looks, and had just said that she looked as well as
ever she had done before her accident.

The first intimation that anything was wrong came
when Vladimir came out of the house as the carriage
drew up, and opened the door before the footman could
reach it. 'Have you . . . ?' he began abruptly. 'No, I see
you haven't brought Vassily with you. Have you seen
anything of him?'

'Not today,' Lev replied. 'Why?'

'His horse came home without him just before dinner,' Vladimir replied. 'Come inside. There's no point in talking out here.' He handed Irina down and kissed her hand in an abstracted manner, a slight frown on his otherwise impassive face. Lev also descended, and Vladimir then lifted Tatya out and carried her into the house. He held her quite securely, and did not appear embarrassed, but she sensed a stiff tension in him as he took her through the house to Rose's sitting-room, where Prince Nikolai, Rose, Olga and Marisha were already assembled.

They all looked eagerly towards the door, and Vladimir said, 'No, he's not with them.'

'Then wherever can he be?' Rose exclaimed, looking anxious. 'It's not at all like him—he's never stayed out without letting us know before.'

'Perhaps he's with Boris,' Prince Nikolai suggested, but he sounded doubtful.

'If he didn't intend to dine here, he would have sent a message.' Vladimir said as he put Tatya down on a sofa, quite gently, but rather as if she was a fragile parcel. 'Elementary courtesy. Besides, why send the horse home on its own? It might have got lost, or been stolen or injured.' He shook his head. 'Something's happened to him. Didn't he say where he was going?'

Rose shook her head and raised her hands in a helpless gesture. 'He went out after luncheon and said he was going for a ride. He often does in the afternoon. I didn't ask where he intended to go, of course, and he didn't say. I've no idea.'

'He came to see me,' Tatya said, her voice sounding odd in her own ears. 'He left me just before Lev and Irina came home. He should have been here in good time for dinner.'

Vladimir turned towards her as she spoke and stared searchingly at her. She met his eyes and realised that he was very worried indeed. 'He didn't mention calling anywhere else?'

'No. He just said he would see me here this evening.'

'He would have passed quite near to Borinka's apartment,' Olga volunteered nervously.

'Who would?' Boris asked, coming in at that moment. He moved across to Rose to kiss her hand, and she said, 'Vassily. Have you seen him?'

Boris looked surprised at this unceremonious greeting and replied, 'Why, have you lost him?' then realised that the others were quite serious and anxious. 'What's happened?'

'The stableman reported that his horse came back without him just before dinner,' Prince Nikolai said. 'There's no sign of anything amiss with the animal, and no message of any kind.'

'Well, he might have . . . I mean, he's gone off on his own before . . . You know, for the night . . .' Boris was trying to convey delicately, in the presence of five ladies, that Vassily might have gone to a brothel.

'I shouldn't think he'd need to go anywhere so urgently that he couldn't send Rose a message,' Lev said. 'He may be odd, but he's not ill-mannered, and he'd not treat a horse like that, either. Besides, he told Tatya he'd be here this evening.'

'There must have been an accident,' Tatya put the cold fear gripping her heart into words.

'Between your house and here? It doesn't seem likely.' Vladimir chewed at his moustache, made up his mind and took command. 'Nikolai, will you go to the police? I'll return to the Fortress and detail a search party to go over the route. Someone may have seen something. Boris, will you try the hospitals?'

'I will too,' offered Lev. 'Save time.'

The men left, and the ladies drew together round Tatya's sofa. Each of them had some sewing, and they worked at it in a desultory fashion, starting at every sound and waiting with growing anxiety. The doors and windows were wide open, but the room seemed airless and the approaching storm made the atmosphere heavy and enervating. A faint growl in the distance made Irina shiver and exclaim, 'Oh, dear! It's going to thunder—I wish Lev would come back!'

None of the men returned until nearly midnight. By then, the storm had broken and the rain was falling in a steady downpour. Irina was kneeling on the floor with her face hidden in Tatya's lap, too frightened by the violence of the storm to care what anyone thought of her, and Olga was obviously nearly in the same state. Rose had rung for candles, and the curtains were drawn over the closed windows, and she was walking backwards and forwards across the room as if she could no longer sit still. Tatya had closed her eyes and was praying silently in a numb, automatic fashion, 'Please, God, please, please!' over and over again. Only Marisha was still stitching her embroidery, but she started at every peal of thunder, and occasionally dabbed her eyes with a small handkerchief.

Vladimir came in first, closely followed by Boris, and Prince Nikolai and Lev were not long after them. They were all drenched, and it took only a glance at their strained faces to see that no-one had any news.

'A porter at the Admiralty saw a man with red hair dismount from his horse and get into a carriage,' Vladimir said in a sharp, strained voice. 'The carriage drove away towards the Palace Quay, and the horse trotted off this way. He couldn't describe the carriage, and he didn't see who was in it, nor was he sure of the time. He only noticed because he thought it was odd, and because the man was hatless, and there aren't many red-haired men in Russia. I've had half the battalion out searching and questioning, and that's all we've discovered. I don't know what to do.'

'The police were no help,' Prince Nikolai reported. 'They sent out a party to question people, of course, but they found nothing. I think we'd better change out of these wet clothes and have something to eat. It would be as well if you all stayed the night here—what there is left of it. I'll tell my major-domo to arrange beds. Lev, what will you need? I'll send a carriage for your valet, and the ladies' maids.'

Lev had gone straight to Irina, helped her up, and was comforting her on one of the sofas. He looked up and said, 'Oh, yes. Thank you. Josef will know what to bring, and I suppose Elena and Masha . . .'

'Tell them we'll need things for the night, and for the morning,' Tatya said quietly. She had managed to achieve a kind of frozen calm on the surface, despite the savage anxiety she felt deep within.

Irina let Lev go to shift his wet clothes, and sat hunched in a corner of the sofa with her hands over her ears until he returned. Prince Nikolai had lent dressing-gowns to him, Boris and Vladimir and changed his own clothes. Vladimir was taller than the Prince, and an expanse of bare ankle protruded from under the hem of his dark red brocade gown, which appeared to worry him, for he sat down on a chair and tried to tuck his feet under it, tugging at the skirts of the garment.

Lev went back to Irina, put his arms round her, and murmured soothingly to her until the storm died away in the distance and she gradually relaxed and began to take more notice of what was going on. Nobody said very much, and for long intervals there was no sound but the drumming of rain outside. A trio of footmen brought in the supper trays, but no-one could do more than pick at the food, and Tatya, unable to manage even a polite pretence, simply declined the offer altogether.

Olga went over to Vladimir and took his hand as he sat staring blankly in front of him. He looked up at her, startled, gave a faint, brief smile, and drew her down on to his lap. She put one arm round his neck and stroked his hair with her other hand, and he buried his face in the lace frills of her falling collar. It was so uncharacteristic of the rather formal and proper way in which he usually behaved towards her that it seemed symbolic of the upset of this wretched, unhappy night.

Josef arrived with Elena and Masha, and Boris's valet Grisha, and everyone retired for what was left of the night. Tatya had a room near Ilya's, and Rose looked in just as she was settling into bed to say that Ilya had been crying because the storm upset him.

'Pyotr comforted him, but he wanted Vassily to explain what made all the noise and the flashing,' she said. 'I told him that Vassily is staying with friends for the night, but I think he guessed that something is wrong. Children are very quick about some things . . . Oh, Tatya! Wherever can he be?'

Tatya shook her head, and said in an unsteady voice that she would listen for any sound from Ilya, and go to him if he called out. Then she turned away and buried her face in her pillow. Rose hesitated, then touched her gently on the shoulder and went away to her own room.

It rained all night, and was still raining in the morning. No-one had slept. Tatya prayed all night, and got up as soon as she heard someone moving in the house, and the others must have done the same, for they had all breakfasted and were back in Rose's sitting-room, racking their brains for some idea of what to do next, when the major-domo brought in a letter for Vladimir, saying that it had been delivered to the Fortress, and the orderly officer had sent it over because it was marked Urgent.

Vladimir looked at it with a puzzled frown as he asked leave to open it. The word 'urgent' and the direction were written in Russian, and the seal was a plain wafer. He opened it, read a few sentences, exclaimed 'My God!' and went as white as a ghost.

'What is it?' Prince Nikolai asked.

'It's from some lunatics calling themselves the Sons of Liberty,' Vladimir replied hoarsely. 'They've got Vassily! They're holding him hostage, "in a safe place", they say, and if I don't do as they ask, they'll . . . Oh, God!' He dropped the letter as if it had stung him and put his hands over his face.

Vassily mounted his horse in the stableyard and set out to ride back to the Volkhovsky Palace, humming a tune, thinking, and taking little notice of anything around him. It was near the most fashionable hour for dinner, and there were therefore very few people about. Apart from a stationary carriage, Admiralty Square was deserted as he turned left across it towards the Isakievsky Bridge. His route took him close to the carriage, and as he approached it, the door opened, and a man inside called out, 'Count Karachev! A moment, if you please!'

Surprised, Vassily drew rein and dismounted, walking the last few feet to the carriage door with his reins looped over his arm.

'You called?' he asked, peering inside. The blinds were down and the interior was dark.

There was a movement inside, and a hand appeared holding a cocked pistol levelled at his head.

'I did indeed,' said the man's voice from the dim interior in rather sibilant French. 'You will loose your horse and enter this carriage, or the results might be unfortunate.'

Vassily hesitated for a second, and saw the finger tighten on the trigger. He shrugged and dropped the reins, then climbed into the carriage and sat down facing the man with the pistol. The door closed with a decisive click, and the carriage immediately moved off, swinging righthanded across the square towards Palace Quay.

'Hold out your hands in front of you,' directed the sibilant voice, and Vassily did so. Immediately, he became aware that there was a second man in the carriage, who seized his hands, clapped them together, and tied the wrists with a thin cord, pulled unnecessarily tight.

'I'd be obliged if you'd tie me a little less tightly,' Vassily said, keeping his usual light, ironic tone despite the sick feeling of fear and anger in the pit of his stomach. There was no reply, and the cord remained painfully tight.

'May I enquire why you have such a pressing desire for my company?' Vassily tried again. It was not by any means the first time in his life that he'd been in an unusual situation, and he'd always found it helpful to make the other people involved talk, for they usually gave away more than they intended.

'You will remain silent, unless you wish to be gagged,' the sibilant voice replied.

Guessing how painful a gag applied by the other man would be, Vassily remained silent as instructed, and listened to the sound of the carriage wheels and the horses' hooves. For a while, they made a grinding noise as they moved over the granite setts of the Palace Quay, and then they turned left, and the sound changed to a hollow drumming on wood. 'Troitsky Bridge,' he thought.

When the sound changed again to a road noise, and they turned right and continued for a short time, he guessed that they were passing behind the little wooden house of Peter the Great. Then followed another bridge, a short piece of road, and then a left turn. 'Now we're on the Viborg side,' he thought. 'Where the devil are we going? Finland?'

They slowed down for the police post at the city boundary, but the carriage was obviously well-known and was not stopped. After that, they drove on for a considerable time—at least an hour, he estimated. No-one spoke, and he became more and more apprehensive. What on earth could they possibly want of him? If it was robbery, he had nothing worth all this trouble. There were a few roubles and kopecks in his pocket, but nothing else, not even his precious watch, which he was not carrying today. It was too dark in the carriage to see either of his captors—they were just vague shapes, menacing in their silence.

Eventually, the carriage turned sharply left. Judging by the jolting and lurching of the last few miles, they were well out in the country, on a corduroy road, and they now turned in to a gravel drive. The carriage stopped, the door opened, and the sibilant voice said, 'Step down, Count.'

Vassily did so. With his hands tied, he was unable to steady himself, and the other man gave him a sharp push which sent him sprawling on the gravel, grazing his hands and face as he tried to save himself.

He lay still for a moment, and then a kick in the ribs accompanied a sharp 'Get up!' in a different voice, and he scrambled to his feet. They were outside a small, four-square house of three storeys and an attic, of a type fairly common all over Russia. The front was symmetrical—a door in the middle, a pair of windows on either side of it, five windows above on each floor, and a central dormer projecting from the roof. A heavy iron gutter ran along the edge of the roof-shingles, with a stout drainpipe at each corner to carry away the Spring thaw.

That was all he managed to see before the pistol jabbed into his back, and he entered the house ahead of his two captors. Further jabs directed him into a room on the left, which was sparsely furnished with four chairs and a large, battered, flat-topped desk. The shutters were closed, and the room was ill-lit by four guttering candles.

Two of the chairs were occupied by men wearing black velvet masks, both rather ordinary-looking and dressed in sober, gentleman's clothing. One was fair, the other dark. As the other two joined them, Vassily saw them for the first time. The one with the pistol was a tall, heavily-built fellow with white streaks in his black hair, who seated himself at the desk and laid the pistol on top of the sheets of paper on its surface.

The other was a thin man of medium height with lank brown hair and disproportionately large, ugly hands, red-skinned, with bitten nails. He seemed nervous and kept rubbing his hands together and licking his lips. These two men were also masked.

Vassily looked round for a chair, but there were only the four occupied ones, so he stood facing the man at the desk and waited, a most unpleasant sensation in his stomach. A trickle of blood was congealing stiffly on his face, which was stinging, his hands were numb, and his ribs throbbed painfully.

The silence stretched on for some time, and he realised that they were straining his nerves, waiting for some reaction. Perversity and experience kept him silent, so that eventually the man at the desk cleared his throat and said, 'Well, Count Karachev. No doubt you are still curious about our "pressing desire for your company", as you put it. You have a brother.'

It was a statement rather than a question, but Vassily cautiously replied, 'I believe so.'

'Your brother commands the Volkhovsky Regiment.'

'He does.'

'The Volkhovsky Regiment at present forms the garrison of the Petropavlovsky Fortress.'

Vassily made no reply and let his face go as blank as his brother's might have done in his place. The sibilant voice repeated the statement in an impatient tone.

'I'm sorry,' Vassily said politely. 'I thought you were telling me, not asking me. To be accurate, one battalion does, or do, depending on whether you regard a battalion as singular or plural.'

Sibilant Voice made an impatient gesture and went on, 'We have written a letter to your brother. It will require your endorsement before we send it to him, so I shall tell you what it contains. You will be well advised to listen carefully, as it concerns your well-being very closely.'

'Do you think I might have my hands untied, then?' Vassily asked mildly. 'I shall lose the use of them shortly if the circulation isn't restored, and then I shan't be able to write your endorsement.'

To his surprise, the lank-haired man laughed, a harsh, grating sound, but the fair-haired man came forward at a nod from Sibilant Voice and cut the cord with his pocket-knife. The pain was excruciating as the blood returned to Vassily's hands and he rubbed them hard together, trying not to show any signs of suffering because the lank-haired fellow was watching him, licking his lips again, but not, Vassily now realised, with nervousness, but avidity.

Sibilant Voice waited patiently until Vassily's hands

were reasonably normal again, and then he said in his curiously stilted, formal manner, 'The purpose of this letter is to inform your brother, Colonel Karachev, that we are holding you hostage in order to persuade him to carry out our instructions. This letter will reach him early tomorrow morning, and it will give him until noon to convey to us his willingness to accede to our demands. If he fails to do so, we shall send him your right thumb to persuade him a little.'

Vassily could hardly take in what the man had said. He repeated 'My right thumb?' in a tone of sheer incredulity, and then felt that he would either choke or vomit as the full realisation came to him.

Lank Hair licked his lips again, and Sibilant Voice repeated, 'Your right thumb. Followed on successive days by other little gifts, until he comes to a proper realisation of his family responsibilities. Each of your fingers, one by one, then your tongue, or a foot, perhaps. They will be —er—removed with great care, of course, and boiling tar applied to the stump each time. It will be interesting to see how far our friend here can go in dismembering a living body before it—er—ceases to be living.'

'Our friend here' was, of course, Lank Hair. Vassily stared at Sibilant Voice in silence, his mind wrestling desperately with the problems of trying to understand fully what the man was saying without showing too much of the horror he was feeling.

And fear. Once he had taken in just what these people intended to do with him, sheer terror gripped him, causing a violent contraction of his abdominal muscles, and a feeling like an icy finger travelling slowly up his spine. He had been in danger of death before, but nothing like this . . . !

'Who—who are you?' he asked involuntarily. For a moment, he almost expected to be told 'The Devil', but Sibilant Voice replied, 'The Sons of Liberty. We are members of a society dedicated to the overthrow of tyranny in all the Russias and the restoration of the

sovereign power of the common people. Once we have
rid the world of the Romanov tyrants and their parasitic
aristocracy, we shall give to all men the freedom and
equality which God intended them to enjoy.' He spoke
in an elevated manner, almost intoning the words, and
the other three stirred and murmured as though they
were deeply moved by some great religious leader.

Vassily had been little more than a baby when the
French Revolution began, but he had heard enough
fanatical talk in various places to recognise the breed.
'Mad,' he thought. 'Jacobins, and quite mad, especially
that lank-haired fellow!' and he heard Prince Nikolai's
voice saying, 'Don't get yourself mixed up with those
lunatics!'

There was silence for a few moments, and then Lank
Hair spoke in a cold, rasping voice. 'I do hope your
brother is fond of you. On a previous occasion of a
similar nature, I succeeded in removing all the extremi-
ties, and the head and trunk died while I was operating
on the genitals. He suffered a great deal.' On the
surface, the voice was coolly impersonal, but there was
an underlying note of gloating which made Vassily
concentrate on a desperate prayer to God for help in
concealing just how terrified he felt.

'No doubt you will wish to know what it is that we
require your brother to do in exchange for your body,'
Sibilant Voice resumed. He sounded almost bored by
the whole conversation, and his apparent indifference
was even more unnerving than Lank Hair's unhealthy
pleasure. 'It is, quite simply, the Petropavlovsky Fortress. He will allow the members of our Society to occupy
the fortress and the magazine, and he will be allowed to
remove himself and his soldiers to safety before we
strike the blow which will begin our revolution.'

Vassily understood only too clearly. The guns of the
fortress commanded all the heart of St Petersburg. They
could close the Neva to shipping, destroy the bridges,
bombard the Admiralty, the Winter Palace, the Bourse
. . . Alexander would have to give in to the rebels, or see

his capital city destroyed in a rain of shot and shell! He forced down the panic, the fury, the revulsion, the fear, and made himself reply with some dignity, 'I think you are mistaken. You're asking my brother to trade his honour for my life, and I know he'll consider the former the more valuable.'

'I hope, for your sake, that it is *you* who is mistaken,' Sibilant Voice replied with a cold smile. 'Now, Count. I'm afraid that three of us must leave you shortly. We have our places in Petersburg, and must be seen in them this evening. You will, of course, remain here, and we shall return tomorrow afternoon to tell you what your brother has decided. You will be well advised to divide your time between prayer that your brother may choose wisely, and sleep, for you may be in too much pain to rest after our return. We have prepared a room for your accommodation. You will not find it comfortable or convenient, but that really matters very little. It is an attic, and you will no doubt be pleased to find that it has a window, so you will be able to see the sky, which I believe has some emotional importance to you decadent romantics. You will also be able to see that this house is extremely isolated, and it will be a waste of time for you to call for help. I should add that the window is extremely small, so there is no danger of you—er—falling from it, even if you could reach it! Your door will be locked and barred, and, in any case, it communicates only with an inner room, the door of which will also be secured. Do not, therefore, allow yourself to waste time or thought on hopes of escape—there are none.'

This rather lengthy speech had given Vassily time to regain his self-control, and he enquired, in a reasonable imitation of his normal manner, 'Will my gaoler be serving dinner? I was on my way to mine when I received your—er—invitation.'

Sibilant Voice appeared disconcerted by this very practical question, and turned to the fair-haired man, who replied, 'There's bread and water. It's not what you're used to, but you can eat like your serfs for a change.'

Vassily, whose serfs ate a great deal more than bread and water, raised his eyebrows a little, but made no comment. He doubted if he would be able to eat in any case—his stomach was churning about most uncomfortably.

'Now,' said Sibilant Voice briskly, 'you will write something on the bottom of this letter . . . just a few words which will assure your brother that we really have you in our custody . . .'

He pushed the paper across the desk to Vassily, who stepped forward, took the pen which the man held out to him, and dipped it in the inkstand which stood on the desk. Then he paused and rapidly glanced through the letter, which was written in Russian. It was addressed to Vladimir, and stated that Count Vassily Sergeivich Karachev was a prisoner of the Sons of Liberty, gave a brief series of instructions which Vladimir was to follow to show that he was prepared to hand over the fortress in exchange for his brother's freedom, and an outline of what would happen to Vassily if he refused or ignored the letter. Vassily wrote a single sentence at the foot of the paper, hoping Vladimir would interpret it correctly, sanded it with the shaker from the inkstand, and returned it to Sibilant Voice.

'What does this mean?' Sibilant Voice asked.

'My brother will understand,' Vassily replied, then closed his lips firmly.

There was a pause, and then the fourth man, who had not so far spoken, murmured something about the time. Sibilant Voice picked up the pistol and motioned to Vassily to move towards the door. As he did so, Lank Hair went in front of him, leading the way across the vestibule and up the stairs, while Sibilant Voice followed, jabbing Vassily in the back with the pistol from time to time. They mounted the creaking wooden stairs to the attic floor, and passed through one room into another, smaller one under the eaves. Before Vassily could take in more than the briefest glimpse of it, Lank Hair turned and hit him hard across the face.

As his head jerked back with the force of the blow, Sibilant Voice seized his arms and held him while Lank Hair drew back and then kicked him in the groin. He gave a cry of pain and doubled up, then was pushed hard from behind and sent sprawling across the floor, fetching up with a crash against the far wall, which knocked the remaining breath out of his body, and as he lay retching and gasping, trying to fight off the red mist of pain which engulfed him, he dimly heard the door slam and the click of the lock, followed by another crash as the door was barred. The sequence of sounds was echoed as the outer door was secured, and then there was silence.

He lay still, gasping and clutching himself as the pain flooded through him and then slowly receded. Somewhere in the distance, he heard the sound of wheels and hooves on gravel, then a distant, menacing growl of thunder.

CHAPTER
NINE

SOME time later, Vassily stirred and painfully dragged himself into a sitting position, leaning against the wall. His whole body ached abominably, and his mouth was full of the sour taste of bile. He held up his right hand in front of his face and looked at it with interest. It was white-skinned and well-cared for, the hand of a man who had never done any hard manual work, with long tapering fingers, unadorned by rings. Then he looked round the room.

The first things he saw were a jug and a wooden platter standing on the floor to the right of the door. He crawled over to them, lifted the jug to his lips and gulped greedily. The water was brackish and stale, but he was too thirsty to care. On the platter was a shapeless lump of black bread, green with mould. He turned away from it, his stomach heaving again, and surveyed the rest of the room.

It was about ten feet square, with a boarded ceiling sloping downwards until it met wooden panelling about four feet high on the opposite side from the door. In the centre of this panelling was a square opening forming a box some six feet deep, which sloped upwards to the dormer window, so that the small area of daylight seemed to be at the end of a short tunnel. Apart from the jug and platter, there was nothing in the room but a layer of dust on the rough board floor.

He pulled himself to his feet by holding on to the door frame, and leaned against it until his head stopped spinning, then straightened up and stretched himself cautiously, feeling his ribs. They were sore like the rest of him, but he began to think that he might recover in time, and even managed a wry smile at the way his mind had phrased the thought.

Another faint rumble of thunder, still very far away, drew his attention to the window, and he hobbled across to the opening. It was very small, barely two feet square. He took off his coat and wriggled into it, hunching his shoulders and inching his way up until his hands, held above his head, were touching the glass. It was a single pane, not double-glazed as it should have been, and filthy, but after rubbing it with his shirt-cuff, he could see out fairly well.

It was darker outside than he expected, and he tried to work out what the time might be—not more than eight o'clock, surely? It should still be broad daylight for several hours yet at this time of year—it would hardly be darker than this at midnight! He peered at the sky. It was heavily overcast, and towards the horizon it was quite black. As he looked, a flash of sheet lightning illuminated the distance, and he saw that the house looked out over a wide area of flat marshland. A few clumps of pine trees and thickets of alder and willow stood starkly against the stormclouds, and the road ran past in a straight line, going out of sight into a stand of pines on his left, and stretching as far as he could see, his nose pressed to the glass, to his right. Below him was a neglected garden bisected by a gravel drive a couple of hundred yards long, which passed through a broken-down boundary fence of wooden stakes to join the road.

The lightning flashed again on the far horizon, and he slid down the narrow chute, landing in a heap on the floor, leaned his head against the panelling and tried to think.

At first, his mind was confused and despairing, running forward in sick anticipation to long hours in this silent, solitary prison, followed by . . . He jerked his mind back from that and tried to think of something pleasant. It had always worked in the past. Whenever his nerves were strained by some unpleasant situation, he had taught himself to concentrate on the inner vision of some beautiful memory—a picture, a scene, a book, home . . . Ash Glade would be at its most beautiful now, with the trees in leaf and the garden full of flowers . . .

Flowers. Roses. A cascade of pink roses behind a lovely head, framed by the pale fragrant blossoms and glossy leaves . . . He shifted to a more comfortable position and closed his eyes, concentrating very hard on that picture. Gradually he relaxed, and actually drifted into a half-sleep, from which he was suddenly wakened by a clap of thunder, very much nearer than the earlier distant rumbles. How fast was the storm approaching? There was a vivid flash of lightning, and he began to count steadily until the thunder rumbled again, a little nearer, but still some way off.

He got into the window aperture again, pushing up to the glass, and looked out. Just below him, the roof sloped down to the iron gutter, which was rusty. Beyond it was a sheer drop over the edge of the roof to the garden below. He bit his lip and frowned, and peered sidelong towards the corner of the roof, where the gutter joined one of the down-pipes, then slid back to the floor and pulled off one of his boots. With it in his hand, he returned to the window and waited until the thunder roared again, appreciably nearer. Almost immediately, there was a second peal, and the faint patter of rain, which grew steadily louder and more intense as the storm approached, and then, quite suddenly, it was overhead and the lightning and thunder were coming together.

A great clap immediately overhead shook the house, and Vassily smashed the heel of his boot into the glass, shattering it, and broke the remaining pieces away as best he could under cover of successive roars and rumbles. He could hardly hear the noise himself, and the drumming rain drowned the sound of falling fragments. Ice-cold rain blew in his face, and he let it run over his cheeks and wet his hair before returning to the floor of the attic, where he stripped off his shirt and trousers and made a bundle of them with his boots in his coat, tying it firmly with the sleeves.

Once more he inched up the sloping opening to the window, pushing the bundle in front of him, then shoved it as hard as he could through the window. It slid down the roof, checked for a moment as it caught on the gutter, then vanished.

He twisted round, inch by inch, praying that he would not stick, until he was on his back, stretched his arms out of the window, and reached up for a grip on the little pointed gable of the dormer. Then he pulled himself out of the window, the jagged glass remaining in the frame gouging into his back and sides. He felt the blood warm on his skin for a moment, and then the cold rain struck his shrinking flesh and made him shiver, and he stopped to get better control of himself, his upper body as far as the waist out in the chill wet air.

'I can't do it,' he thought. 'On the other hand, Volodya'll be in a devil of a predicament if I don't. So shall I, for that matter!' He shut his eyes and prayed briefly, thinking that he should have thought of that before he started, then shifted his grip on the gable and heaved himself upwards and outwards. His drawers snagged on the glass, and he wished he had taken them off, then decided that if Lank Hair was going to find him down on the gravel with his neck broken tomorrow, he would prefer not to be stark naked. It was an illogical thought and he smiled grimly to himself, pulled harder on the gable, and felt the fine linen tear.

Next, he stuck with the upper edge of the window-frame pressing jagged glass into his belly and had to shift his grip and let the sharp edges score his flesh until he could pull himself up far enough to get his legs out of the opening. Then he balanced for a moment, pushing down hard on the top of the dormer with the point of it pressing into the pit of his stomach and his arms shaking with the effort, collected himself to change the direction of the thrust, and lowered himself until he could slide down the slope of the roof and hang there, his hands still gripping the top of the gable. Cautiously moving one hand at a time, he felt for and gripped the bottom edge of the window frame, and let himself slide further, the glass cutting into his fingers and palms and the rain sluicing down his back, which was stinging all over with cuts and scrapes.

After a few moment's rest, he turned his head and looked down the length of his body. The gutter was still a good yard beyond his feet. Would it give way? He let go and slid, trying to brake himself with his hands on the rough wooden shingles.

His feet struck the gutter, which gave a little, coinciding with another peal of thunder which brought his heart to his mouth, thinking it was the sound of the gutter collapsing, for he had forgotten about the storm. He stopped, spreadeagled on the roof with only the sagging gutter between him and the long drop to the ground, and remained there, afraid to move, while the storm continued and the rain poured down, showing no signs of diminishing, and he soon felt so cold that he thought he had better move before he shivered himself over the edge.

Once he started to slide himself sideways towards the corner, the fear left him and he was able to think what he was doing again. After all, he'd climbed things before—cliffs, trees, even a few buildings . . . Despite ominous creaks, the gutter held, and he reached the corner of the roof fairly easily. There was nothing to hold on to in order to get down to the pipe, which began under the gutter, and he was afraid to let himself slip over the edge in case he could not stop in time, so he turned sideways, somehow contorting himself with one foot wedged in the gutter and reaching down with outstretched hand until he was lying horizontally along the edge of the roof. After that, it was comparatively easy to grasp the top of the down pipe and lower himself until he could grip it with his knees and climb down to the ground.

Once there, he sat down on the wet ground and leaned against the wall of the house, shaking with released

tension and cold. He felt bruised all over and half-flayed,
and had to force himself to get up and walk on trembling
legs to the gravel drive, where he found his bundle of
clothing lying neatly in the middle of the turning-circle
before the doorstep of the house. He picked it up and
retired round the side of the building to pull his clothes
and boots on. They were all soaking wet, but better than
nothing.

Restraining an impulse to run—hobble—as far away
as possible, he crept up to the window of the room in
which he had talked with the Sons of Liberty. It was
shuttered, but there was a tiny gleam of light through a
crack. He peered in, but could see nothing, and the noise
of the rain drowned any sound. He turned away and
limped over the grass beside the gravel drive to the
broken gate, looked back once, then turned right and,
hobbling with pain and stiffness, set out into the grey,
rainswept night on the long walk back to St Petersburg.

Boris picked up the single sheet of paper which Vladimir
had dropped and read the letter aloud, his voice reflect-
ing his mounting horror as he came to the part describing
what would happen to Vassily if Vladimir delayed in
obeying instructions. Tatya listened in a numbed state of
shock, unable to believe that this could really be happening.

'Surrender the Fortress to them!' Lev exclaimed.
'Good God! How much of Petersburg could they destroy
with the guns?'

'More than enough,' Vladimir replied grimly.
'There's enough powder and shot in the magazine to
destroy half the towns in Russia, and food and supplies
for a year . . . What the devil am I going to do?'

'Go to the Emperor!' Boris said urgently.

'He's at Czarskoe Selo. It would be past noon when I
got there . . . If they haven't heard from me by then,
they'll . . .' Vladimir choked. 'He's my brother! I
can't . . .'

'What's this sentence at the end?' Lev was looking at

the letter. 'It says "You must carry out their instructions as accurately as Blanche shot Damkov". It's Vassily's writing, but what does it mean? Who's Blanche? Wasn't the Colonel before you called Damkov?'

Vladimir's white face suddenly flamed crimson, and it was Boris who answered 'Yes, he was, and Blanche was someone we knew years ago, in Paris.' He looked at Olga, who was staring at him with anxious eyes. 'She died, so why on earth . . . Vladimir, when she shot Damkov, she wasn't aiming at him, was she?'

'No.' Vladimir suddenly pulled himself together. 'No, she wasn't! In fact, she shot him by accident, but the authorities pretended she did it on purpose to save an international scandal, because the person she meant to shoot was . . . well, never mind! Give me that letter!' Lev passed it to him, and he read Vassily's message again. 'Well, either he means carry them out, but make a complete muddle of it, or he means pretend to carry them out while really doing something else . . . I suppose I could fool them somehow, for a time, at least . . .'

'You won't need to,' said a very unsteady voice from the terrace door. 'I've come back.' They all turned in amazement and saw Vassily standing in the doorway, holding on to the frame and clearly in a state of exhaustion. He was soaking wet, with water dripping to form a puddle round his feet, his face was livid white against his rain-darkened hair, and a black bruise stained one cheek, with a savage red graze running from eye to chin.

Tatya's whole body jerked with her impulse to go to him, but she could only sit and stare as Vladimir half-carried him to a chair. Boris ran to the far end of the room, where a tantalus stood on a side-table, and came back with a brimming glass of brandy, which he pressed into Vassily's hand. He was shaking so much that it rattled against his teeth as he gulped the spirit, then choked a little.

'Steady, old fellow,' Vladimir said gently. 'Are you all right?'

'I'm still complete,' Vassily replied in a pale ghost of

his usual light, ironic manner. 'Apart from a few acres of skin. You'd better go and report all this to Alexander Pavlovich, Nikolai. They're a covey of lunatic Jacobins, and they'll have to be arrested today or you'll lose them.'

'Let me help you out of that wet coat first,' Prince Nikolai said. Vassily was too near collapse to think of anything but passing on his information, and he let Prince Nikolai and Vladimir remove his sodden coat without remembering the state of his shirt, until a cry from Tatya jerked him out of his preoccupation. He looked at her and saw that she was staring at him in horror.

There was silence for a full second as everyone realised that his shirt was not just wet, but stained with blood over most of its surface. Tatya's body again jerked with the urgency of her longing to go to him, and she half-rose to her feet, forgetting her helplessness, then fell back again as her leg gave way under her. 'Oh, Vasya!' she whispered.

'I'm all right.' he said, looking at her. 'Only cut and scraped, nothing worse.' He briefly described his escape, making it sound an easy matter of breaking a window and sliding down a drainpipe, and purposely omitted to say that the window was a dormer in the roof.

Vladimir had pulled his shirt open and briefly surveyed the damage. 'How did you get so cut about?' he asked, noticing the bruises, but not mentioning them as he buttoned the shirt again.

'Very small window. Jagged bits in the frame. There were four men.' He described them as well as he could, and shivered uncontrollably when he came to Lank Hair. 'They took me to a house on the road north—have you a map, Nikolai?'

Prince Nikolai fetched a map from his library, and Vassily showed him where the house was situated. 'You can't mistake it,' he said. 'It's the only one—quite isolated, with a broken fence . . . the attic window is smashed as well.'

'*Attic?*' Vladimir began, then bit the question off as he realised the implication.

'They're going back there this afternoon, fairly late. You'd better be there to receive them,' Vassily went on, then repeated what Sibilant Voice had said about revolution and overthrowing the Romanovs.

'Very well, old fellow,' Vladimir said. 'That's enough for now. Nikolai, we'd best ride out to Czarskoe Selo and tell the Emperor all this. Rose, will you look after Vassily?'

'Of course.' Rose went over to Vassily as her husband and the other man hurried off to see the Emperor. 'What should we do first, Vassily?'

He managed a lop-sided grin. 'Ring for my valet, I should think. François will see to me.'

'Hot bath,' Rose said briskly. 'Salve, bandages . . . food?'

He shook his head and looked rather sick.

'You'd better go to bed afterwards. You must be tired.' Rose, oblivious of the fact that she had just achieved the understatement of a lifetime, glanced sidelong at Tatya, then went on, 'Olga and Marisha, would you please go and see what Ilya is doing for me, dears? I think he's in the nursery. Irina, perhaps you'd come and help me?' She crossed to the door, almost shepherding the others through it, and they went out looking a little mystified. Rose glanced back over her shoulder and said, 'I'll just set everything in train, and perhaps you'll come when you're ready?' before going out and shutting the door.

Tatya had been all this while in a state of total frustration. Every nerve in her body seemed to be screaming with longing to help Vassily, to comfort him and tend his injuries, but she could do nothing. Other people could go to fetch salve and bandages and hot water, but all she could do was sit helplessly on this *damned* sofa and look on. She gave a sob as the door closed behind Rose, and put her hands over her face.

'Don't cry, *dushenka*!' Vassily said. He got up out of

his chair with an effort and staggered across to her, dropping on to the sofa beside her as if his legs had given way. He went to put his arms round her, checked, and said, 'I'm filthy and wet—I'll ruin your gown!'

Tatya turned to him, put her head on his shoulder and cried like a heart-broken child. He put his hands on her back, trying not to smear blood on her silk gown, and whispered, 'You mustn't, *dushenka*! There's nothing to cry about. I'm safe, and not much hurt. I'm cut about by the glass, that's all.'

'I want to help you!' she sobbed. 'I can't do *anything*! I'm so useless!'

'I know,' he said soothingly. 'Don't worry about it, François will clean me up and I'll be as good as new once I've slept a while.' He winced as she moved her head and pressed one of the deeper cuts, and she raised her head to look at him.

'You're in pain?'

'A little. Some of the cuts are rather deep, and I've a few bruises.'

She made an effort to calm herself and fumbled in her reticule for her handkerchief. When she found it, Vassily took it from her and wiped her eyes as he had done twice before.

'There, that's better. I must go, Tatya. I'm beginning to feel most peculiar. I expect it's the brandy.'

She let him go, and watched longingly as he limped from the room. There was nothing she could do but wait until Rose and Irina came back to sit with her, while the two younger ladies played a complicated game with counters and dice with Ilya at the far end of the room.

François, Vassily's French valet, came in some time later, and reported that his master had taken a bath and been anointed with Rose's herbal salve and the worst of his cuts plastered or bandaged, and he was now safely in bed and asleep. As the man had once been a Trappist monk and was habitually very sparing of the spoken word, Rose had to drag an account of Vassily's injuries out of him, and discovered little more than that there were many cuts and grazes on his back and chest and hands, and bad bruising on his ribs and 'elsewhere'.

'Oh!' said Rose, guessing what he meant. 'Do you think we should summon a doctor?'

François looked horrified, and intimated that Josef and Pyotr had been consulted, and that they agreed that the various injuries were not serious. 'A doctor would bleed him and make him worse!' he said.

Rose, who also had a poor opinion of doctors, told François to be sure to tell her if Vassily needed anything, thanked him, and allowed him to make his escape.

'I suppose we'll just have to wait until the men come home now,' she said. 'It's very frustrating, being a woman.'

The day dragged by wearily. The rain ceased at about noon, but the sun only managed a watery appearance, and the atmosphere was damp and chilly. Rose had the stoves lighted, which made them more comfortable, and the five ladies sat talking and waiting until dinner-time, when the men at last returned, all four with expressions of grim satisfaction.

'We caught them,' Vladimir said. 'Alexander Pavlovich insisted on coming with us, and brought a dozen Cossacks. The fellow they left on guard was dead drunk—didn't even know Vassily was gone!' He gave a sardonic grin. 'The news sobered him quite remarkably! We hid the horses and the Emperor's carriage at the back of the house, and waited inside, and the other three had a shock when they walked in and found the Emperor sitting there with a pistol in his hand!'

'Where are they now?' Rose asked.

'Where they wanted to be. How's Vassily?'

'Feeling better, thank you,' Vassily answered for himself from the doorway. He was dressed and did indeed look much better, but he was still pale, and one side of his face was swollen and purple. Everyone seemed inclined to make rather a fuss of him, and he smiled in a self-deprecating manner as he said, 'Really, I'm much better, François, Josef and Pyotr held a committee over me, and bathed, salved and plastered me, and I've had a very welcome sleep. I'm just a little stiff and battered, that's all. I gather that you caught them all?'

'Indeed,' replied Prince Nikolai, 'and they kindly gave us the names of their other members on the way back to Petersburg. It was quite a small organisation, and they'll all fit quite neatly into a dozen cells in the Fortress until they leave for Siberia!'

'Exile?' said Marisha, surprised. 'I thought they'd be executed!'

Prince Nikolai shrugged. 'Alexander Pavlovich says they're entitled to their opinion, but can go and hold it elsewhere.'

Rose told the men that they were excused changing for dinner as it was already so late, and they had missed their luncheon. Vassily went across to Tatya with the obvious intention of carrying her up to the dining-room, but Boris intervened and took her instead. Vassily caught Tatya's eye and gave her a faint, lopsided smile.

Later in the evening, they were all sitting round the stove while the men gave a more detailed account of the day's events, when Prince Nikolai's major-domo made a portentous entrance and announced, 'His Imperial Majesty!' flinging open the double doors and standing aside as Alexander limped into the room.

'No ceremony!' he said in a nervous, hurried manner. Everyone but Tatya had risen, and the ladies curtseyed in a rustle of silk as the men bowed. Tatya made a seated obeisance which was both dignified and graceful, and Alexander gave her a particularly pleasant smile and nod, to convey that he knew why she remained seated and was satisfied with her effort.

After the usual conventional greetings and remarks, he turned to Vassily and spoke quietly and sincerely to him about his abduction and escape, thanking him with a great depth of feeling for his courageous service to his country.

'It was more a service to myself,' Vassily replied smilingly. 'For I'd no wish to stay there, you know—I didn't care for their hospitality, and the proposed entertainment had no appeal whatsoever!'

'I was not thinking only of your most recent service,' Alexander replied. 'I have long felt that I should make some public acknowledgement of your services, but my advisers have always expressed a fear that to do so would curtail your further usefulness. Now, however, they feel that it would be unreasonable to call upon you to the same extent in future, and this present occasion gives me the opportunity to award you the Order of St Anne, ostensibly for this particular adventure, but you and I know that it really conveys my gratitude for much more.'

Vassily looked distinctly taken aback, but it was not clear whether this was due to the news that he was to be allowed to retire from whatever it was that he did for the Foreign Ministry, or because of the Order. His expression was a curious mixture of pleasure and embarrassment as Alexander produced the diamond-studded star, red-enamelled gold cross with its central picture of the saint, and the vivid red, yellow-bordered ribbon, and solemnly performed the investiture, then placed his hands on Vassily's shoulders and formally kissed him on either cheek.

The others crowded round, loud and cheerful in their expressions of pleasure and congratulation, but once again Tatya had to undergo the frustration of sitting alone watching, wishing that she could shake his hand and kiss him with the other ladies. She was particularly touched by his thoughtfulness when he came over to her, gave her both his hands and bent down to receive her kiss on his cheek, suddenly turning his head as he did so, so that the kiss landed on his mouth. Then he sat down beside her so that she could look more closely at the star and badge.

'May I stay for a while?' the Emperor asked in an oddly shy, hesitant way when the excitement had died down a little, and of course, he was assured that he would be very welcome to do so. He took a chair and leaned back in it with a sigh, as if he was relieved to relax in an informal way with a few friends.

Lev asked him if he knew anything about the Sons of Liberty, but Alexander shook his head and lifted his hands in a helpless gesture.

'There are so many!' he replied. 'There must be dozens of these political societies of various kinds. Some of them are quite sane and sensible, and I find their reports and minutes of great interest—even of practical value. No doubt, when things are more settled, we may be able to implement some of their ideas. I have great sympathy for people of liberal views, so long as they are sensible and law-abiding, like yourselves. Unfortunately, the world is so disturbed and unsettled, with all these extraordinary Jacobin hotheads stirring up trouble all over the place, it is impossible to institute even the most desirable reforms for fear of unloosing further revolution about our ears. Those so-called Sons of Liberty appear to have been quite insane and certainly violently destructive in their aims. I shudder to think what might result if such people ever achieved control of this empire!'

'I'm sure your Imperial Majesty would rather talk of something more pleasant,' Rose put in smoothly, seeing that Alexander was looking quite distressed, then, remembering that Prince Nikolai had mentioned the Emperor's addiction to weak China tea, 'may I offer you tea?'

Alexander beamed with pleasure, and the business of ringing for the footman and then the arrival of the tea equipage and the handing of cups and trays of tempting little delicacies provided a diversion which enabled the conversation to move on to more comfortable ground, and the Emperor was heard to laugh several times at various witticisms, mostly from Vassily. He obviously enjoyed his informal visit, and stayed very late.

By the time he left, everyone was doing their best to stay awake and stifle their yawns. There was a certain strain in talking to such an Elevated Personage, however relaxed he tried to be, and Tatya thought pityingly that it must be a hard life for an Emperor, when no-one could feel completely at ease with him.

After he had gone, the party broke up for the night. Vassily forestalled Boris and had picked Tatya up before anyone else thought of it. As he carried her to the waiting carriage, she touched his cross of St Anne and said, 'I'm glad he gave you that—you deserve some recognition.'

'Isn't it typical of the man, though?' Vassily replied. 'All his good intentions turn into disasters! I'll never be able to wear the thing in public!'

'Why ever not?' asked Vladimir, who had followed close behind in case his brother showed signs of fainting or dropping Tatya.

'The ribbon clashes with my hair!' Vassily replied ruefully.

CHAPTER
TEN

HE CALLED on Tatya the next afternoon, as she had hoped he would, coming across the garden with only the slightest limp, and taking her in his arms without a word until after he had kissed her.

'I had to tell Rose I was coming here,' he said. 'I must say she didn't seem surprised.'

'I told them you'd been here when . . . when . . .'

'When I was missing?'

'Yes.'

She looked at his face anxiously, and he replied to the unspoken question, 'I'm quite all right, my dear. The cuts are mostly superficial, and the bruises not as bad as they look. Don't worry.'

'I'm sorry. I was so afraid . . .' Her voice broke on a sob.

'Yes, I know, but it's all over, and no harm done.'

He made a slight movement as if to stand up, but Tatya clung to him, and after the briefest hesitation, he squeezed himself half on to the daybed beside her and held her with one arm round her shoulders. She leaned against him and closed her eyes, and they were silent for a time, and then Tatya said, 'Did Rose say anything?'

'No. Oh, yes—she sent you her love.'

'It's very odd that no-one says anything about you coming here. Lev and Irina never mention it, but they must know that you come.'

'Lev knows all about it.'

'What, about the game?'

'Yes.'

Tatya digested this, then asked hesitantly, 'Did he—did he ask you to do it?'

'Well, yes—in a way.'

'So it's just something you're doing to oblige a friend.'
She sounded bitter and unhappy.

'No. It's something I'd already decided to do, but he
had the same idea and gave me his blessing, that's all.'

'Why?'

'Because he thought it might both entertain and help
you, I suppose.'

'No, not that. I mean, why had you decided to do it?'

'For the same reason. I thought it would amuse us
both for a few weeks, and perhaps help both of us.'

'Us?'

'I need help as well, *dushenka*.'

'Does it help you?'

He hesitated, then said, 'In a way. Does it help you?'

'More than I can ever tell you, and I'm so grateful to
you . . .'

'Stop worrying, then.'

They were silent again, and Vron, who had been
stretched out on the window-sill, rose from his recum-
bent position, plumped to the floor, stretched and
yawned, and then strolled over to the daybed, leapt
nimbly on to the high curved head, and sniffed at
Vassily's hair.

'Now what can I do for you?' asked Vassily.

Vron made a brief statement and nuzzled Vassily's
face, attracted by the salve which he had put on the
grazed cheek.

'Get off!' Vassily exclaimed, trying to evade the rough
tongue, but Vron persisted, and in his efforts to escape,
Vassily moved too violently and fell off the daybed, at
which Vron said something which sounded remarkably
coarse and ran under the table at the far end of the room.

'Are you hurt?' Tatya asked anxiously.

Vassily started to laugh. 'This is a lesson to me not to
try to make love on a daybed—they're not intended for
such activity!' He scrambled up and kissed Tatya, and
then sat beside her on the edge in a safer position.

'You did look a little ridiculous,' Tatya said.

'No more than usual. I can't help it, with this hair.'

'Was your father red-haired?'

'No, my mother. Father was dark, like Volodya. There's a very strong resemblance, in character as well as looks.'

'Who was Blanche?'

'A Frenchwoman. He met her during the war, and saw quite a lot of her while we were in Paris. He was really quite infatuated with her for a time.'

'You said that someone told you he's an excellent lover—was that Blanche?'

'Yes.'

'And did she really shoot Colonel Damkov?'

Vassily hesitated, then said, 'Not exactly. It was rather complicated.' He looked at Tatya's enquiring expression, then went on reluctantly, 'She aimed a pistol at . . . at someone, and Volodya thought it was Alexander Pavlovich, so he got in the way and took the bullet. Then someone else tried to disarm her, and the second barrel went off in the struggle and killed Damkov. She was tried for murdering Damkov and attempting to murder Volodya to conceal what she really intended.'

'Was—was she executed?'

'No. She died before . . .'

Tatya digested this in silence, then asked, 'But whom did she intend . . . ?'

'State secret,' Vassily replied firmly. 'I told you it was complicated. It was in '14. We'd just beaten the French so no-one thought it odd that a Frenchwoman shot two Russians, and it saved a deal of trouble, because if she'd hit the man she aimed at, there'd have been a fearful imbroglio! Now let's talk about something else.'

When he took his leave some time later, he said, 'I daren't be late for dinner, or Volodya will have the whole Regiment out looking for me, and leave the Fortress open for the first-comer to occupy!' He left Tatya a little parcel in his usual casual fashion as he went. It was a tortoiseshell comb this time, of the Spanish variety just coming into fashion, with an

ornamental top decorated with piqué work. Tatya put it
in her hair and admired the effect in the nearest mirror.
She was surprised to see how well she looked—quite like
her old self!

By the beginning of the following week, Vassily
appeared to have recovered from his injuries. The bruise
on his face had faded to a mottled grey and yellow, and
his cuts had healed to pink scars. His name-day fell in
mid-week, and Prince Nikolai had arranged a celebration for him, inviting a number of people for dinner at
the Volkhovsky Palace, with dancing to follow in the fine
ballroom.

There was some discussion between Lev and Irina
about suitable gifts for him, but Tatya had already
decided on hers, and ordered the two volumes of Ter-
laich's *A Short Guide to the Systematic Understanding of
the Civil Law of Private Property in Russia* from Belizard's, bound rather austerely in black morocco with a
matching slip-case. She had Vassily's monogram tooled
in gold on the covers, and felt that they needed no
further embellishment, as their plain appearance was in
keeping with the contents.

She also gave a great deal of thought to planning what
she would wear for the occasion, and when the day
arrived, she sat in front of her mirror, surveying the
result, and was satisfied that, considering her age, it was
really quite successful.

Her gown was of rainbow silk gauze over white sars-
enet, and shimmered with changing colours as she
moved. The boat-shaped neckline was low-cut and revealed her smooth white shoulders and a moderate
amount of bosom, framed in a lace-trimmed ruching of
the gauze, and a collar of fine opals encircled her throat,
showing the same kaleidoscopic shifting of colours as her
gown. The skirt was a little longer than was fashionable,
the deep, lace-edged frill just reaching her slippers and
concealing both her mis-shapen ankle and the band of
silk-covered horsehair which gave the necessary weight
and belled shape, but was easier to manage than the

usual stiff padded rouleau. A beaded reticule, long white gloves and Vassily's fan completed the ensemble. Her hair was parted in the middle and drawn smoothly to just above her ears, where it fell in ringlets, and was swept up at the back into a pile of curls trimmed with a bow of the gauze and an opal ornament.

She carried flowers as well. They arrived in a square box covered with pretty flowered paper and tied with silver ribbons, and inside was a posy of little tight rosebuds arranged in concentric circles, deep red in the centre and shading through pinks to white on the outside, and mounted in a gilt holder of a design similar to her fan, with a chain to hang it from her wrist. There was no note, but she guessed who had sent it.

As the carriage turned into the semi-circular drive of the Volkhovsky Palace, she had a sudden qualm of fear, remembering her last visit, when Vladimir had come out, but this time it was Vassily who was standing waiting as the footman opened the door and let down the step.

He was wearing green velvet Court dress with a most elegant cravat and his Order and ribbon of St Anne, despite its colour. He greeted Lev and Irina, complimenting her on her pale blue barège gown, and then entered the carriage to lift Tatya, greeting her with, 'Good evening, Iris.'

She was disconcerted for a moment until she recalled her Greek mythology and replied, 'Good evening Apollo,' and thanked him for the flowers.

'Thank you for the books,' he replied.

'I'm afraid they're a little dull,' she said, with a touch of misgiving.

'Not in the least. I find them most interesting and useful, particularly the section dealing with serfs, as I expect you intended.'

Tatya smiled and admitted that the thought had occurred to her.

The entrance hall of Prince Nikolai's house looked like something out of a fairy-tale. The huge central chandelier with its hundreds of crystal drops blazed with

the light of a thousand candles, making the honey-
coloured translucent marble of the walls and staircase
glow. The balustrades and the first-floor gallery were
lined with a hedge of flowers, and trails of ivy twined up
the hand-rails. Liveried servants stood impassively waiting to attend the guests, who were mounting the stairs in
chattering, beautifully-dressed groups to where Rose
and her husband were waiting to receive them.

It was amazing how many acquaintances Vassily had
in St Petersburg, considering that it was midsummer,
when so many people went to the country, and he spent
so little time in the capital himself. Some fifty people sat
down to dinner, and more than a hundred more were to
attend the ball afterwards, and they all seemed very
pleased to see Vassily and congratulate him on his St
Anne.

Questions about it and his recent adventure began as
soon as he had carried Tatya into the salon, and she
noticed that he seemed very reluctant to say anything
about either, fending off enquiries with joking remarks
and rapidly changing the subject by asking the question-
ers about something else—Are you staying in Petersburg all summer?—How is your father these days?—
anything that seemed appropriate.

The dining-room had recently been redecorated in a
very pale, misty green with white plaster garlands on the
walls and light satinwood furniture. The vast white
damask tablecloths were looped up with green ribbons,
and the gold vases down the centre of the table were
filled with roses and ivy, arranged to cascade downwards
without impeding the diners' view of people opposite.
The wall-sconces and chandeliers were ablaze with candles and crystal, and the gold flatware gleamed softly in
the light. The food was served on porcelain from the
Imperial Factory, the plates edged with gold in a border
composed of the initials of Rose and Nikolai. Tatya
pointed this out to Vassily, for she had been seated next
to him, and he replied that the service was a wedding
present from the Emperor.

She was having a little difficulty in managing her posy as well as fan, reticule and gloves, and laid it on the table by her place with reluctance as she feared that the flowers might be crushed. Vassily picked it up and smilingly showed her that the holder was ingeniously fashioned so that three little legs opened out to enable it to stand upright.

'All eventualities foreseen,' he commented. 'Didn't you know that posy-holders do that?'

'I've never had one before,' she replied.

'I've never bought one before, for that matter. The fellow in the shop showed me how it worked.'

He was distracted by a question addressed to him from further down the table, and looked at the speaker, his smile fading a little as he saw that it was Sergei Dmitriev.

'I'm sorry—I didn't quite hear . . . ?' he said.

'I asked,' Prince Sergei repeated more loudly, 'who it was that abducted you, and what purpose they had for doing it.' The question was a reasonable one, but something in his tone made it disagreeable.

'I understand that they were members of one of the more extreme political groups,' Vassily replied equably. 'Their purpose was to hold me hostage and use me as a bargaining counter to persuade my brother to do as they wished.'

'Oh, I see.' Prince Sergei apparently lost interest, for he bowed with a sarcastic smile and did not ask any more questions. The conversation once more became general.

'Why is Sergei Mikhailovich here?' asked Tatya quietly. 'Surely he's no great friend of yours?'

'As he's Nikolai's brother-in-law, we could hardly not invite him,' Vassily replied. 'I could wish him to the devil, but Nikolai seems to feel some responsibility for him.'

After dinner, the guests moved to the ballroom, which Tatya found all too unpleasantly familiar, and as Vassily carried her in, she gave an involuntary shiver.

'What is it, *dushenka*?' he asked.

She hesitated, then replied reluctantly, 'I first met my—General Kalinsky here.' She always found it difficult to say 'my husband', and at the moment it seemed impossible.

'Did you know you were to marry him?'

'No. My father presented him during a ball which Nikolai's father gave, and it wasn't until a few days after that he told me that he had chosen the General for me. I didn't like him from the first.'

Vassily put her down on a sofa which Nikolai or Rose had provided, where she would have a good view of the dancers, and said, 'Don't let your memories spoil your evening, Tatya. I do want you to enjoy my name-day ball. I don't have one very often.'

'Of course I shall enjoy it,' she said resolutely. 'It's a very beautiful ballroom.'

Vassily looked about him. 'Yes. I like the painted ceiling—I see it has the Petersburg skyline round the cornice. How clever to do it in that grey silhouette against a pale blue ceiling. It looks like the city in the early morning, with just a touch of sea-mist.'

'I've never seen five very large chandeliers hanging from the sky over the Neva,' Tatya observed pensively.

'It would be rather interesting . . .' Vassily sounded equally pensive. 'One could suspend them from captive balloons, I suppose, and the heat from the candles would keep the balloons aloft.'

They had conducted this exchange in very serious tones, but now they looked at each other and burst out laughing. Lev, standing nearby talking to the City Governor, General Miloradovich, turned in surprise at hearing Tatya's clear, merry laugh, which had been a rare sound for far too long.

Presently, when Vassily had gone to open the ball with Rose, he sat down beside his sister and said, 'You seem to be enjoying yourself, and you look very pretty this evening.'

Tatya thought to herself with amusement that, although Lev had always managed to find the most gallant complimentary remarks for other ladies, his sister was never anything better than 'very pretty', but she thanked him all the same.

'Pretty flowers,' he said, admiring her posy.

'From Vassily,' she felt obliged to say.

'Er—yes,' Lev failed to meet her eyes.

'He says you know about it.'

Lev rubbed the side of his nose and said awkwardly, 'Yes, but it's all right, you know. I mean, he's a good fellow.'

'He's very kind.'

'Yes, though he always pretends he isn't.'

'Why did you ask him to pay attention to me?'

Lev looked startled, then replied as honestly as he could, 'I thought it might cheer you up a little, to have someone pleasant to flirt with again. Nothing wrong with that, is there?' He sounded slightly defensive.

Tatya smiled, 'I used to enjoy a little flirtation,' she admitted. 'And so did you.'

'Still do,' Lev said with an unashamed grin. 'But now I only flirt with my wife.' He looked sidelong at Tatya, hesitated, then asked, 'You're not upset about it, are you?'

'About what?'

'My knowing that Vassily visits you.'

'No, not really. It's only that . . . Oh, I suppose it all seems very childish.'

'Why should it? People play games all the time. It's only a little amusement.' He gestured towards the gay, colourful scene before them. 'It's no sillier than this— people dressing in fine clothes and prancing about more or less in time to a rhythmic noise. We all enjoy it—why shouldn't you enjoy something? It's perfectly harmless, and it seems to be doing you good.'

'It is harmless, isn't it?' Tatya sought reassurance.

Lev took her hand and gave it a comforting squeeze. 'Yes, pet, quite harmless, and no-one else's business, even if you choose to take Vassily for your lover in reality! I don't expect either of you want to go to those lengths, though, so enjoy your game and don't give a fig for what anyone else thinks!'

Tatya smiled and felt reassured, as he had intended, and presently he went away to dance, and Vladimir took his place, smoothed his moustache with one finger, cleared his throat, and said gruffly, 'Thank you for talking to Olga Mikhailovna.'

Tatya had almost forgotten her conversation with Olga, but she managed to recall the gist of it, and said, 'I didn't really tell her anything more than she had already worked out for herself. She's had a very dull life, and it's hardly surprising that the sudden change made her a little silly. Are things better between you now?'

Vladimir's impassive face broke into a very charming smile. 'Much better. She seems to have decided that perhaps I'm not as dull as I look. She's stopped fluttering her eyelashes at Dmitriev too, though I don't think he's very pleased about that.'

Tatya felt a twinge of anxiety. 'Is he still paying her attention?'

'Yes. He behaves correctly enough, and I do believe with some seriousness. I've no liking for the fellow, and I suppose that prejudices me against him. Still, she don't like him, so there's no point in worrying about it.'

'She likes you well enough.'

Vladimir tugged at his moustache, sank his deep voice to a confidential rumble, and said, 'I've written to her mother!'

Tatya was delighted. 'Oh, Vladimir! I do wish you every good fortune! Does Olga know?'

'Yes. I asked her if I should write. I didn't say what about, but there's really only one reason for a fellow to write to a lady's mother, isn't there? Er—you'll keep it to yourself, won't you?'

'Yes, of course. Thank you for telling me.'

He fidgetted with his gloves, and then said abruptly, without looking at her, 'Vassily's paying you a lot of attention, isn't he?'

'Yes. He's very kind,' Tatya replied cautiously.

'That attitude of his—you know, laughing at everything, never seeming to be serious about anything—it's only on the surface. He's not really a cynic.'

'I know.'

'He was badly hurt once, and he's never really recovered from it.'

'He told me about it.'

Vladimir was so startled that it actually showed in his face. '*Told* you? Vassily?'

'Yes.'

'Good Lord! I'm sorry—I didn't mean . . . I've never known him speak about it to anyone before! Well, you'll understand why he'll never marry, then.'

'Yes,' Tatya replied more calmly than she felt. 'I don't suppose he will. You're very fond of him, aren't you?'

Vladimir grinned. 'And you're very perceptive! Most people think we don't like each other much!'

After a while, Vladimir went to dance, and he was replaced by a succession of gentlemen. Tatya was not surprised that Prince Nikolai and Boris took a turn at sitting out with her, but there were several others she did not expect, and it was quite like old times to find herself sought out, complimented, and clearly still attractive to four or five men who were not old friends, or likely to feel any obligation to be kind to her.

Vassily, as guest of honour, was much in demand—all the more as he was such an accomplished dancer—but he found time to sit with Tatya again, commenting mischievously 'I see "Tatya's beaux" are still gathering round the honeypot! I shall soon have to take my turn in the queue, I suppose!'

'I think you might be considered privileged, so you've no reason to be jealous.' She replied in the same humorous vein. 'Did you receive many interesting gifts?'

'A great many! To tell the truth, I was overwhelmed to find how kind and generous people are! I had this from Ilya.'

He pulled a folded piece of paper from his pocket and gave it to her. She opened it and found that it was a drawing executed in coloured crayons of a large purple object surrounded by bright blue squiggles. Sundry fish-like shapes disported themselves here and there, and across the top was a band of lighter blue with some white blobs, and a large yellow spider.

She considered it for a few moments, turning it first one way and then another as she puzzled over the purple object, and then said, as light dawned 'Oh, of course! It's a whale!'

Vassily regarded her with pleased approval. 'Oh, excellent female! I knew you wouldn't betray my good opinion of you! He copied it from an engraving in Nikolai's big atlas, but, of course, the engraving wasn't coloured. He says it the Emperor of Whales—that's why it's purple.'

'Are the white things clouds or gulls?'

'A little of each—interchangeably, I think. It's very good for a child of six.'

Tatya agreed and returned it to him. He refolded it and put it safely back in his pocket.

'What was Volodya looking so deedy about when he sat with you? Not while he was talking about Olga, but later, when he started fiddling with his gloves,' he asked.

'How did you know he was talking about Olga?'

'One—he kept looking at her. Two—he was actually smiling! What did he say after that? Something he didn't much like saying, from the way he was fidgetting about.'

Tatya occupied herself with smoothing her own gloves, keeping her eyes on them as she replied, 'He was making sure that I realise that you don't ever intend to marry,' in as calm a voice as she could manage. Because she was looking down, she failed to see the sharp, searching glance Vassily gave her as he replied, 'The devil he was! I hope he didn't think I'd been attempting to deceive you about my intentions!'

'Of course not!'

'Well, it sounds as if he did, or why bother to put himself to the embarrassment of mentioning it at all?'

'But I don't . . . I know what your intentions are!'

He looked at her serious face for a moment without comment, then said smilingly, 'Shall we go out to supper? Everyone else seems to have done so.'

After supper, Olga joined Tatya on her sofa and chattered away for a little while, and then said confidingly, 'Vladimir has told you, hasn't he? About writing to Mamma, I mean.'

'Yes. He told me earlier this evening. I'm very happy for you.'

Olga dimpled shyly and smoothed the skirt of her green and white striped silk gown in a complacent manner. She looked very pretty and demure with her green velvet slippers set neatly side by side below the stiff padded rouleau, criss-crossed with silver ribbons, at the bottom of her skirt. 'I hope Mamma doesn't make any objections,' she said. 'I can't think why she should, for he's a very good man, perfectly suitable in rank and fortune, and quite old enough to be reliable.'

'You're certain that you want to marry him?'

'Oh, yes!' Olga turned large, dark, earnest eyes on Tatya. 'I'm not really a silly little fool, even if I have behaved like one!'

Tatya suddenly became aware that two gentleman were heading towards them in a purposeful manner. One was Boris, the other Prince Sergei.

Boris arrived first, and said to Olga in a firm and slightly reproving tone, 'I've just been talking to Aunt Dorya. She tells me that you haven't been to visit her since before Pentecost!'

Olga looked guilty and murmured 'Oh dear! No I suppose I haven't.' She caught sight of Prince Sergei, who was now standing behind Boris, listening to the conversation with a bored expression, and said to Boris, 'Shall we talk about it while we're dancing?'

'There's not much to say,' Boris replied. 'I've told her that we'll both call on her tomorrow afternoon. I'll bring my carriage for you as soon after three as I can manage . . . Olga, are you listening?'

Olga was apprehensively conscious of Prince Sergei's presence, but she switched her attention back to her brother and said in a hurried, nervous voice. 'Yes, Borinka. You'll send your carriage at three tomorrow. Oh, please—shall we dance?'

Boris looked puzzled and glanced at Tatya, who indicated with a slight movement of her head and eyes that there was someone behind him, and he swung round to face Prince Sergei, who gave him a contemptuous look and said in his usual drawl 'I was about to ask Olga Mikhailovna to dance.'

'I've just asked her myself,' Boris replied both truculently and untruthfully.

'Oh, have you?' Well, it's very kind of you to take a brotherly interest in seeing that she's not left by the wall, but I'd be quite happy to relieve you of the necessity.' Prince Sergei's tone was not quite insulting to either Boris or Olga, and had Olga been a fool, and plain into the bargain, she might even have thought he meant to be kind, but she flushed and Boris stiffened with anger, and they both answered more or less together, 'I'm quite content to dance with my brother,' and 'Countess Kalinskaya doesn't require your condescension,' Boris then took Olga's hand and whisked her out on the ballroom floor with quite a visible jerk.

Prince Sergei looked a little taken aback, and Tatya, secretly filled with delight at his discomfiture, said coolly, 'Neither of the Countesses Kalinskaya, in fact, require it. I've no doubt you'd find my middle-aged company very dull, Sergei Mikhailovich, so I'll be happy to excuse you to find another partner.' He bowed and walked away, his back stiff with annoyance.

The ball ended at four in the morning, and Tatya leaned a sleepy head close to Vassily's as he carried her out to the carriage in the early morning sunshine. A blackbird was singing on the top of one of the trees in front of the Palace, and they stopped for a moment to listen.

'It's so clear and beautiful,' Tatya whispered.

'Yes. Better than a nightingale,' Vassily agreed. 'Have you enjoyed yourself, *dushenka*?'

'Yes, very much. Thank you, Vasya.'

'For what?'

'I didn't enjoy anything much before I met you.'

'Well, I told you that you needed a lover. You were quite the most beautiful female at the ball, you know.'

'And you were the handsomest man.'

He laughed aloud at that, and was still looking very amused as the carriage drove away from the Palace.

CHAPTER
ELEVEN

TATYA returned to the Volkhovsky Palace after luncheon. Lev and Irina had arranged to visit some friends at Gatchina and did not expect to return until after midnight, and, as Tatya had no wish to travel so far and go through the fuss and embarrassment entailed in being moved about among comparative strangers, Rose had invited her to spend the afternoon and evening with her, and stay the night, enabling Lev to give all his servants permission to visit the Midsummer fair. Tatya had also given Elena leave to go, providing that she rejoined her mistress at the Volkhovsky Palace before midnight.

It was another dull, damp day, not exactly raining, but too chill and unpleasant to go out on the terrace, so Tatya and Rose sat in the latter's sitting-room, stitching their embroidery and talking. Prince Nikolai was closeted with his man-of-business, and Olga was upstairs trying on all her bonnets to see which was the most suitable for a visit to her Aunt Dorya. Vassily was sitting with Tatya and Rose, reading.

Prince Nikolai had appointed his valet's brother Shura to look after Ilya, with the idea that he would become the boy's valet later on, and they had been out in the stableyard for Ilya's riding lesson when Tatya arrived, but the child came in soon after to make his stiff little bow to the visitor, and told her confidingly that he had been learning to trot.

'Are you going to teach your pony when you've learned yourself?' Vassily enquired from behind his book.

Ilya thought about that, then said, 'Alexander Nevsky and I are learning together.'

'Alexander Nevsky!' exclaimed Vassily. 'Not that fat little barrel with a leg at each corner? Good Heavens!'

'It's a very good name for a pony,' Tatya said with every appearance of sincerity. 'It gives him something to aim at. That was a very good picture that you drew for Vassily Sergeivich's name-day, Ilya.'

The boy gave a little wriggle of pleasure. 'Did you like it? I'll draw one for you if you'd like me to.'

'That would be very pleasant,' Tatya replied.

'What shall I draw for you?'

Tatya's mind immediately went blank, and she could think of nothing which might be within the child's experience and capability.

'How about an elephant?' Vassily suggested. 'We found a very good picture of one the other day. In the red book, you remember?'

'Yes. It's in the schoolroom. I'll fetch it.' Ilya ran off purposefully and soon returned clutching a large leatherbound book which required both his arms to carry it. He put it down carefully on the table near where Vassily was sitting, and then took his papers and crayons from the drawer where they were kept and set to work, the tip of his tongue sticking out as an aid to concentration. Vassily caught Tatya's eye over the top of his book and gave her a solemn wink.

Olga came down dressed ready to go out, and pirouetted in front of the ladies, enquiring if they thought she looked suitably clad for her visit, for 'Aunt Dorya is very particular.'

She was wearing a blue velvet pelisse over a paler blue muslin gown, high at the neck, with a lace ruffle. Her bonnet was large, the brim lined with velvet to match the pelisse, and trimmed with a number of silk roses and a magnificent ostrich plume. Tatya and Rose both gave their approval, and Vassily raised his eyes from his book long enough to say, 'Charming, my dear,' in a benevolent and avuncular tone.

'I've time to go and change if you're not sure . . .' Olga began, but at that moment a footman arrived to announce that Count Kalinsky's carriage was at the door, and Olga went out in a flutter of feathers, lace and velvet.

'I thought Boris said he would come for her,' Tatya remarked. 'And surely it's not yet three o'clock?'

'A quarter before,' Vassily said, consulting his watch. Ilya promptly got down from his chair and went to look at it, and Vassily obligingly pressed the repeater and let it play its little chiming tune for him. When it finished, he gave a little sigh of satisfaction and returned to his drawing.

Vladimir arrived on the stroke of three, and Vassily reluctantly laid aside his book in order to exert himself a little in conversation. Tatya caught sight of the cover of the book as he put it down on the table, and realised that it was one of the volumes which she had given him the previous day, and was pleased that he obviously found it so interesting.

'Has Olga gone already?' Vladimir asked. 'Boris must have grown wings, then. He was still at the Winter Palace when I left there at two. Still, I've been to the Fortress, so I suppose he could just have managed . . .' He looked puzzled for a moment, then shrugged in dismissal, and looked over Ilya's shoulder at the child's drawing.

'Can you tell what it is?' Ilya asked anxiously.

'Well, it looks like a green elephant . . .' Vladimir replied cautiously, clearly wary of hurting the boy's feelings.

'Elephants is really grey,' Ilya told him, 'but grey's not very pretty.' He gave his drawing a last careful inspection, and then took it to Tatya and said, 'For you, Tatya Petrovna.'

'Thank you, Ilyusha,' she said. 'It's a very good elephant, and I'll take great care of it.'

'Vassily Sergeivich rode on an elephant,' Ilya informed her solemnly.

'Did he?' Tatya exclaimed. 'I've never seen one! I don't believe there's a single elephant in the whole of

Russia! Where did Vassily Sergeivich find it?'

'In Paris,' Vassily said with a tender, reminiscent smile. 'A charming beast—I was very fond of it.'

'Ilyusha, will you ring for tea, please,' Rose said. 'And then go and knock on the study door and ask your father if he will come here for tea, or if he would like it sent in.'

Ilya shut his eyes and murmured the message over to himself, and then trotted to the bellpull by the door and gave it a tug before going out of the room in a very important fashion, closing the door carefully behind him. He returned in a few minutes with Prince Nikolai, who had finished his business, and went to stand by Rose while she poured the tea. His father greeted his friends, then went to hand the cups for his wife.

'Would you like to hand the cakes?' Rose asked Ilya. He picked up the plate of little sugar-cakes and went round with them, and then returned to Rose with the depleted supply.

'You may have two,' she said, and he selected a pink one and a white one, thanked her, and retired to his chair to eat them.

The others drank their tea and were talking about the previous night's ball, when Boris was announced, and came in looking both anxious and puzzled. He kissed the ladies' hands in an unusually hurried manner, and asked, 'What's this about Olga going off in a carriage?'

'You sent your carriage for her, as you said . . .' Rose began, and then the expression on Boris' face stopped her. 'Didn't you?'

'No I didn't say that. I said I'd come for her with my carriage as soon after three as I could manage, and here I am,' he replied. 'But your footman tells me that Olga left in a carriage which was supposed to be mine some time ago.'

'At a quarter to three,' Vassily said, standing up. 'There's something amiss here, Nikolai.'

'Yes.' Prince Nikolai agreed, going to the door. 'Something I don't like the sound of.' He went out and returned in a few minutes with the footman. 'Now,

Yakov Igorovich, will you tell us exactly what happened when the carriage came for the younger Countess Kalinskaya?'

The footman allowed a fleeting expression of surprise to cross his face, and replied, 'A carriage drew up outside, sir, and the driver came to the door and said it was Count Kalinsky's carriage, come to fetch his sister. I told him to wait and came to inform the Countess. She was ready, so she went out, I helped her into the carriage, and she drove away. That's all.'

'What was the carriage like?' asked Boris.

'Just a gentleman's small town carriage, sir. It was black or dark blue, I think, with a yellow line. There was no crest on the door. Otherwise, it was very like the one in which you just came, sir.'

There was a puzzled silence, which began to take on an air of anxiety as the five friends glanced at one another.

'Did you notice anything odd or unusual?' asked Vladimir.

'No, Excellency. Oh, well—there was one thing—I was surprised to see the driver.'

'Why?' asked Boris sharply.

'I didn't know that he'd passed into your service, sir, and, in fact, I wouldn't have thought you'd wish to employ him. He's not altogether honest.'

'You know him?'

'Why, yes sir! He was Prince Dmitriev's driver— Prince Sergei, that is. I suppose the young gentleman no longer keeps his own carriage . . . I mean . . . er . . .' The footman cleared his throat as if to convey that he knew and they knew that Prince Sergei was in financial trouble, but it was not his place to mention the matter.

'Sergei Dmitriev!' exclaimed Boris. 'My God! You don't think . . .' He broke off, and waited until Prince Nikolai had made sure that the servant had no more relevant information and dismissed him, then he said in a less explosive manner, 'You don't think the little fool's gone off with him, do you?'

'Of course not!' Tatya said at once. 'She was obviously expecting to go to your aunt's. Wait a moment . . . I must just try to remember . . .' She put her hands to her head and thought back to the previous night. 'When you made the arrangement with Olga—do you recall? Sergei Dmitriev was about to ask her to dance, and he was standing just behind you. He distracted Olga's attention, and you asked her if she was listening. She repeated what you had said, but she had it all wrong, and before you could correct her, Sergei interrupted. You said you would *bring* your carriage soon after three, but she said you would *send* the carriage *at* three. He must have heard . . .'

'And earlier, at dinner,' Vladimir suddenly picked up the thread. 'He was plaguey interested in Vassily's abduction . . .'

There was silence, as no-one wanted to voice the fear that was in all their minds, then Vassily said quietly, 'That swine's abducted her!'

Vladimir went quite white, but Boris reddened and spluttered, 'I'll kill the rat . . .' and Prince Nikolai cut in sharply, 'Be quiet, Boris! Losing your temper won't help. We must find her and get her back with as little fuss and noise as possible, for her sake. Never mind Sergei— I'll deal with him.'

'Can't deal with him till we've found him,' Vladimir said laconically. 'Where would he take her?'

'We must think this out,' said Prince Nikolai. 'Calmly,' he added, with a sharp glance at Boris. He began to pace slowly about the room, and Tatya remembered that both Vladimir and Boris had served under his command before he was wounded at Borodino—clearly, old habits persisted, for both men watched and listened as he said, 'Now, has he copied Vassily's abductors slavishly? If so, he'll have taken her out of the city.'

'Not in a town carriage,' Vassily put in. He was right, of course. Such a small, light vehicle would have been impossible on the rough corduroy roads beyond the wooden pavé of the city.

'Except the Moscow road,' Vladimir pointed out. 'That's a possibility, but surely she'd have the sense to call out, and there's so much traffic in that road that someone would hear her!'

Prince Nikolai nodded. 'Yes, I don't think he'd risk passing the police post, and I think he's more likely to stay in the city—he hasn't any money, remember. Of course, he'll have to get her off the street as soon as possible in case she manages to attract attention to her situation.' His head jerked suddenly, as if something had just occurred to him, and he turned to Boris.

'Take your carriage,' he said briskly, 'and go straight to the police post by the Moscow gate and check with them whether a town carriage has passed. If not (and I don't think he'd risk going that way), go to the Dmitriev Palace and enquire there, but for Heaven's sake be discreet! If he's not there, come back here. Vassily, will you go with him? Don't let him do anything foolish! A duel, or anything of that sort, would be a disaster!'

Vassily nodded, seized Boris by the arm and propelled him towards the door. Boris pulled back for a moment to ask, 'What will you do?'

'We'll try one or two other possibilities,' replied the Prince, who had turned to Vladimir, whose mouth had opened to protest, but had been arrested by the Prince's firm and significant stare. He closed his mouth and waited until his brother and Boris had left, and then said, 'Why Vassily? I should have gone!'

Prince Nikolai shook his head. 'They won't find him there. His father told me in confidence a day or two ago that he's thrown him out, and he's living in a small apartment in the Italianskaya, with barely a kopek to his name. I'm sure he'll have taken her there, but I wanted Boris out of the way. Rose, will you come with us? She may need a female's help . . .'

'Of course.' Rose had already risen to her feet, but she checked and turned back. 'Tatya?'

'I'll be all right,' Tatya replied. 'I'll stay here with Ilya. Shall I send to Olga's aunt to say that she's indisposed?'

'Please.' Rose turned to Ilya, who was watching with a puzzled expression, not understanding the adults' concern. 'You'll be a good boy and look after Tatya Petrovna?' She spared time to kiss him. 'Papa and I have to go out for a while.'

'Yes, Mamma,' he replied docilely, and returned to his drawing, losing interest in the inexplicable behaviour of the adults.

By the time the carriage was ready, Rose had donned her bonnet, and she set off with Prince Nikolai and Vladimir, who was chewing the edge of his moustache and scowling in a manner which made Rose wonder what he would do to Sergei Dmitriev when—if—they found him.

The inactivity of the drive across the city filled all three with frustration, until they drew up outside the building which Prince Nikolai knew to be Prince Sergei's new address, and they went into the entrance lobby, where a sleepy porter replied to their enquiry that Prince Dmitriev's apartment was on the third floor, but he could not say if the Prince was in or not.

They mounted the stairs quickly, and Vladimir ran ahead, tried the door, which was not locked, and burst in. Prince Nikolai followed, and Rose stopped at the door and looked back down the stairs. There was no sign of life below.

Inside the small vestibule, there were three doors. One stood open and revealed a dining-room with long sash windows, the central one was closed and gave on to the kitchen quarters, and the third was also closed, but a shuffling sound came from behind it, so Vladimir charged it with such force that he overturned the chair which Prince Sergei was trying to wedge under the doorhandle, and sent the Prince sprawling across the floor, where he scrambled out of Vladimir's way with undignified haste and made a quick lunge past him for the door. Prince Nikolai intercepted him and took a firm grip on his collar and one arm.

The room was simply furnished with a couple of

cabinets, a washstand and a brass bedstead. There were
two chairs, one on the floor, and Olga was sitting in the
other, her ankles tied together and her arms tied behind
her back. Her bonnet had been tossed on to the wash-
stand, her pelisse lay on the bed, and her muslin gown
had been ripped open at the front. She was gagged, and
her dark eyes were so full of terror that it was doubtful if
she understood what was happening.

Vladimir came to a halt in front of her and drew his
sword. The sound and sight seemed to penetrate her
fear, but only to make her shut her eyes and give a little
strangled moan, as if she expected him to run her
through. He cut the cords which fastened her, then
fumbled with the knot of the gag and gently removed
it.

Prince Nikolai called Rose, who ran in and went to
Olga, taking the girl in her arms as she began to sob in
near-hysteria.

'Take him out!' Rose said to Vladimir. 'Leave her
with me for a few minutes.'

Vladimir nodded, paused for just a second to look at
Olga, his face strained with anxiety, then he went out,
seizing Prince Sergei and pushing him along in front of
him. Prince Nikolai followed, and they went into the
dining-room, where Vladimir almost threw Prince
Sergei into a chair, and stood scowling down on him.

'I haven't . . . I didn't mean any harm!' Sergei said, his
voice rising and cracking. 'I want to marry her . . . on my
honour . . . I only wanted to make her agree, and then
make her parents give their consent . . . as God's my
witness . . . !'

Vladimir was silent, standing there broodingly, staring at the wretch as he squirmed and babbled in-
coherently.

'Have you raped her?' he asked coldly, cutting across
the other's torrent of excuses.

'No! Oh, God! No!'

Vladimir said nothing more, but took a single step
nearer to Sergei, who gave a squeal of terror, looked

from Vladimir to Prince Nikolai like a hunted animal, his eyes staring and his face distorted. The two tall, menacing figures towered over him, blocking any chance of escape through the open door. He gave another squeal, then bolted for the window, knocking his chair flying.

'Don't come near me!' he panted, backing up to the windows. He stood silhouetted against the light, for the long windows reached almost to the floor. The one behind him was open at the bottom, the sash pushed up as far as it would go. Vladimir noticed it, then realised that Sergei was still moving backwards. He uttered an involuntary 'Don't . . . !' and took one step forward. Sergei started back, went too far, and the backs of his knees came up hard against the window-sill. He made a convulsive effort to save himself, but his momentum carried him on and he fell backwards out of the window. There was a cry of sheer animal terror, and a horrible sound which made Vladimir turn even paler and gasp with horror.

'Stay there!' Prince Nikolai said sharply. He crossed to the window, looked down, and said quietly, 'Oh, God! I think he's dead! Look after the ladies, Vladimir. I'll go down.'

Vladimir nodded, and stood where he was while the Prince left the apartment and went down the stairs. He was still standing there when Rose brought Olga into the room about ten minutes later. The girl had stopped crying, but she avoided looking at Vladimir. Her pelisse was buttoned over her torn gown, completely hiding the damage, and her bonnet was on, the ribbons tied under her chin.

'She's not harmed in any way,' Rose said at once. 'Just shocked and frightened. He threatened her, but nothing more. He wanted her to marry him, and if she refused, he said he'd—well, he'd make it necessary for them to be married.'

Vladimir shut his eyes for a moment and sighed with relief. 'Olga?' he said softly, trying to catch her eyes, but she turned away with a sob and clung to Rose, who looked concerned and shook her head at him.

'Where is he?' she asked.

Vladimir jerked his head towards the window. 'He fell out. He was frightened, and didn't realise that the window was open . . .'

'That cry . . . ? Is he . . . ?'

'I think so. Nikolai's gone to see.'

They waited in silence until Prince Nikolai returned. 'He's dead,' he said abruptly. 'Broken neck. We carried him into the porter's lodge, but the porter's half-drunk and so confused that he doesn't remember anything much. He didn't see Sergei come in, so he didn't see Olga either. We'll say that we all came to see Sergei's new apartment—it's a natural enough thing, as he's my brother-in-law, and we all know him quite well. No need to mention whether or not we all arrived together, unless the matter is specifically raised, in which case we'll say that we agreed to meet here. Apart from that, we tell the exact truth—he backed towards the window while he was talking to Vladimir and me, waiting for the ladies to—er—tidy themselves. None of us realised that the window was open until it was too late, and he went too far and fell out. Can you all remember that?'

Vladimir and Rose nodded, and Rose added, 'Olga and I didn't see anything, as we were in another room.'

'Yes, that's right. What about Olga?'

'I didn't see anything,' Olga replied. 'We heard a cry, that's all.' She gave a little sob. 'I'm all right. I understood all that you said.'

Prince Nikolai nodded in a kindly way. 'I must stay here and see the police when they come. Vladimir, please take the ladies home and stay there. Rose, will you please tell Boris what's happened as soon as he returns, then bring him back here in our carriage, not his own, and we'll go together to Sergei's father. He'll have to know the whole truth.'

'Shouldn't I . . . ?' Vladimir began.

'No. Your place is with Olga. You've really nothing to do with what happened.' Prince Nikolai looked closely at Vladimir. 'That's the truth, you know. You didn't so much as threaten him—his fear was due to his own conscience—and you tried to warn him. Don't blame yourself, man!'

Vladimir nodded again, looking a little less troubled, and went with Rose and Olga, following them down the stairs in silence, and they drove home, with Olga clinging to Rose and sobbing at intervals.

Boris and Vassily were in the entrance hall of the Volkhovsky Palace, having just arrived back from their abortive visit to the Dmitriev Palace, and Boris started towards them with an exclamation of, 'What . . . ?' which Rose cut short by saying swiftly, 'Oh, Boris, Vassily! Sergei Mikhailovich has met with a dreadful accident! He fell from the window while we were there, and broke his neck! Olga's upset, as are we all, that's why she looks so white! Boris, will you please come back with me? Nikolai particularly asked that you should go with him to see the old Prince Dmitriev.' Quite half a dozen footmen were listening with interest.

'Yes, of course.' Boris hesitated, looking at Olga. She raised stricken eyes to him and whispered, 'I'm quite all right, Borinka. It was such a shock . . .' Boris patted her on the shoulder, and went with Rose.

'Come to Rose's room,' said Vassily, after exchanging a glance with his brother. He took Olga's hand, and she let him lead her to the sitting-room, where Tatya was still waiting after what seemed hours. Shura had taken Ilya away some time ago, and she had tried to pass the time by reading, but to her despair, vivid black and white zigzags had obtruded themselves across her vision of the pages of the book, heralding the imminent onset of the migraine, and she could only wait helplessly for it to begin.

As they entered, she made one of her abortive efforts to stand up, then sank back, saying, 'Is she safe?' She could only just recognise the three figures who had entered through the interference of the fortification patterns across her eyes.

'Yes,' Vassily replied, sitting the girl down on one of the sofas, where she hid her face in a diminutive handkerchief. Vassily looked at Vladimir, who said, 'She doesn't seem to want to speak to me.'

Vassily looked at Olga, who was crying again, then sat down beside her and again looked at Vladimir, who pushed his own much larger handkerchief into the girl's hand, then gave a succinct account of the finding of Olga and the events leading up to Sergei's fall, and what Nikolai had said afterwards. 'It was a genuine accident,' he finished.

Neither Vassily nor Tatya expressed horror at the outcome of the afternoon's events, Tatya because everything around her was rapidly taking on the air of unreality common in a migraine attack, and Vassily probably because he considered the living more important than the dead.

'Now, Olga!' he said. 'What's the matter with you?' He untied her bonnet-ribbons and set the bonnet aside, then put his arm round her and began to talk quietly to her. Vladimir stood and watched.

Tatya tried to relax. The jagged lines were fading now, but everything seemed to be happening a long way away from her, at the far end of an invisible tunnel, and Vassily's voice had acquired an odd resonance.

'He didn't rape you, then?' he asked in a matter-of-fact way.

'No. He said he wouldn't if I agreed to marry him. He said I must give him a written promise by midnight, or he'd . . .' Another sob.

'What else did he say?'

'He boasted about how clever he'd been. He said that what happened to you gave him the idea, and when he heard Boris say that he'd send his carriage for me, he thought he'd send his just a little earlier . . . He said he'd only just taken that apartment, and no-one knew he was there, and anyway, you'd all think he'd taken me out of the city, like those people did with you, and by the time you found me, I'd be so compromised that I'd have to marry him, because no-one else would have me.' She sobbed again.

'Why won't you speak to Vladimir?' Vassily asked quietly. Tatya thought with painful clarity that the situation must be serious—Vassily had called his brother Vladimir!

'I can't! I'm not good enough for him any more!'

'Why not?'

'That man . . . he tore my bodice and pulled up my skirts . . . he made me feel dirty . . . he touched me, and . . .' She dissolved into tears again.

Vassily looked up at Vladimir, and the two brothers silently changed places. Vladimir put his arms round Olga, and said softly, 'I love you, Olga. I love you very much, you know.'

She sobbed.

'Little goose,' Vladimir went on fondly. 'Just because that scoundrel put his hands where he shouldn't . . . You don't really think that would stop me wanting to marry you, do you? Whatever he'd done, I'd still want you!'

Olga buried her face in his shoulder and cried as if her heart was broken. Vassily watched as Vladimir soothed her with gentle words, and Tatya wished she dare break into Vassily's preoccupation to draw his attention to her own needs, for the blood was beginning to pound in her temples, and everything about her appeared out of focus and distorted, as if she was looking through a thick sheet of glass.

Olga calmed down after a while, and Vladimir said firmly, 'Now, listen to me! Whatever Sergei Mikhailovich did doesn't alter anything between you and me! You understand?'

Olga nodded, sitting up and staring at him, apparently mesmerised by his sudden assumption of command over her.

'Good. I have every intention of marrying you as soon as possible, and from now on, if you want to flirt with anyone, it will have to be with me. You understand?'

Olga looked at him with huge, adoring eyes, a tear still hanging on her lashes. She nodded again, and the tear ran down her cheek. Vladimir took his handkerchief from her and carefully removed it. She had a little sniff, and said, 'I didn't know it was his carriage. I wouldn't have gone anywhere with him. I love you, Vladimir, and I'd marry you this minute if you like.'

Vladimir's face broke into its rare, charming smile, he gathered her into his arms, and he kissed her in a very unrestrained fashion. Her eyes opened even wider and assumed a look of amazement, which turned to a dazed and incredulous delight. When he eventually broke off the kiss and had regained his breath, he said, 'Now we're going to take a walk in the garden, and I shall probably behave rather improperly!'

He stood up and pulled Olga to her feet, put his arm round her, and took her out through the terrace doors. Olga gazed adoringly up into his face, and neither of them bothered to look where they were going. Vassily watched them go with a cynical grin which was a complete failure, and then stared into space with a wistful, lost expression on his face.

Tatya could barely see anything at all now, and the throbbing in her head had intensified to a violent stabbing which suddenly made her gasp and clutch her head with both hands. Vassily swung round at the sound and went to her side with a concerned, 'What is it, *dushenka*?'

Another stab like a sharp knife jabbing her temple made her sob and grasp his hands. 'Oh, my head!' she exclaimed. 'It's the migraine! Oh, Vasya! I can't see, and it hurts so much!'

'What can I do?' he asked quietly.

'Take me home! Oh, please take me home!'

'Can I get you anything first?'

Another stab. 'No, there's nothing. I can only lie down in the dark . . . Oh!'

'I'll call a carriage. I'll only be a minute.' He squeezed

her hands comfortingly and ran out of the room. Through the pain and blindness, she vaguely heard him speaking to someone in the corridor, and then he came back to her. She was aware of his arms about her, of being carried, lifted and set down in the carriage. She thought vaguely that she should leave a message of apology for Rose, that she should put on her bonnet, that there was some reason why she could not go home, and she stirred in Vassily's arms, moaning as the pain beat through her head.

'Hush!' he said. 'Everything's under control. Just relax and leave it all to me.' She let her head drop against his shoulder, closed her eyes and tried to will the pain to go away, but it had now become a continuous pounding, filling the whole of her mind and body.

Somewhere, a long way off, someone who was herself, and yet not herself, someone outside the universe of stabbing pain, was carried from the carriage and into her own home, and heard voices—Vassily's and another— the dry tones of Josef—speaking in vague, disjointed phrases. 'Out,' she heard. 'Midsummer fair . . .' 'Midnight . . .' 'No-one else?' 'Tisane . . .' 'Look after her.'

Then she was moved again. A door opened and closed and gentle hands unpinned her hair, removed her slippers, unbuckled the garters below her knees and took off her silk stockings. She lay limply, like a rag doll, while someone moved her about, unfastening the buttons of her gown, slipping it off, unlacing her stays, then lifting her again and laying her on the yielding softness of the bed. She turned her head and tried to bury the pain in the cool, smooth pillow, but it still beat and pounded unbearably. After an unknown length of time, she was half-lifted again, and something warm and moist touched her lips. 'Drink this,' said a soft voice, and she sipped obediently. It was fragrant with the sharp taste of thyme, and something else—something bitter.

When it had all gone, she was lowered again and lay still, turned on her left side with the firm pillows supporting the intolerable burden of her head. Gradually, very slowly, the warmth of the steaming liquid seemed to seep through her, rising into her head like a mist, creeping through her skull and gently smothering the pain, wrapping it in a shroud of grey nothingness and drifting with it further and further away, until it became a sharp pinpoint in the distance, surrounded by pitch darkness. For a time—seconds?—hours?—it hung there like a visible, glowing dot of blindingly bright light, and then it was suddenly extinguished and the blackness was absolute. She slept.

CHAPTER
TWELVE

SEVERAL hours later, Tatya began to dream. At first, it was no more than a vague consciousness of feeling very comfortable and safe, but gradually the dream became clearer and more real, and she felt that she was with Vassily, lying in his arms with her head on his shoulder, and it seemed that they had been there for a long time.

'I'm dreaming that I'm in bed with Vasya,' she thought. 'How strange—I'm not in the least afraid! Of course not—I'm never afraid with him!' She wondered if they were in the beautiful room at Oranienbaum, and whether it would be possible to open her eyes and look without waking herself. She was very reluctant to risk waking, so it was some time before she could make up her mind to open her eyes the merest crack. All she could see was a dim white mist.

Puzzled, she opened her eyes completely, and saw that she was lying on her own bed, although she felt so drowsy and confused that it took her a few moments to realise it. The muslin curtains were drawn round it, and the early morning light shining through them gave the misty effect, but where they had not quite met, she could see a glimpse of the Chinese brocade wall-covering and one of the windows. It was broad daylight outside, but that meant very little at this time of year.

But then, it could be any time in a dream, or no time at all.

It seemed odd that she was lying on the bed, not in it, and even odder that she was wearing her chemise and petticoats instead of her nightshift, and Vassily was dressed in shirt and trousers . . .

'Is your head better?' he asked softly.

'My head?' She was very confused, but after a few moments, she remembered that there had been a migraine . . . when? 'Yes, quite better,' she said vaguely. 'What a very pleasant dream . . .'

'You're not dreaming.'

It was a full second before the meaning of the words penetrated her delightful drowsy feeling, and then she gasped and sat up, suddenly wide awake, and stared down at Vassily in horror.

He was lying on his back, his red head on the pillows and a faint smile curving his mouth, but his eyes were watchful and a shade anxious as he looked at her. She was suddenly conscious that her shoulders and arms were bare, and the low-cut chemise hardly more than half-covered her breasts. Her hair was tumbling about her shoulders, and her feet and legs were bare under the long petticoats.

'There's nothing to worry about,' he said calmly. 'Lie down again, and I'll tell you all about it.'

She hesitated. Her head still felt foggy inside—the aftermath of the migraine, she supposed. It would be very pleasant to do as he said, but what on earth would he think of her if she did?

'You won't be raising any false hopes in me,' he answered her unspoken question. 'I've no designs on your virtue at the moment, so stop looking as if you've found a great black spider on your pillow, and lie down again.'

He reached up to her, and it was so easy to let him draw her down and rest her heavy head on his shoulder again.

'You had the migraine,' he said. 'Do you remember?'

'I think so.'

'I brought you home, as you asked, but only Josef was here—Lev had given all the other servants leave to go to the fair until midnight. You were obviously in great distress, so it seemed to both of us that the best thing was to put you to bed. Josef prepared a tisane and we put laudanum in it—I expect you feel a little confused as a result, for it was quite a large dose.'

Tatya thought for a few moments, then said, 'Who—who undressed me?'

'I did. Well, I took off your shoes and stockings, your gown and your stays. I didn't think you'd like me to go any further, and that was enough to make you more comfortable. Oh, I unpinned your hair, too. That's all.'

Tatya thought it was more than enough, and yet . . . She hastily diverted her thoughts from this dangerous path and said, 'I think I remember the tisane, but not much else.'

'There was nothing else to remember.'

Again, it took Tatya's drug-slowed wits a few moments to appreciate his meaning. 'Whatever must Josef have thought?' she asked inconsequentially.

'That the best thing to do was put you to bed, and stay with you in case you needed anything. He said there was no point in calling a doctor, as he couldn't do anything, and you've had these attacks two or three times a year for most of your life.'

'Yes.' Then a horrifying thought struck Tatya. 'But he'll tell Lev!'

'Yes. He told him when he came home.'

Tatya gasped. 'Lev's home!'

'Yes. Irina came in about an hour ago, to ask if she could do anything. You were asleep, so we thought it best not to disturb you, and she went away again.'

Tatya digested this in silence, and then he said, 'She didn't offer any opinion about my presence, and Lev hasn't been in with a horse-whip, so I shouldn't worry about it.'

'But what will he think . . . ?'

'What do you imagine? Do you believe that I've taken advantage of your helpless state to have my wicked way with you?'

'Of course not!'

'Then I expect Lev and Irina will do me the honour of thinking the same! Really, *dushenka*! You don't think

Lev would have let me stay here for a second if he thought you were in any danger, do you?'

'I—I suppose not.'

'Then stop worrying about what people think! I should have left as soon as you fell asleep, I suppose, but you were in such a state that I was worried about you. I made myself comfortable, and then I'm afraid I fell asleep too.'

She was silent for a while, and he gently stroked her hair and then caressed her shoulders, and she found that the tremulous, fluttery feeling which he stirred in her made it quite difficult to breathe.

'I—I really thought I was dreaming,' she said at length.

'That was the drug. Did you enjoy the dream?'

'Y-yes.'

'Was it better than waking up with your late, unlamented husband?'

'I—I didn't . . .' She hesitated, then began again in a rush, 'I didn't ever wake up with him—he never shared my bed . . . not at all . . .'

Vassily said nothing, but his body gave a slight jerk. Tatya shivered and pressed close against him, then continued in a hurried half-whisper, 'I've never told anyone . . . When he . . . wanted me . . . he'd send for me to go to his study . . . It was dreadful, for all the servants knew what he wanted me for . . . and he'd tell me to take off my clothes . . . and then he . . . he would beat me . . . with a l-leather strap . . . until I cried and b-begged him to s-stop . . . and—and then he would be . . . excited, I suppose, and he'd . . . do what he w-wanted to me . . . on—on the floor . . .' She began to cry, and the last few words were almost incoherent. 'Then he'd get up and go out of the—the r-room and leave me . . .'

'He hurt you,' Vassily's voice was hard and cold.

'Y-yes. He couldn't enjoy it if he didn't . . .'

'I hope he's burning in Hell!' Vassily said between his teeth. '*Dushenka moya!* Listen to me! He wasn't a normal man! I can't promise you that you'd never find another man like him, but they're few and far between, and it's unlikely! That's why you've never dared to try again with someone else, then?'

'Yes. I was so afraid . . . I'd no idea how it would be until after we were married, and I thought I might marry again and find it starting all over again . . .'

'It won't—I'll see to that! Any man you think of marrying is going to be thoroughly investigated by me! How long did he have you?'

'You mean, how long were we married?'

'If you can call it that!'

'It was only just over three weeks, but it seemed a lifetime! Father died two days after the wedding, quite suddenly, and Lev was away in Austria with the Army. I wrote to him, but he never received the letter . . . Then he—the General—was recalled and went to Austria too. I was going to run away before he came back, but he was wounded, and then he died, and—oh Vasya! I was so grateful to God for taking him! I couldn't believe it was wicked to thank Him!'

'Of course it wasn't! He spared you from enduring a life that wouldn't have been worth living! You must learn to believe that very few men are like that, and it's perfectly possible for you to marry again and be happy.'

'I do believe it now. You've taught me so much in these few weeks, and all my fears of—of trying again seem foolish now . . .'

'Not foolish, *dushenka*. Understandable, for so few people are able to speak freely about intimate matters like the relationship between a man and his wife. I wish I'd met you years ago—if I've helped you, that is.'

'Of course you've helped me! No-one else ever took so much trouble to help me and show me how it could be . . . Oh, if only I had known you years ago!'

'We nearly did meet once. It was when Lev came home at the end of 1812—he travelled back to Petersburg with me, and invited me to stay here while I was in the city, but I had to go to the Foreign Ministry, and they sent me straight off to Paris, so there was no time even to call . . . But still, perhaps the time wasn't ripe then, for either of us! I was still very bitter against females then.'

He sighed and lay still and silent, remembering, perhaps. Tatya snuggled against him and felt all the tension flowing out of her and being replaced by a glow of peace because at last she had been able to tell someone about those nightmare weeks of her marriage. She closed her eyes and gradually drifted into a deep sleep.

When she woke again, Vassily had gone, and Elena was quietly moving about the room, putting away the things she had worn the day before and getting out fresh clothes for her to put on. She sat up, yawned and stretched, and greeted the maid with a serene smile and a happy, 'Good morning'.

'Oh, Tatya Petrovna!' Elena exclaimed. 'I'm so sorry about last night! I went to the Volkhovsky Palace, and they said you'd come home ill, and I was so upset! To think you wanted me, and I was out enjoying myself!'

'It wasn't your fault—you weren't to know,' Tatya replied soothingly. 'Did you enjoy the fair?'

'Yes, madame, but your poor head . . .'

'Count Karachev brought me home, and he and Josef concocted me a tisane and a sleeping-draught, and I slept for hours. Now my head's quite better, so don't worry about it!'

'Well, that Josef! I wouldn't have thought he'd know what to do, and when I got home, do you know, he wouldn't let me come in to you! He said you mustn't be disturbed! As if I'd have disturbed you! He takes a deal too much on himself, if you want my opinion . . .'

'He was very kind, and I *was* asleep,' Tatya replied soothingly. 'Now, don't think any more about it, Elena.'

Elena gave a final sniff, apparently directed at Josef in his absence, and assisted Tatya with her toilet, making rather a lot of unnecessary fuss, which her mistress bore patiently, knowing that it was the woman's way of making up for being absent the previous evening.

Irina was alone in the breakfast-parlour when Tatya entered it, and she rose to kiss her sister-in-law and ask how she felt.

'Quite better now, thank you,' Tatya replied. 'I—I don't know what you must think . . .'

'Nothing to worry about,' Irina replied calmly. 'Vassily acted very efficiently, I think. Most people wouldn't have the slightest conception of what to do for someone with the migraine! It was very sensible to bring you home, and to stay with you. In any case, it's entirely your own business. Lev and I both want you to be happy, that's all.'

'I suppose you think Vassily is my lover,' Tatya said miserably.

'I've known you for nearly eight years,' Irina replied. 'And I've a fair idea of what you would and would not do, you know! You always enjoyed flirting, but you've always known where to draw the line! Lev and I both know that you and Vassily are only playing a game—a sort of elaborate flirting game—and in any case, it's entirely your own business, as I said, and if you want to take a lover, . . . Not that I think you have!' she added, then stopped, realising that over-elaboration was likely to undo any good she might have managed to do so far.

'Is Lev angry?' Tatya asked, thinking that Irina was perhaps protesting a little too much.

'Of course not! You know very well that if he was, he'd have come in and dragged Vassily out by the hair! Do stop worrying, Tatya!'

It was unusual for the gentle Irina to take such a strong line, and this convinced Tatya more than anything else could have done that she was, in fact, making too much fuss altogether, so when Lev came in, all she said, after answering his enquiry about her health, was, 'Did you see Vassily before he left?'

'Yes. He came to give an account of himself,' Lev replied cheerfully, squaring up to his modest breakfast of a moderate helping of everything available—devilled kidneys, a little cold roast beef, cheese, ham, croissants, raspberry conserve and some *blini* with *smetana*. 'He left in one piece, and I refrained from pursuing him across Siberia with a horse-whip. I didn't even challenge him!' He suddenly caught sight of the expression on his sister's face and hurriedly added, 'I'm joking, pet! I actually thanked him for taking such good care of you. I dare say some scandal-mongering busy-bodies who don't know you both as well as I do might make something out of the night's events if they tried, but something of the same sort happened to me with Irina once, so I do have a little understanding about how it came about. The whole point of Vassily flirting with you is to amuse you, not to worry you into a decline, so enjoy yourself, and the Devil take anyone who thinks ill of it!'

After Lev had gone away to write some letters, and Irina to her daily conference with Pavel Kuzmich, the major-domo, it occurred to Tatya that she had not said a word to them about the previous day's other events, and she decided that it would be better for her to remain silent on the subject until Boris, or perhaps Prince Nikolai, had an opportunity to tell them, for she was not at all sure what had actually happened, and had only the vaguest memories of Vladimir's telegraphic account. In any case, Lev's man-of-business called during the morning and stayed to luncheon, preventing any private conversation by his presence.

Just as he was leaving, Boris arrived, and Tatya said to him, 'I haven't told the others anything. How is Olga this morning?'

'Quite well, and a little subdued, which won't do any harm. We've decided not to tell our parents—it would only upset them, and to no purpose. Nikolai will be here directly, and we'll tell Lev and Irina all about it then, for he's just clearing up the last details with the police.'

Prince Nikolai came in a few minutes later, and he and Boris between then gave a full account of Olga's abduction and rescue, which made both Irina and Lev exclaim in concern.

'Oh, poor Olga!' Irina looked very upset. 'She must have been terrified! And poor Vladimir, wondering what had happened to her!'

'Did you have the task of breaking the news to Sergei Mikhailovich's father?' Lev asked Prince Nikolai.

'Yes. He took it very well. I think he's been expecting Sergei to come to bad end for some time,' Prince Nikolai replied. 'He was thankful that it was an accident, with no scandal attached, as he'd been afraid it would be a duel or a drunken brawl.'

'Was there any difficulty with the authorities?' asked Tatya.

Prince Nikolai shook his head. 'We told them exactly what happened—not the real reason why we were there, of course, but otherwise we were completely truthful, for there was no reason not to be. Apparently something similar happened recently in another apartment further along the street, and they've been complaining about those windows ever since. It's a dangerous arrangement, with the sill below knee-height and no rail or balcony to stop anyone falling out. As it turned out, once the police Inspector realised that Rose and Olga were not in the room when it happened, he said he had no need to put them to the trouble of an interview.'

There was silence for a few moments, and then Tatya said, 'Poor Sergei! I don't suppose anyone is really sorry that he's dead. Isn't it sad?'

They all looked suitably grave and thoughtful at this, and then Lev said, 'Well, at least some of us should go to his funeral—the men, that is.'

'I'd be grateful if you and Boris would,' Prince Nikolai said. 'Vassily too, if he wishes, but not Vladimir, I think. Under the circumstances, it would hardly be appropriate, and I think it's too much to ask of him. I shall go, of course, as he was my brother-in-law, and I feel I should support the old Prince.'

Boris then changed the subject by asking Tatya if she was quite recovered from her migraine. 'I feel very badly about that,' he said. 'Everyone was so táken up with the problems of the other Countess Kalinskaya that nobody even noticed that you were unwell.'

'It came on quite quickly,' Tatya replied. 'You and Rose and Nikolai were not even there at the time.'

'It's lucky that Vassily was about,' Prince Nikolai observed. 'He's a very sensible, reliable fellow in an emergency.'

Irina, perhaps to avoid any further mention of Vassily in connection with Tatya's indisposition, suggested that there was no need for them to remain sitting in the garden-room as it was such a fine afternoon—why did they not go out into the rose-garden? There was a general movement to the iron garden chairs which had been set out round the little fountain in the midst of the flower-beds, and Boris obligingly carried Tatya out. He did it quite safely, but she felt her body stiffening in anticipation of disaster and told herself severely, 'You're a nervous, stupid creature, Tatya Petrovna! You're always worrying about silly things that will probably never happen. However did you come to be such a ninny?'

Rose, Marisha Olga and Vladimir arrived shortly after, and Tatya looked beyond them, an undeniable feeling of disappointment welling up inside her when there was no sign of a slim, red-haired figure following.

'How are you, dear?' asked Rose, kissing her in greeting. 'Is your poor head better? Such a horrid thing, the migraine! My old great-aunt suffered from it, and there was never anything at all we could do for her.'

Tatya made a slightly distracted answer, straining to hear something Vladimir was saying to Irina about Vassily coming later, when he had finished writing an important letter. Everyone was making a fuss of Olga, who was looking pale, with dark rings under her eyes. As everyone spoke kindly to her and it was clear that no-one thought she had meant to go off with Sergei Dmitriev, and Vladimir was standing protectively beside her, she soon cheered up and began to look better.

'You were right about that man!' she confided to Tatya. 'I can't imagine how I ever thought there was anything exciting about him!'

'Was I right about Vladimir too?' Tatya asked mischievously.

Olga blushed and laughed for reply, and gazed adoringly up at the Colonel, who smiled back at her with a great deal more expression in his face than usual.

Gradually, people wandered further afield, Rose and Marisha walking round the garden with Irina to look at the roses, Prince Nikolai and Boris with Lev to look at the alterations he had made to his sawmill plans, and Olga and Vladimir into a private little world of their own, although their physical presences remained in two chairs near where Tatya was sitting.

After a while, Vassily came out of the house and crossed the garden towards her. As she had begun to think that he would not appear that afternoon, she greeted him with a radiant smile and forgot that she had expected to be embarrassed at seeing him again after last night.

'Are you quite well now?' he asked, kissing her hand formally, and then, after a glance at Olga and his brother, who were quite oblivious, he kissed her palm, and then her lips, laughing and whispering, 'Did you miss me when you woke up? Laudanum sometimes makes people forget things . . .'

'Lev said he saw you . . .' she whispered back. 'Was he . . . was it all right?'

'Yes, perfectly amicable,' Vassily replied lightly. He drew up a chair and sat down at her gesture of invitation. 'He was only concerned about your state of health, my dear. Don't worry.'

'I've come to the conclusion that I do worry too much, and usually quite unnecessarily,' Tatya said with a sigh. 'Am I a very fussy creature, Vasya?'

He considered the matter seriously, and then said, 'No, not fussy, but you are rather a worrier. You need more important matters to occupy your mind—a hus-

band and half-a-dozen children, for example. I'm sorry I
was late this afternoon. I had to write a letter, which I'll
tell you about some other time.' He had obviously
intended to tell her at once when he began the sentence,
but the other ladies had returned from their stroll among
the roses, and he had to rise to greet them. Vladimir also
returned from wherever his silent communing with Olga
had taken him, and was despatched to summon the other
men while Irina sent for tea.

'That sawmill should be quite a picturesque feature as
well as being useful,' Boris commented when they were
all assembled and had been served with tea. 'It's a very
good idea to make a manufactory look attractive if one
possibly can.'

'I wish someone would tell that to the Tula ironmas-
ters,' Vassily said. 'Even allowing for the necessary
smoke and dirt, the foundries could be much less of an
eyesore than they are.'

'Perhaps you could disguise them as little volcanoes,'
suggested Rose with apparent seriousness.

'Or Chinese pagodas,' Tatya volunteered.

'Pagodas don't smoke,' Vassily objected solemnly.

'I don't know what makes you think you are compe-
tent to offer an opinion on architecture,' Vladimir remarked in the austere tone which he generally employed
towards his brother. 'You haven't even a dining-room at
Ash Glade!'

'No dining-room?' Marisha expressed the surprise
which they all felt. 'Why ever not?'

'Well, I *had* a dining-room,' Vassily replied, lounging
comfortably in one of the less rigidly upright chairs, 'but
somehow my books started to overflow into it, and then
my uncle died and left me his library . . . I mean to build
a new wing on to the house, when I can find the time, but
meanwhile, the books must go somewhere, and it's not
good for them to be packed in boxes . . .'

'So the dining-room walls are lined with bookcases,
with more across the room, leaving no room for non-
essentials like a dining-table,' Vladimir finished for him

in an expressionless voice which gave a misleading impression of stern disapproval.

'Where do you dine, then?' asked Rose.

Vassily shrugged. 'Oh, anywhere I can find an odd corner.'

'Is your house entirely filled with books, then?' Olga looked as if she thought him rather odd.

'Not entirely. I believe there's an attic in the west wing . . .' Vassily began, then, more seriously, 'A great deal of the house is shut up. If I need a dining-room, I use one of the salons, if we can find it under the dust-sheets, but I don't entertain much, I'm afraid.'

'It's a great pity,' Prince Nikolai said. 'It's very fine building, one of the best in the province. Your grandfather built it, didn't he?' He seemed to have forgotten that most of his own town-house had been shut up for years before he met Rose.

'Most of it. There was a much smaller one there before, and that was incorporated into the east wing. It's far too big for me, but I expect Olga and Volodya will manage to fill a few corners.'

'Don't call me Volodya,' Vladimir said mechanically from the habit of long years.

'What's it like?' asked Rose, who was interested in architecture.

'The central block is modelled after the Parthenon,' Vassily replied. 'At least, the back and front ends of it, but with a Russian dome over the middle. It's four floors high, counting the attics, and the colonnade keeps all the light out of the rooms, particularly in the front, which faces north. There are symmetrical wings on either side, one floor lower, and a stable wing which sticks out at the southwest corner. I intend to build a matching one on the other side sometime, though it's not exactly necessary, with the central block unused. It offends me as it is, though—it's unbalanced, like a three-legged horse.'

'Or a one-legged female.' The thought dropped into Tatya's mind like a little piece of ice, and she realised something which had escaped her attention before. If

Vassily had removed her shoes and stockings yesterday evening, he must have seen her scarred, deformed leg! Bad enough that anyone should see its misshapenness decently veiled in white silk, but revealed naked . . . ! Vassily, of all people, with his fastidious dislike of anything ugly . . . Involuntarily, she looked at him and found that he was watching her face with a thoughtful, curious expression. The conversation had passed on to a general discussion of country houses, and Irina was describing the barn-like structure in which she used to live with her aunt. Tatya was vaguely conscious of her voice, but not of what she was saying, as she stared at Vassily, her beautiful eyes filled with a stunned unhappiness as she waited for his gaze to slide away with the evasiveness of a man who has found a female unattractive after all.

Instead, he gave her one of his deliberate, caressingly admiring looks, and then a little frown of concern.

'Are you not feeling well, Tatya?' he asked quietly.

Irina broke off and they all looked at Tatya, who flushed and said, 'I'm just a little tired, that's all. I expect it's the aftermath of the migraine.'

'Why don't you lie down for a while?' Irina suggested. 'An hour's rest now, and perhaps you'll feel better by dinnertime.'

They were to dine with Boris that evening, and he looked very concerned at the thought of his carefully-planned arrangements being thrown out, so Tatya said wearily, 'Yes, I think perhaps I will. I'm sorry to be so silly.'

A chorus of voices assured her that she was not being silly at all, but Vassily removed her from them by picking her up and taking her indoors. As soon as they were out of earshot of the others, he said, 'What is it, Tatya? Something upset you, didn't it?'

She hesitated, half afraid to tell him in case he confirmed her fears, and then she blurted out, 'You said you took off my stockings last night, didn't you?'

'Yes. Is it something to do with that?'

'Yes.'

He crossed the garden-room with her, managed to open the door, and as they passed through it, said, 'I had to unfasten your garters, but I give you my word that neither my hands nor my eyes went above your knees. Is that what was worrying you?'

'N-no.'

'What then?'

'My leg.'

He mounted the stairs in silence, took her into her room, then said gently, 'It would obviously be untrue to say that it isn't ugly, or that it doesn't matter. Yes, I saw it. I looked at it, I kissed it, and I damned near wept over it. It doesn't make you any less desirable. What else can I say?'

'Nothing,' in a small voice.

'What made you think of it?'

'You said that your house offended you, like a three-legged horse.'

'Oh, damnation! I didn't mean . . .' He put her down carefully on the bed. 'It doesn't matter in that way. I mean, if I . . . if a man wanted to marry you, he wouldn't be put off by it. It's a trivial thing from that point of view, though not, of course, from others. I'm not expressing myself very well.'

'Yes, you are,' she said. 'I understand, and thank you, Vasya.'

'I'd better not stay here any longer,' he said. 'May I call your maid, or fetch you anything?'

'No, thank you. I'll just rest for a while.'

'Oh—your crutches . . .'

'I'll ring for Elena when I want them, but not yet—she'll only fuss. Thank you, Vasya.'

'At your service,' he replied with a smiling bow, then went out, closing the door quietly behind him.

CHAPTER
THIRTEEN

'IF A MAN wanted to marry me . . .' she thought after he had gone. 'But I don't want to marry any man. I want Vasya. I love him.' It was so simple, once she had admitted it to herself, and it explained her confused and odd feelings in the past few weeks, yet at the same time it opened up an appalling vista of the future.

How long could she hope he might continue his game of pretending to be her lover? Not much longer, surely. In a few weeks, at the most, he would go back to Ash Glade, or off abroad somewhere, and when would she ever see him again?

'I'm a fool,' she thought. It's been plain enough all along—he said himself that he could never love a female, and Vladimir told me that he'll never marry. What am I to do?'

The answer was only too obviously *nothing*, and it was no use crying over it, so she made a silent resolve to enjoy his company and his kisses while she could, and then find some useful and time-consuming occupation for herself after he had gone, and stop wasting her life in regrets and feeling sorry for herself. An orphanage, perhaps, she thought. At least she would then have children to care for—'but not Vassily's', a sad little voice in the back of her mind reminded her.

Elena came in plenty of time to help her to change for dinner, and she took care to make herself look as well as she could, and even enjoyed the evening at Boris' comfortable apartment. At the end of it, Vassily carried her down to the carriage and whispered, 'You're very beautiful, *dushenka*. It's as well that you've one little blemish, or the goddesses would be jealous.'

'I shan't worry about it any more,' she replied. 'Vasya—Irina and Lev are going to Borovikovsky's tomorrow . . .'

'Where do you think I shall be going, then?'

The weather had changed again by the next afternoon, and turned misty and overcast, causing Lev to shake his head gloomily over the prospects for their second visit to Peterhof, planned for next day, but the ladies exchanged smiles behind his back, for his weather forecasts were always wrong. Tatya had the stove lit in the garden-room, and Vron materialised in front of it directly in the second-sighted manner of cats.

Vassily arrived soon after Irina and Lev had left, and Tatya tried not to respond too eagerly to his kiss for fear of betraying her feelings.

'What's wrong?' he asked.

'Nothing. Why?'

'You seem a little unbending. Are your stays laced too tight?'

'Vasya!'

He laughed. 'I'm a shocking fellow, aren't I! Quite unfit for decent company! What is it, *dushenka*? Have you grown tired of me, or is it just maidenly modesty?'

'I'm not tired of you.'

'Let's begin again, then.'

He kissed her again, and she made no attempt at restraint this time. Afterwards, he held her closely for a few minutes, his face buried in her hair, and then he said, 'That's better,' and moved to a chair.

'I meant to tell you yesterday about the letter I had written, but there was no opportunity. It was to my man-of-business in Tula about my serfs. I've instructed him to start the procedure for freeing all those on the Ash Glade estate, and two other estates in Tula province. I think that totals a fraction over half of all I own, but we won't quibble over the odd hundred or two.'

Tatya stared at him aghast. 'But I didn't . . . !'

'I said I should free them if you spent a night in bed with a man, and you did. The fact that I didn't specify what you were to do there is neither here nor there—you've fulfilled the letter of the bargain, and so must I.'

'But that's not fair . . .'

He laughed. 'If that troubles you, you know what to do about it!'

'It would be so easy . . .' she thought. 'If I said "yes", at least I'd have that to remember, but he'd guess . . .'

Even as the thought and the regretful rejection of it passed through her mind, Vassily was saying, 'There's something else I've made up my mind to tell you this afternoon, but I hope you'll forgive me if I ferret about for an opening, for I've no idea how to begin.'

'Yes, of course,' she replied, pulling herself together.

'Er—it seems to me that you don't—er—that you don't think any less of Ilya because he's—because of the circumstances of his birth?'

'Of course not.'

'Or of Nikolai?'

'No. It was understandable, even in a man as moral as I know him to be. I suppose men who are lonely or unhappy tend to . . . I know Lev had several mistresses before he met Irina—not all at once, of course!'

'But no bastards?'

'No.' Tatya resolved not to be embarrassed. 'One understands that a gentleman takes precautions . . .'

'Oh, under normal circumstances, of course one does,' Vassily replied impersonally, then paused and thought for a moment before continuing abruptly, 'I've already told you that I haven't led a particularly virtuous life, but I haven't left a trail of red-haired Vassilieviches across Europe.'

'No.' Tatya only replied because he seemed to expect her to.

'Only one.' He watched her face as he said it.

She stared at him in silence, feeling a shock deep inside her of—yes, it must be—jealousy! Somewhere there was a woman who had borne Vassily a child!

'I'm sorry if I've upset you by mentioning the matter,' he said, apparently worried and misled by her silence. 'I rather hoped I might be able to tell you about it, because I've never managed to speak of it to anyone else, but I won't go on if you'd rather . . .'

'Please tell me,' she said, much more calmly than she felt.

After another hesitation, perhaps in case she changed her mind, he said, 'It was an odd business altogether. You know I was in Paris in 1814—I had rooms in an old house in the Rue de St Honoré—its former owner had been guillotined in the Terror, and the house was divided into apartments. There was a concierge—a fat, lazy creature, but pleasant enough. She had a niece come up from the country to stay for a few weeks, and she gave the girl all the work to do, and kept her scrubbing and polishing all day long.

'She was a poor little wretch with a shapeless body and great red hands, and the ugliest face . . . it might have been pretty once, but it was pitted and distorted by smallpox scars . . . I've never seen a worse case!' His own face had become very sad, and Tatya guessed that he was reliving the sight of that poor girl's face, which must have filled him with a mixture of pity and loathing.

'I was sorry for her,' he continued, 'because she had nothing, you see, and she'd given up all hope of ever having a husband—well, there was a shortage of young men in France at that time, as you can imagine, but even so, had it been otherwise, I doubt if she'd have found anyone . . . Sometimes she looked after a neighbour's baby, and it was clear enough how much she longed for a child of her own. When the time came for her to go, I thought I'd give her a present—she'd earned one for all the work she'd done, and I'm sure her aunt gave her nothing but board and lodging. I asked her what she'd like, expecting she'd say a trinket of some sort, but she misunderstood me and said "a child",' he stopped and looked sidelong at Tatya, then went on uncertainly, 'So I gave her one.'

She was silent, thinking how like Vasya it was to be so

sorry for a poor little peasant girl, just as he had been so kind to herself . . .

'That's all,' he said lamely.

Tatya suddenly realised that he had mistaken her silence for disapproval, and hastily asked, 'Did she—I mean, was it a boy or a girl?'

'A boy. I—we only made the one attempt, but it was successful.'

'Is he like you?'

'She says so. Red hair and green eyes, at least.'

'She says . . . ? Haven't you seen him?'

'No. He's entirely her child. I've no claim on him. My lawyers send her money for him, of course.'

'Isn't she at Ash Glade, then?'

'Oh, no. Hélène—that's the mother—has a farm at Chantilly, near Paris. They live there.'

'He must be much the same age as Ilya.'

'A year younger.'

'And you've never seen him?'

'No, nor ever shall. She writes to me sometimes, but she's almost illiterate, so it's never more than a few words, just to say that he's well and growing—nothing much.'

'Aren't you sorry?'

'That I did it?'

'No, of course not! That you'll never see him.'

'I suppose I am, but he's all she has, you see. I couldn't take him from her or share him in any way. It's better as it is.'

'Better?'

'For both of them.'

'And you?'

'I?' he shrugged. 'It costs me a few roubles a month. What do you expect me to say, Tatya? That I'm ashamed that I gave a peasant girl the child she wanted so desperately?'

'Of course not! It was a good, compassionate thing to do. I only thought . . . He may be all she has, but what do you have?'

He looked her straight in the eyes, all his cynicism and his smiling mask gone, and she saw a very lonely man. 'As much as I deserve,' he said bleakly.

Her eyes filled with tears, and she burst out, 'That's not true! You're a good, kind man, and you deserve to be loved and cherished . . .' She choked and started to cry.

Vassily stared at her for a moment, then said coaxingly, 'Please don't cry, *dushenka*! I seem to be for ever plunging you into tears, and it makes me feel guilty!'

'I'm sorry,' she gulped, and fumbled at the clasp of her reticule, which had the lace edge of her handkerchief caught in it and refused to open. 'You looked so lost and wretched . . .'

Vassily gave her his large clean handkerchief and took her reticule from her, busying himself with freeing the clasp while she dried her eyes.

'If I am lonely,' he said at length, 'it's my own fault. If I hadn't been fool enough to play out the tragedy of the betrayed lover, I might have had a Bluebeard's castle full of wives, and a whole regiment of children by now. I'd rather not be pitied, even by you, because I don't deserve it, and I don't want to cause you distress. Do you condemn what I did?'

'No, of course not. I mean, under the circumstances . . .'

'The circumstances make the result acceptable?'

'Yes.'

'That's all right, then.' He suddenly resumed his normal light-hearted manner, as if from relief, and said, 'See what I've brought you today. I did think of bringing you a castle in Spain, but I couldn't carry it, and I thought it might prove an embarrassment, so I brought this instead.' He went over to the chair by the door as he was speaking, where he had left his coat as he came in, and returned with a oblong parcel about a foot long and half as wide, and four or five inches deep.

He put it in Tatya's lap, and sat down again, watching

her with amused interest as she untied the green ribbon
and unwrapped the white tissue paper.

Inside was a box made of sandalwood, its unmistakable spicy scent apparent as soon as she opened the
wrapping. It was inlaid with mother-of-pearl in a design
of pagodas and willow trees in the Chinese style, and
Tatya immediately exclaimed, 'It's a Chinese iron
foundry!'

Vassily laughed. 'Well done! I hoped you'd guess! I
believe it's intended for gloves,' and indeed, it contained
half a dozen pairs in white kid.

'It's beautiful!' Tatya exclaimed, fascinated by the
workmanship of the fine joints and the delicate inlay.
'Oh, thank you, Vasya! Is it Chinese?'

'I believe so.'

'You're very kind to me!'

Vassily pulled a face, but he responded to her outstretched hand by going to collect her kiss of thanks,
which he returned with interest, and presently suggested
a game of chess.

When Irina and Lev came home, they found a silent
scene in the garden-room of a contented cat stretched
along the curved end of the daybed like a miniature
sphinx, watching two people in close concentration
over the chess-board.

'Who's winning?' asked Lev.

'We're very evenly matched, but I think I am,' Vassily
replied, moving a piece.

'Checkmate!' said Tatya, and it was.

'Ah, but you have a very unfair advantage,' Vassily
said good-humouredly, putting the pieces away in their
box. 'Half my attention is taken up with admiring your
beauty, so the odds are weighted against me.'

'A specious excuse,' said Irina. 'Will you stay to
dinner, Vassily? There's no need to dress—it's only us.'

'Thank you—I'd like to,' Vassily replied, 'but could
someone be sent to tell Rose? She'll call out the entire
Army and Navy if I don't turn up again . . .'

'Yes, of course.' Lev went out to send a servant over

to Vassilievsky Island with the message, and Irina settled down to amuse them with an account of Borovikovsky's latest fit of artistic temperament, which had caused him to daub crimson paint all over Lev's figure in the painting, and throw a copper teapot out of the window.

'Fortunately it was empty,' she added.

'Why did he do that?' Tatya asked.

'That's what we wondered,' Irina answered, 'but in the end, he announced that he didn't like Lev's waistcoat. He said it made him nervous.'

Lev returned at that moment, and Vassily went over to him to hold open his coat and inspect the offending garment.

'I must say that it doesn't exactly have a calming effect on me, either!' he commented.

'It's nothing to the enervating effect of scarlet hair!' Lev replied, raising a playful fist, and the two fell to a friendly wrestling match like a pair of schoolboys, while the two ladies and the cat watched indulgently. It ended with Lev flat on his back, with Vassily sitting on his chest and making him recite 'Red hair is best' twenty times.

After dinner, they all sat talking until quite late, and then Vassily carried Tatya up to her room before he left, and she took the opportunity to say 'I haven't thanked you yet for freeing your serfs. It was a very generous thing to do, particularly as you were cheated into it.'

'I should have done it long ago, for I'm as much aware of the iniquity of the system as Lev or yourself, but I've soothed my conscience by thinking that they're happy with what I've given them. However, just lately I've found out that nothing makes a person happy if he isn't free, and it only needed something to spur me into taking action. I should be thanking you. I hope you'll soon be giving me a good reason for freeing the rest of them, although I shall do it in any case, of course, as soon as the first lot of processing is finished.

Wretchedly aware that it was unlikely that she would ever be able to give him the reason he meant, Tatya covered her lack of an answer by kissing him, and his response carried them up the rest of the stairs and into her room, where, fortunately, Elena had not yet arrived. He set her down in what would have been a standing position if she had been able to stand, and continued to kiss her for several minutes.

He eventually desisted, possibly because he heard Elena coming, but Tatya wondered if he had guessed how near she had come to losing her self-control.

'I hope it's fine tomorrow,' she said distractedly. 'Though I don't suppose it really matters if it snows—I mean, rains . . .'

'Not in the least,' he replied, obviously amused by her attempt to take refuge in a safe topic of conversation. He put her down on the bed and kissed her hand as Elena entered, added, 'Don't lose any sleep over it! Thank you for listening to me,' and then left with a smiling 'Good-night' for the maid.

She did, in fact, lose a great deal of sleep, but not over the weather. She fought a long and losing battle over her sharp envy of the Frenchwoman who had the joy of bringing up Vassily's son, and told herself frequently and ineffectually that there was no reason for jealousy as Vassily had obviously never loved the woman, and clearly had no intention of ever seeing her again. Nevertheless, there was a boy with red hair and Vassily's eyes in the world, born of another female, while she, Tatya, had no child, and now would never have one. It was very difficult not to give way to utter despondency.

No-one except Lev was particularly surprised when the next morning turned out fine and sunny, with a clear blue sky and a very slight breeze to keep it from being uncomfortably hot. The expedition set off for Peterhof quite early, with the ladies in two carriages and the gentlemen on horseback, the servants (the Orlovs' this time) going ahead with the luncheon appointments in order to have everything ready in good time.

It was a pleasant drive along the wooded ridge over-looking the Gulf of Finland, with occasional glimpses through the trees of sparkling sea, sailing ships of all kinds, and the dark bulk of Kronstadt brooding in the distance. On either side of the road were the fine country houses of various high-ranking members of the Court, set in landscaped grounds, interspersed with odd patches of scrubby marshy country, as yet unfit for any form of agriculture. The carriage hoods were down, and the ladies chatted merrily among themselves, calling across to the other carriage, or to the riders, who drew ahead or fell behind as the course of the conversations dictated.

There was time on arrival to visit the church pavilion at the eastern end of the Palace, both to see the exuberant Baroque of Rastrelli's decorations and to pray and light candles, and then luncheon was served *al fresco* in the formal gardens at the back of the Palace, sheltered by its yellow and white bulk from the sea-breeze and cooled by the shady trees and the splash of the Neptune fountain, a large, circular basin with the standing figure of the sea-god in the centre, raised on a high plinth and carrying his trident nonchalantly behind his back in a diagonal across his buttocks. The base was surrounded by sea-nymphs and tritons, and little boys riding dolphins and sea-horses, all spouting water as though their existence depended on it, which it did.

'It has an odd history,' Vassily observed, gesturing towards Neptune with a chicken-leg. 'It was made for the market-place in Nuremburg, but they hadn't enough water to do it justice, so it was put up for sale, and the Emperor Pavel Petrovich bought it—the only sensible thing he ever did!'

After luncheon, they entered the Palace and ascended the great *Escalier des Marchands* to the State rooms on the first floor, passing through a whole succession of them, each beautifully furnished and kept carefully swept and dusted, but only used now on one day a year, when the Emperor invited the merchants of his capital to a fête.

Eventually, they reached the throne-room, where they gathered before the portrait of the Empress Ekaterina II, mounted on a dappled horse and wearing military uniform. Olga asked if the Empress often dressed as a man.

'Quite often,' Vassily replied. 'She had a shapely pair of legs, and liked to show them off. She's dressed so in this portrait for a special reason, though. Lev, you should tell the story—it was your family which brought it about.'

Lev grunted and rubbed the side of his nose with one finger—he was not particularly proud of some of his Orlov connections. 'I expect everyone knows about it,' he said.

'I don't,' said Marisha. 'At least, I don't remember all of it. Please tell us.'

There was a murmur of agreement, so Lev began, 'Well, Ekaterina Alexeievna was the wife of Peter III. He wasn't a very good husband, nor a very good Emperor, for that matter, and eventually the Guard Regiments decided to revolt against him. It was organised by Grigor Grigorovich Orlov and his brother Alexei—Grigor was Ekaterina's lover—and they planned to imprison the Emperor and put her in his place.

'Everything was carefully planned, and one morning in the June of 1762, Alexei woke Ekaterina and told her to dress and go with him to Petersburg—she was living here, in Monplaisir, at the time—and they went first to the Ismailovksy Barracks in the city, and the soldiers took the Oath of Loyalty to her, and then they all went to the Winter Palace and she was proclaimed Empress.

'After that, she dressed in the uniform of the Semenovsky Guard, as you see her in the portrait, and led all the Guard regiments back here, where they sent for Peter—he was at Oranienbaum, I think—and they told him to renounce all his titles and his throne, which he perforce did, and that was that.'

'What happened to him?' Olga asked.

Lev looked acutely embarrassed, knowing that Alexei Orlov had killed Peter in a drunken quarrel, but Prince Nikolai cut in smoothly, 'He was murdered, or perhaps killed by accident—no-one knows for sure, but it's not a subject for discussion. The portrait was painted by a Dane, I believe, and it's a very good likeness.'

They all contemplated the face of the Empress who was deservedly called Great, but had not a drop of Russian blood in her veins, and then moved on.

CHAPTER
FOURTEEN

THE best room had been saved until last, and when they saw it, they all agreed that it was indeed the best. It was called the Partridge Room, because the walls were hung with a patterned silk of pale blue covered with garlands of barley and flowers, which framed groups of partridges among rocks and more flowers. The figures were woven, but in such fine detail that they appeared to be painted. The curtains and chair-covers were made of the same silk, and it gave a light, cool look to the room, well set off by a white dado lined with gold, and a very light white and gold cornice.

It was a small room by Palace standards, sparsely furnished with a few chairs, a small table with ormolu mounts, a very fine mirror in a gilded Rococo frame, and a clock mounted on a gold chariot drawn by black lions, which drew Vassily's attention, and he left Tatya on one of the chairs while he went to look at it.

'French,' he observed to Boris, who was using the mirror behind it to make some small but vital adjustment to his cravat. 'It's an odd thing, but if ever one sees an interesting clock, it's sure to be French, never Russian.'

'Why bother to make clocks ourselves when the French make them so much better?' Boris asked teasingly. 'There's quite a good clock at the Ekaterininsky which I believe was made in Novgorod. I thought we might go to Czarskoe Selo next week, if everyone isn't surfeited with palaces, and you'll see it then.'

'Mm. That's a pity. I'd like to see the inside of the Ekaterininsky,' Vassily said regretfully, 'One doesn't often have the opportunity to look at anything properly there when one's with the Emperor, so to speak, but I shan't be here next week, so I'll have to hope for another chance at some time.'

'Not here?' Boris was surprised.

Tatya could hear what they said quite clearly, but the rest of the conversation seemed to come from an infinite distance, each word dropping into her mind with cold clarity like the drips from an icicle, freezing her inwardly until she could hardly breathe for the chill, dead weight in her chest as Vassily said calmly, 'I didn't mean to stay so long, you know. I shall return to Ash Glade at the end of the week to sort out a few problems, and then I'm off back to Norway, in pursuit of my whale.'

'Oh. I thought you'd be here all summer.' Boris glanced inadvertently at Tatya, who was sitting quite still and staring straight in front of her, wondering if her heart had stopped beating. Obviously not, or she would be mercifully dead by now, and not feeling this dreadful aching sense of loss and hopelessness. Of course he must go soon, but not *so* soon . . . not at the end of the week . . . not in only a few more days . . .

'Have you seen enough, Tatya?' Vassily's voice enquired in her ear. 'The others have gone on.'

She started and looked up at him, on the point of bursting into an hysterical plea that he might stay just a little longer . . . just another month—a year—for ever . . .

'Are you tired?' he asked gently, his face concerned and his eyes watchful. 'Perhaps you'd like to rest for a little?'

She closed her eyes for a moment, made an effort to control herself, and replied quite calmly, 'It's rather hot in here with the sun on the windows. Perhaps it would be better in the gardens.'

'Of course.' He picked her up and took her to rejoin the others at the foot of the great staircase, where they had left her wheelchair. He put her in it and pushed her out into the garden, where they all strolled about among the formal flower-beds, and were presently served with tea under the trees.

The journey back to St Petersburg was accomplished in plenty of time for everyone to change for dinner. They were to dine at the Volkhovsky Palace again, and went straight there, having arranged for maids and valets to join the guests there with their evening clothes. Elena had brought Tatya's lilac-grey velvet, and as she put it on and sat before the mirror while Elena brushed and arranged her hair, she thought how much had happened to her since she last wore it for Prince Nikolai's wedding.

'I was different then,' she thought. 'A timid, frightened creature, afraid of being seen, convinced that I had nothing left to look forward to in life, and now I know that there could have been so much . . . I could have been so happy and contented, if only . . .'

There was no opportunity to talk to Vassily again that evening. Even when he carried her out to the carriage, she could do no more than touch his lips with her finger-tips in lieu of a kiss, for Irina was already in the carriage and Lev was close behind. She looked back as the carriage drove away, and saw him standing on the portico steps, one hand raised in a gesture of farewell.

It was fortunate in some respects that she had not slept well the previous night, and was tired after a day of fresh air and sight-seeing, for at least it meant that she fell asleep very quickly and did not lie awake all night tormenting herself. However, she woke early, and was forced to endure a couple of hours of the misery of going over and over the same track in her head, trying to think of some way of at least keeping contact with Vassily in the future.

Perhaps if she begged him to stay a little longer . . . but that would almost certainly lead to him wanting to know why, and she would probably break down and tell him, and that would only make things worse. He would pity her at the best, and perhaps be all the more eager to leave to avoid any further entanglement.

She went through their past conversations in her mind, and at last an idea occurred to her, and because she was now in such a state of despair that she could no longer think clearly, she resolved on a course of action which at any other time would have horrified her by its sheer insanity, and then spent the remaining time before Elena came to her in working out exactly what she would say to Vassily when he came.

Waiting for him to come was nerve-wracking. Having made up her mind what she would ask of him, she wanted to get it over before her courage failed her, and the interval between the decision and the opportunity seemed an eternity.

Eventually, she was alone and hearing his tuneful whistle as he emerged from the stableyard, stepping lightly in his soft leather boots as he crossed the garden. He greeted her with his usual kiss and she clung to him, afraid that it might be the last if he rejected her request.

'Shall we go into the garden, *dushenka*?' he asked.

'No, not just yet, thank you,' she replied breathlessly. 'I—I want to ask you something, Vasya.'

'By an odd coincidence, I want to ask *you* something, but you shall have first say. What is it?'

'It's—it's serious, Vasya.'

'Of course.' He drew up a chair and sat down, regarding her with only the faintest of smiles, his head cocked a little and his eyes watchful and interested.

She took one long look at him, then lowered her eyes and fixed them on her own hands, twisted together in her lap, as she began in a low, nervous voice, and found that all her carefully rehearsed words had left her and everything seemed to come out wrongly.

'I know you don't really love me,' she began.

'But I adore you, *dushenka*!' he said lightly.

She shook her head. 'No, you don't. I'm not playing the game any more, Vasya. I'm serious.'

'By all means.' His smile vanished, leaving his thin face alert and intelligent, but she still did not look at him.

'I know you're going away soon—I heard you tell Boris—and perhaps I'll never see you again, so I have to ask you now, before it's too late.' Having reached the crucial point, she stuck for a moment, and then blurted out, 'Will you give me a child, Vasya?'

There was horrifyingly long silence, and she dared not look at him, and then, at last, he said coldly, 'Are you out of your mind, Tatya?'

'Oh, is it so much to ask?' She was nearly in tears. 'You did it for that poor French girl—why not for me?'

'I don't make a habit of it! In any case, the circumstances are different.'

'Why are they different? Don't you think I want a child as much as she did?'

'I've no doubt that you want a child—children—but you can marry and have your family in the conventional way. She was an ugly little wretch with no hope of marriage, but you're beautiful. You'll have no difficulty in getting a husband and as many children as you want.'

'I want *your* child.' It was a frantic plea, but his voice was quite calm as he replied, 'My bastard? What do you think I am, Tatya? A stallion at stud? Where's your common-sense? How could a female in your position bear a bastard? You'd be ostracised, forced out of Society, and you'd lose any hope of marriage! What do you think Lev would have to say about it? We've both some responsibility to our families and friends, you know, and I do have a few shreds of honour left! Lev has trusted me with you, and if I got you with child, what do you think he'd feel—more to the point, what do you think he'd do?'

'I wouldn't tell anyone it was you,' she said miserably.

'Red hair isn't exactly common in Russia—hadn't you noticed? It's madness, Tatya—utter madness! What on earth possessed you to think of such a thing?'

It had been hard enough to ask him in the first place, but this calm, reasoned rejection was more than she could bear. She made a pathetic clutch at the last rags of dignity and self-respect, but her bitter unhappiness welled up and broke through in a sobbing outburst of pleading. 'Oh, Vasya! When you go, I'll lose you and I'll have nothing! I want your child to love because I can't have you! I c-can't bear it!' She put both hands over her face and burst into tears.

In a moment, he was beside her on the daybed. He seized her wrists and pulled her hands away from her face, saying urgently, 'Stop it, Tatya! You're being hysterical! Stop it at once!'

She choked and fought for self-control, knowing that all he had said was true—the whole idea was utter madness, and she was indeed being hysterical, and nothing was any use . . .

'That's better,' he said, his voice losing its sharp note. 'Now, tell me quietly and reasonably why you want this so desperately.'

She shook her head silently.

'But you must tell me! You can't face me with an outrageous proposition like that without having some most urgent reason! What is it?'

He was holding both her hands in his own, and she looked down at them, seeing his long, flexible fingers which were so much stronger than they looked, and she clutched them convulsively.

'You're going away,' she said with reasonable calm. 'It was only meant to be a game, but you see, I've fallen in love with you, and I can't ever marry anyone else now. I know you don't love me, and you'll go away and forget all about me, but I thought—if I had your child, he'd be something of you that I could have and love. Please don't be angry, Vasya! I know it's madness, but I can't help it—I love you so much . . .'

'I'm not angry,' he said gently. 'You realise yourself now that it would never do, so we'll forget you ever asked such a thing. Now it's my turn to ask you something. May I speak?'

Tatya was surprised that he could turn so quickly to something which was probably trivial after such an emotional scene, and she was too wretched to understand fully what he was saying, so when he asked, 'Will you marry me, Tatya?' she looked at him blankly for a full second.

His face was completely serious and more than a little anxious, and he repeated, 'Will you marry me, *dushenka*? I'll give you as many red-haired brats as you please, as long as you keep their sticky fingers away from my books.'

'But—but you don't . . . You said you couldn't love anyone!'

He gave a twisted smile. 'That was weeks ago. Things have changed since then. You don't really believe I've been pretending all this time?'

'I thought . . . You said it was only a game . . .'

'I think I've loved you from the first moment I saw you, and you say that you love me, so will you have me, Tatya?'

The door of the room suddenly opened and Lev walked in. He stopped dead in his tracks, staring at Tatya's tear-streaked face, and Vladimir and Boris, coming in behind him, collided with him and stood bunched together in silent surprise.

Vassily glanced over his shoulder and said, 'Why the devil couldn't you have come five minutes later? Tatya, yes or no?'

'Yes,' she replied with unmaidenly promptitude, shaken out of her surprise by the new arrivals.

His face lit up with a radiant smile of pure relief and happiness as he slid his arms round her and they kissed, not in the least constrained by their audience.

After several seconds, Irina came in, threaded her way between the still, stunned figures of the three men, and looked at the couple embracing on the daybed with pleased satisfaction. 'I've sent for tea,' she said, 'but I suppose it should really be champagne.'

Vassily reluctantly broke away from the kiss and said vaguely, 'Oh, water, tea, ambrosia—who cares? They'll all taste alike . . .'

Lev cleared his throat and enquired what the devil was going on.

'What do you think?' Vassily asked acidly. 'It's the usual sequence, you know. One falls in love, proposes and becomes betrothed, then marries. We've just arrived at the third stage.'

'You mean that you're betrothed to Tatya?' Lev sounded faintly disbelieving.

'He doesn't seem very pleased,' Vassily remarked to Tatya. Her cheeks were still wet, and he absent-mindedly dried them with the end of his soft silk cravat. 'Perhaps he's going to refuse his consent, and we'll have to elope. The others don't approve either, and we'll probably have to live abroad, in lonely exile. Shall you mind very much, my dear?'

'I don't mind.' Tatya sounded dazed, and she was quite unable to take her eyes off Vassily's face.

'Of course I'm pleased!' Lev exploded. 'I'm delighted! I was just surprised, that's all!'

'We all thought you didn't ever intend to marry, you see,' Boris explained reasonably.

'Intentions have nothing to do with it,' Vassily assured him. 'One doesn't intend to drown in a quicksand, but it happens.'

Vladimir, who had not said a word or shown a flicker of expression, crossed to the daybed, pushed his brother out of the way, and bent to kiss Tatya.

'I hope you'll be very happy,' he said. 'I expect he'll make quite a good husband now he's made up his mind to it.' He sounded doubtful, but Tatya knew him well enough to realise that he was really very pleased.

'Scenes of wild enthusiasm,' Vassily commented. 'Overwhelming congratulations! People dancing in the streets! I'm very moved.'

'Of course everyone is pleased,' Irina said comforting-ly, coming forward to kiss him and Tatya. 'Rose and I knew that there was more to it than a summer flirtation, but you can't expect men to be so percipient. You must give them time to recover.'

The tea-tray arrived at that moment, supervised by Pavel the major-domo himself, who made a short speech of congratulation and good wishes on behalf of all the servants, thereby confirming Lev's suspicion that one of

the servants at least had the ability to see through solid
oak doors. The business of serving and drinking tea gave
everyone time to get over the shock, and then there were
very genuine hearty congratulations, well-wishing and
kissing.

'Why are you back so early?' Vassily asked at length.
'Has Borovikovsky finished the portrait?'

'No!' Irina exclaimed. 'When we arrived at the studio,
we found he had just cut his finger, and you never saw
such a to-do! He was prostrated with shock, and the
servants were running about with hartshorn and burnt
feathers and bandages, so we came away again. We met
Boris and Vladimir on the way back, and brought them
home with us.'

'Well, it was very inconvenient. You nearly ruined
everything.' Vassily put down his tea-glass and stood up.
'Tatya and I are going for a walk in the garden to finish
my proposal, so I'll be obliged if no-one sets foot outside
until we return—if you don't mind, that is!'

He picked Tatya up and went out through the garden
door with her, walking rapidly between the rose-beds to
the gate and through into the water-garden, where he sat
down with her under the willow-tree and said, 'I'm not
dreaming, am I?'

'No. At least, not unless I'm dreaming too.'

'Let's agree not to wake up, then. I'm sorry I was so
harsh, *dushenka*.'

'Harsh?'

'So cruel and cold. You took me by surprise, you see.
I've known for a long time that I love you, but I wasn't
sure about your feelings. Sometimes I thought you might
love me, but then . . . oh, I suppose it was my stupid fear
of making a fool of myself, building up my hopes only to
see them destroyed again. The doubts and fears were
becoming intolerable, so I decided to stake everything
on one throw, and find out one way or the other. I told
Boris I was going away, making sure that you could
overhear me. I thought I would be able to judge your
feelings by your reaction, but you didn't seem to have

heard me—I suppose the over-warm room made you feel unwell, and you didn't realise what I'd said.'

'Oh, but I did!' Tatya interrupted. 'It wasn't the heat in the room, it was the shock of hearing you tell Boris . . . So silly, really, for I knew very well that it couldn't go on for long. I thought you'd grown tired of the game, and I felt so wretched, and afraid I might show you my true feelings . . . That's why I thought of that mad scheme—out of desperation at the thought of losing you.'

'It seems to me that I've made a clumsy mess of everything. I decided during the night to come and tell you straight out that I loved you, and ask you to marry me, but as soon as I arrived, you came out with your own request, and I didn't know what to think. I assumed that you meant that you just wanted a child, and not me at all.'

'Like Hélène.'

'Yes. I suppose one always goes by past experience. That's why I was so harsh with you—to make you tell me the reason. I daren't ask you to marry me until I was sure there was a chance that you loved me. Once you said you did, everything was all right.'

'Oh, Vasya!' She put one hand to his face and stroked his cheek lovingly. 'I'll make them wash their hands a dozen times a day, I promise.'

He laughed. 'I'll build that new wing and put my books in it, and then they can be sticky all over the rest of the house without restraint.'

They both enjoyed a little silent imagining about their future family, and then Vassily took Tatya's left hand in his. She had worn her marriage ring on the third finger of it ever since the day the General died. It stuck, but he eased it gently over the knuckle.

'Do you want to keep it?' he asked.

'No.'

'I'd like to banish all memory of him from your mind. He doesn't deserve to be remembered, and I promise you that I'm not in the least like him.'

He threw the ring into the pool, where it disappeared with a plop and a flurry of golden fish. Then he produced another ring from his pocket and showed it to her. It was gold and formed two clasped hands, delicately chased with flowers and leaves, with a motto engraved among them saying 'I love you' in Russian. As Tatya looked at it, she saw that the motto was repeated and ran once along the top of the band and again along the bottom, and there was a distinct line between the two.

'It comes apart,' Vassily said, and twisted it somehow between his fingers. The ring parted and became two, each with a motto and an outstretched hand, and they were so fashioned that one was a little larger than the other. 'There, now. You wear one and I wear the other, and they'll come together on our wedding day. You're quite sure you want to marry me?'

'Quite sure.'

He slipped the smaller ring on to the third finger of her right hand, and gave her the other to put on his finger. They both fitted tolerably well.

'That's that, then, and very satisfactory,' he said, and kissed her.

When they eventually returned to the house, Prince Nikolai, Rose, Olga and Marisha had arrived and everyone was dressed for dinner, but Irina said that Tatya and Vassily might be excused from changing as the meal had been waiting to be served for some time.

The new arrivals had obviously been told the news, for they crowded round with a great clamour of congratulations and exclamations of surprise and pleasure, and turned the dinner into a celebration which Vassily accepted with resigned good humour, clearly in the best of spirits about the new state of his affairs.

'I thought you were going back to Norway next week,' Boris remarked.

'Oh, no hurry. I'll go next year. You'd like to see a whale, wouldn't you, Tatya?'

'Yes, and an elephant,' she said bravely.

'You see what excellent taste I have,' Vassily boasted.

'She's beautiful, intelligent, in love with me, and as complete a lunatic as I am!'

'A well-matched pair,' said Vladimir solemnly.

They all spent a merry and convivial evening, but eventually the time came for the visitors to leave, and Vassily lingered over saying goodnight to Tatya, whispering, 'I can hardly bear to leave you.'

'Nor I to let you go,' she replied, but the others were waiting, and he left her with a last kiss on the ring on her finger, and she suddenly realised that she was very tired, and although it was not yet midnight, she went up to bed.

Of course, once she was undressed and between the sheets, she was quite unable to sleep. The moon had risen and was shining in at the window, adding a cool lustre to the twilight of the summer night. It was still very warm and the far window was open to allow a slight current of air to freshen the room a little—a practice of Tatya's which Elena deplored in view of the known dangers of exposure to the night air. She lay watching the play of light on the golden sheen of a lacquer cabinet, and thought about the incredible events of the afternoon.

Last night—how wretchedly unhappy she had been, not dreaming that Vassily really cared for her after all. She had been so convinced by his own words, by all she had ever heard about him, by Vladimir's clear warning, that he would never marry, and yet somehow she had achieved the impossible and won his love and trust . . .

And he had done the same for her. She trusted him completely, and could look forward to their life together without the slightest qualm of fear or uncertainty.

A scraping sound interrupted her reverie, and she tensed, listening, wondering what it could be. It came again, and she realised that it was outside. Something—somebody in the garden, below her window.

The sound came again, much closer, and she sat up with a jerk as a dark figure suddenly appeared, outlined against the far, open window. Someone was on the little balcony, was coming into the room . . .

She opened her mouth, her mind racing . . . what if it was a burglar? What if he cut her throat? Would it be sensible to pretend to be asleep? She put a hand to her throat and said 'Who is it?' in a sharp whisper.

'Only me, *dushenka*,' Vassily's voice replied. 'Thank goodness you spoke! I was afraid I might have the wrong room. Too embarrassing for words if I'd come upon one of the maids!'

He came into the room and sat down on the edge of the bed. There was enough light to show that he was smiling, and she put her hands on his shoulders and said, 'How did you get to my balcony?'

'There's a convenient drainpipe. It's a fine night for climbing in and out of bedroom windows, so I descended from mine, walked over here, and ascended to yours.'

'But Vasya—this is the second floor!'

'Well, it's a good stout drainpipe, much better quality than the last one I climbed.'

'Do you often climb drainpipes?'

'Only occasionally. The last one belonged to the so-called Sons of Liberty.'

She shuddered, remembering. 'But the second floor . . . !'

'I pursued that one all the way down from the roof. I thought you'd decided to stop worrying about trivialities, my dear. I'm here, safe and sound, so why are you anxious?'

'You might have fallen.'

'If there had been any danger, I'd not have attempted it. I'm not a fool.'

'No. I'm sorry.'

'Sorry I'm not a fool, or sorry I came?'

'Sorry to make a fuss.'

'Ah—so you're not sorry I came?'

'No,' shyly.

'You don't sound very sure. Shall I go away again?'

Thinking of the drainpipe, Tatya exclaimed, 'No!'

'You know what will happen if I stay?'

'Yes.'

'You're not afraid?'

'No, Vasya. I'm not afraid of you.'

'And the morality of it? I believe your request this afternoon was very much out of character in that respect.'

'Yes, it was. I was so desperate . . . but that's over. I'm quite calm and sensible now. I know what I'm doing, and I understand all the implications. I'm betrothed to you, Vasya, and to me that's as binding as marriage.'

She said it with deliberate intent, knowing him well enough to understand that there would probably be one last, lingering doubt in his mind until she could give him absolute certainty.

'And to me,' he replied after a moment's silence while he took in all the aspects of what she had said. 'You're as much my wife now, in my sight and, I believe, in the sight of God, as you will be when the Church has blessed us. Shall I stay, then?'

'Yes, Vasya.'

She felt the tension go out of him, and then he whispered, 'So this is our wedding-night! We'll do things properly,' and he went to draw the curtain over her icon before pulling off his boots and then stripping off his clothes, his movements swift and certain without being unduly hurried. She watched in the half-light, admiring his slim, lithe body, and as he came to her, she pulled at her silk night-shift, and he helped her with it, drawing it over her head and tossing it on to a chair, where it hung for a moment, then slipped to the floor.

She turned towards him as he slid between the sheets and stretched out beside her, his hands closing on her shoulders and drawing her into his arms as he kissed her and then began to caress her warm, soft skin.

As he had promised, he was not in the least like the General, and when she eventually fell asleep in his arms, she was happier than she had ever been in her life before.

And Vassily? He held her closely and murmured

drowsily, *'Now I begin to know what love is,'* in the satisfied tones of a bibliophile who has found the perfect quotation for a very special occasion.